About the author

Liselotte Roll is a freelance journalist and has previously worked for Sveriges Radio as a scriptwriter. She is a qualified Marine Archaeologist, and while working on a dig uncovering a pre-Incan settlement in La Rioja, Argentina, she discovered the story of the military junta's reign. These memories eventually came to form the book you are now holding. Liselotte's books have been translated to half a dozen languages and have piqued the attention of crime fiction aficionados. Critics have described her as one of the most exciting debut writers in recent years and the next Nordic queen of crime.

About the translator

Ian Giles currently divides his time (often unequally) between translation and his doctoral research at the University of Edinburgh in Scotland. He also sits on the managing committee of the Swedish-English Literary Translators' Association. He has translated a wide range of Scandinavian works for publication or performance, including August Strindberg's *Dance of Death*. In 2015, Ian was shortlisted for the Crime Writers' Association International Dagger for his translation of Andreas Norman's *Into A Raging Blaze*. This is his first book for World Editions.

D1418766

Good Girls Don't Tell

Liselotte Roll

Good Girls Don't Tell

Translated from the Swedish
by Ian Giles

World Editions

To my family,
who always lift me to the next level.

Have you ever dreamed that you're dying?

No, you haven't. You've thought: I'm going to die now. Then you've taken a deep breath and woken up. You didn't experience the actual moment of death or what came after. The second before, you opened your eyes, gasped for breath and felt relief that your heart was still beating.

No one has dreamt their own death and told the tale.

Why is that? Why shouldn't a dream about death continue? The imagination is limitless. But perhaps you're not meant to know, not until you truly are dying. Then you find out—but you won't be able to explain.

For some people, that day comes sooner than they expected.

PROLOGUE

Lying on his back on the kitchen table, Erik Berggren awoke from the final bender of his life. His eyes blinked in confusion at the pitch-black room. It was so dark he couldn't see his hand in front of his face—or, that is to say, wouldn't have been able to if he could get his hand free. Both of his wrists were in fact tightly lashed together above his head. He gave a cry and stared around, wild-eyed. However much he tried, he couldn't see anything ... but he could hear. Someone was breathing very close by. Watching him. Examining him.

Still fuzzy from the gin, it took a while for the words to take shape—and when his voice eventually emerged it was cracked and shrill: 'What are you doing? Who are you?' No reply. Just silence. Then someone roughly taped his mouth shut. The rank smell of plastic penetrated his nostrils and panic rumbled through him like a runaway freight train.

He awkwardly wrenched his arms to try and get free, but it only made the ropes dig even deeper into his skin, puffy from the alcohol. He writhed. His breaths were becoming gasps and his red-rimmed eyes were—for the first time in many years—filled with salty, burning tears. The darkness was somehow akin to a dreamlike vacuum, where the only thing that was real was the cutting pain he felt. It was dead silent, yet at the same time there was a hum of uncertain danger in the atmosphere—as if anything could happen.

His big body shook in a fit of shivers. He wanted to scream. Make the person there stop. But he couldn't. Not a sound came out of his lips—and it wasn't just the tape that was stopping him. He was paralysed with fear. The only movement was from the beads of sweat slowly seeking their way down from his grey hairline. It was as if the whole room was waiting for what was going to happen next. Erik wished the searing pain would go away. Nothing else mattered any more. Nothing. He listened to his own breaths—each one was a tiny, agitated squeak from his nose—together they sounded like a weird tune. And somehow he almost found the noise soothing in the silent darkness.

But then there was a sound. A low clicking and a ... a fan? He froze. The sound intensified, then it slowly began to howl, as if it were taking a run up at a roaring fit of madness. But all that happened was that something reached the boil. Bubbles burst like small, aggressive firecrackers somewhere in the black darkness. It took him a while to realize what it was, but once he finally understood, his heart turned to stone.

In a last, hopeless attempt to get free, he tensed his body into an arc, lifting himself off the table. The pain hit him like a bomb blast. His limbs were strained to their limit. His skin was being torn apart, but the nylon rope wasn't budging—not even by a millimetre. With a tormented groan, his body fell back onto the tabletop. Now he had given up. Time no longer existed—all that was left was pain.

He waited. And that was when it came. The water. The sensation as his skin was boiled to shreds was so sweeping that it made his body shake. The tape muffled the scream, but somewhere deep down it still sounded like he was crying.

Erik closed his eyes, then he sank away. Against his will, he vanished—numb—swirling like a leaf in a stray autumn wind. He was freezing, but the lethargy washed away. It was the memories that were surging forth instead, rebounding off the walls like fireflies in the expansive darkness.

He was back on the farm again—just like in many other

dreams. Standing there on the gravel looking toward the red-painted wooden cottage. The black cat gently rubbed against his legs. The mist had thickened into a dim grey fog and there was a raw chill hanging in the late autumn air. Above the roof, nuances of sulphuric yellow slowly wandered across the sky. The sun would soon be setting. It went down early at this time of year, sometimes before he had even got back from school.

Erik bent down and stroked the cat's back. It was a beautiful little cat with round cheeks and calm eyes. Not like him, with his angular appearance and his wavering gaze. As he ran his fingers through the depths of the animal's fur, he reflected that if he had been a feline he would probably have been a worm-infested alley cat. He let the soft hairs twirl between his fingers. She was so soft, like cotton wool.

The cat purred contentedly, its eyes half closed, and he was about to bury his face in all that cuddliness when he heard something. Someone was crying, quiet whimpering sobs. He stopped for a moment, then he slowly—hesitantly—began to move toward the sound.

The gravel crunched underneath the soles of his shoes as he walked toward the barn, but he paid no notice to it—all he could think about was the crying and the anxiety that had now begun to gnaw away at his insides like a frenzied rat. What was in there?

Erik took a deep breath and grasped the handle. He stood quite still for a brief moment before slowly pushing the barn door open. Of course, he had anticipated what he would see, but he couldn't help himself.

Troubled kids always end up in trouble. It's impossible to feel alive if everything is normal all the time—not if you're used to everyday life being hell. And for him it was. Every day was a new hell.

It was dark in the barn, but the light that pierced between the planks of wood made it possible to make out shapes. He blinked a couple of times before he realized what he was seeing.

The girl was sitting on a chair, her face sodden with snot and tears. He so desperately wanted to run away, but even when he took a few clumsy steps back he couldn't let go of her terrified gaze.

Then came the blow; there was a flash in his head and his legs folded as if they were made from paper. He fell headlong onto the stable floor—prostrate—and scraped his hands in the gravel. He knew he couldn't get away. Out of the corner of his eye, he had already glimpsed the familiar figure and it frightened him more than anything else.

'You stay!' The voice was harsh and sharp as it cut through the darkness. It was too late. Erik had never understood why he had turned out the way he had. Now, tied up on a table, he understood, and he thought it was a shame. He blinked. The dream about the barn disappeared and a glaring light furiously sought its way in through his closed eyelids. His head was pounding and it felt like he was going to throw up. Who had left the shopping bag filled with booze on the step yesterday? Two bottles of Gordon's London Dry—he had barely been able to believe his eyes ... but who would do something like that? He didn't know. Somewhere inside him there was a faint warning bell telling him not to open his eyes, telling him it was best to keep his eyes shut.

But his befuddled brain couldn't remember why, which was why he—with great effort—opened his eyes and immediately recognized the allotment hut. A candle had been lit behind him and he could just make out the contours of the furniture. He had never been happy, but now that life was hanging by a thread he was arrested by a strong will to live.

Tears stung his eyes as the figure approached in the flickering light. Another figure, another time, but the same scene. It was over now—there was nothing left. He was looking at the damp stain on the ceiling when he was stabbed through the heart. And then there was nothing more.

PART 1

1

Magnus and Linn didn't get to bed until a little after midnight. They lay there for a long time, twisting and turning silently under the bedclothes. The chilly night air wafted through the open window and reached them as a series of small, refreshing puffs. Magnus rolled over onto his side. He could feel the tension beneath Linn's skin as she lay beside him. She wasn't moving, but he knew she was awake—he could tell from her short breaths and the fact that her body was tense.

He reached out and touched her with his hand. Her nightie was warm and silky. He carefully let his hand rest on her hip for a minute or so and then allowed it to go on a slow caressing voyage of discovery across her body. She gave a tired murmur. The scent of her hair was incredibly arousing. He kissed her mouth, cheek, and throat and soon they were lying facing each other under the duvet. They could be interrupted any second now by the kids bursting in, but they still couldn't help themselves. Even though they had been through so much over the last few years, the passion was still there.

Not long after, they were lying side by side, exhausted. Linn kissed Magnus on the cheek. His stubble stung her lips lightly. A narrow ray of moonlight penetrated through the blinds and revealed his beautiful face, the big green eyes that could appear so determined and the tousled, dark hair that was beginning to be mixed with fine streaks of grey. There wasn't a trace of the skinny little guy with thick glasses that he had been once upon a time. He had all the attributes of a man. Linn's own mother had once described him as a real man's man, and that was probably how most people perceived him. All Linn saw was a person she loved. She had never been particularly interested in masculinity or femininity.

'Go to sleep, we'll probably get woken up soon,' he whispered softly.

'Hmm ... ' Linn already had her eyes shut. The beautiful, tiny crow's feet around her eyes made her look happy even when she was sleeping.

Magnus set the alarm clock. He was going back to work tomorrow. He sighed in disappointment. Every time he had been at home for a few days, it was always tough to go back to work. He somehow had a feeling that he had done himself some harm. It was a feeling that often began somewhere around his stomach before gently settling on his chest and applying pressure. Where had all the motivation gone? He had been proud to be a policeman and felt joy in helping people. Now it just felt like he was rowing up and down shit creek without getting too much of it on himself.

His emotions turned into a sticky mess. The disappointment and anger about people's selfishness got mixed together with sorrow about all the hurt people out there. How had a normal boy from the suburbs ended up here? How naïve his dreams must have been. The only thing time had shown him was that nothing got better. He couldn't get at the evil. It was like pruning an apple tree—the next season saw even more new shoots than there had been before. Disturbed parents continued to bring up disturbed kids, and it all carried on for eternity. Criminals who didn't have a disturbed upbringing to blame their actions on were even worse—they were generally really fucking disturbed. But if he weren't a policeman, what would he do instead? He had no idea.

He pulled the duvet tighter round himself and turned toward Linn in resignation. A blonde lock of hair had fallen across her cheek. He carefully pushed it to one side. It was so good that he had her. That he had met a proper person. She was more intelligent than he was, but that didn't bother him. She excited him with her wild temper and fresh perspectives on practically everything, and he gave her calm in return. That was their unspoken deal and it worked.

2

'Moa and Elin have got streptococcal infections.' Magnus spread his hands apologetically.

He was twenty minutes late and his colleague Roger Ekman looked at him grumpily as they walked in through the entrance to Forensic Pathology.

Magnus's dark hair was all over the place and he had dark bags under his eyes. He had the impression that this somehow delighted Roger.

'This is apparently not much fun,' said Roger.

'What? Is it worse than usual?'

'Yes, the body was found in an allotment hut. I guess you've heard that. But there was something about the way he was lying and so on. Tortured. Tied to the kitchen table with a rope.'

'Oh really.' Magnus looked gloomy.

Roger looked down at his dirty trainers.

'But at least you're here now ... or do you need more time off to look after the kids?'

'No, Linn is at home for the rest of the week.'

Magnus suddenly felt completely exhausted by Roger's sulky allusions. They had worked together for almost twelve years and their relationship had come in waves. At his best, Roger could be a good friend, but he was often a tedious bastard and Magnus preferred to avoid him in the corridors. But that was probably just relationships—he had never managed to get things running like clockwork. If anyone got too close to him, he would often be stiff and unsure of himself. Apart from with Linn, that was.

Roger coughed.

'Well, to update you a bit. The victim's name is Erik Berggren and he's just turned forty. He's signed off from work, an alcoholic, some learning difficulties. He seems to have been living in the hut, which belongs to his old mum.'

Magnus nodded.

'What did the neighbours make of it?'

'They've apparently made a few attempts to get rid of him, but he doesn't really seem to have been bothering anyone.'

'People are so damn picky. Well, they don't have to worry any more.' Magnus gave an askew smile and opened the door to the autopsy room.

The light in the room was cold, but forensic pathologist Eva Zimmer was beaming like a hot sun when she looked up from the body she had in front of her. The broad smile exposed her charmingly crooked teeth.

'Lovely day, isn't it? Lovely sunshine!'

She took a big bite out of a cinnamon bun.

'Do you want one? I bought plenty.'

Neither Magnus nor Roger felt especially tempted by a bun at this juncture.

'As you wish—but these aren't dry things from the supermarket. They're from the patisserie.'

The inspectors smiled.

The forensic pathologist swung round toward the bier behind her and pulled away the sheet with a dramatic tug.

Magnus felt a brief flutter in his stomach. On the bier was a naked man, his skin covered in fluid-filled blisters. The skin had fallen off in places, revealing the red flesh below.

'Terrible, isn't it?' Eva shook her head in consternation.

'The person who killed him poured boiling water onto him before he died. He's basically been blanched.'

Magnus forced himself to focus on the body, which was pale as a wax doll.

'Only around the lower parts ... ' he interjected with a look of disgust.

'What's that?' Roger pointed at a stab wound on the chest.

'Yes, well, that must be what killed him,' Magnus suggested.

'I meant the shape, of course. It's unusual.'

Eva tossed her head.

'I've not had time to check it yet, but it certainly is an unusual shape. I'll get back to you on that ... as well as how long he's been dead. I'm leaning toward a week or so.'

Roger bent over the wound and inspected it. Behind his wide-rimmed glasses there was a gleam of interest.

Magnus spent the rest of the morning on routine tasks like trying to get hold of Erik Berggren's keys, passport and ID. Normally, he would have checked up on activity on the victim's credit cards or calls on their mobile, but in Erik Berggren's case there was no mobile or credit cards. Erik seemed to have been a man living completely outside normal society.

Magnus had just sat down at his desk again when he felt the niggles in his legs—worse than usual. He really ought to make an appointment to see the doctor to find out what it might be, but in spite of the fact that the unpleasant sensation had been there for months by now, he had no desire whatsoever to go to the doctor.

He glanced at the mobile on his desk, which showed three new messages. All of them were from Linn and her voice sounded more and more strained in each call she made. He wanted to go home and help, but Roger would probably flip if he even mentioned it, so he gritted his teeth and did nothing.

Magnus was quite aware that he was already at the limit of what was reasonable at work. He almost always arrived late, left early, and always took long breaks just to get out of the office. It wasn't that he was a bad policeman—it was just that he was so awfully tired and worn out. It was a miracle that he and Linn had been able to have sex last night, he thought. A complete miracle.

3

At lunchtime the sun began to make its presence known from behind the thick clouds. Magnus passed a couple of crowded restaurants before choosing an Indian on Kungsholmen. The colourful strings of fairy lights on the walls immediately transported him into something not dissimilar to the atmosphere at Christmas. The scents of the aromatic spices hung over the restaurant like mist, while you could almost cut through the muffled murmur of conversation with a knife. He felt satisfied despite knowing he would have a stomach ache later. There was something about the chilli—but it tasted so good that he didn't care.

Even though he always ate lots of everything, he was constantly hungry. Probably something to do with his metabolism. At school, he had been the shortest, thinnest kid in class right up until high school. The others had called him the Skeleton. But plenty of hot chocolates and loaves of bread had yielded results, and although the school nurse claimed he would only manage the bare minimum on the height curve, he had run away as a teenager, reaching two metres. Now all that gave away his original build were his skinny calves.

Shaking with hunger, he eased his stout body into the busy

restaurant and took a seat at a small, round table at the back.

He had just received a piping hot tikka masala when Roger called.

'We've just received the forensic pathologist's report. We're having a meeting straight away.'

'But ... I've only just got my food.'

'Chew fast—the others are already here.'

Magnus rubbed his face in resignation.

'Okay, I'm on my way.'

He took three quick bites, got up, and paid.

4

Magnus, Roger and the relatively new Detective Inspector, Sofie Eriksson, were already crammed into the meeting room—each with a boiling cup of coffee to hand—when Superintendent Arne Norman entered. He looked satisfied. His hair shone white in contrast with his chocolate brown tan thanks to his recent return from the Canary Islands.

'Welcome everyone. The conference room was double booked. It's a bit of a squeeze in here, but it'll do,' said Arne, before smiling.

Sofie gave him an appreciative glance and Magnus couldn't help thinking that she approached her work a little too energetically. But since Arne loved brown-nosers, she'd very probably become a favourite.

'I'll try and summarize,' Arne began.

'If you have questions, keep them for later. I get so distracted when I'm interrupted. Firstly, I want to praise the vanguard. They did a good job over the first twenty-four hours after the body was discovered, which means that now we're taking over we have really good foundations to build on. Unfortunately, there are only four of us—everyone else is working on the murder of that former neo-Nazi last week. I'm going to try and release another investigator as soon as possible if I can.'

Arne picked up a pen and began to write on a large white-board on the wall.

'So, the victim's name is Erik Berggren and he was found in his mother's allotment hut in Eriksdalslunden a little over twenty-four hours ago. The man who found him is a retired computer technician called Lennart Wingedahl. He has the next allotment along and there was nothing else to connect them apart from being neighbours—that we know of.'

Magnus raised an eyebrow.

'How was he found?'

'Wingedahl says the door to Erik's hut had been banging in the wind for several days, and that he eventually went there to check what was up.'

'When was that?'

'Yesterday morning. He was at his allotment hut to pick his winter apples, apparently. Anyway, when he arrived he decided to take a look inside, which was when he saw the victim tied to the kitchen table. This is all according to the witness statement he provided yesterday. He's coming in this afternoon and then we'll hear what he has to say again.' Arne looked at Roger expectantly who reluctantly groaned.

'Of course, I'll take it.'

'Good. Wingedahl claims he didn't take more than a couple of steps inside the hut, so the crime scene still has something to offer. The whole office and part of the gravel road outside is cordoned off and forensics have been in, of course.'

Magnus took a gulp of coffee and tried to look more interested than he was. Alkies being put to death wasn't particularly uncommon and even if he didn't want to admit it, he had an internal ranking system. Worst was obviously when children came to harm. Dead, middle-aged addicts rarely made him weep tears of blood.

Arne continued.

'The body has been there for around a week. The autopsy indicates that he probably died as a result of the stab wound, but that he was tortured prior to that with boiling water around his genitals—he has serious burns. We don't know whether he was unconscious or not when he was killed.'

'Okay, anything else?' Roger leaned forward.

'Yes, they've tested the decomposition liquid in the eyes too. Erik's blood alcohol level was sky high, but part of that is of course because of the body's bacteria—they create a lot of alcohol post-mortem.'

Magnus looked disgusted.

'Why did they need to dig around in his eyes—there must be rotten liquid elsewhere?'

Arne shrugged his shoulders.

'Apparently it's cleanest there. Anyway, we can assume that Erik was drunk as a lord when he died. His neighbour, Lennart Wingedahl, claims that wasn't unusual.'

Arne cast his gaze over the group. To his dismay, Magnus was fiddling with the edge of his notepad in disinterest while Roger was staring longingly toward the door.

He sighed.

'Yes—Eva Zimmer has checked the chest wound. She's not certain yet, but the murder weapon isn't a knife and it isn't a screwdriver. She'll get back to us on that. Apart from that we don't know much yet. Forensic analysis is being done right now. I suggest we continue interviewing people.'

He turned toward the group.

'Sofie, can you look for similar cases in our records and continue checking out who Erik Berggren hung out with?'

Sofie nodded.

'Roger, interview Wingedahl, as I said, and then you might as well take the other allotment holders while you're at it.'

'It'll take ages, there's around one hundred and forty huts,' Roger protested.

'Do you have something better to be doing?'

Roger pushed his chair back violently and got up.

'No.'

'Well then.'

Arne arranged his facial expression. He didn't want the others to see how nervous small controversies like this made him.

'Magnus, can you inform the victim's mother? She's called Gunvor Berggren and lives in the Vårdbo old people's home in Åkersberga ... see if you can get any information out of her as well,' he added lamely.

5

Despite the sunshine, there was a biting chill in the air. It was as if winter was biding its time, as if it were waiting to grab hold of the red glow of autumn with its iron fingers and wring the life out of it. Magnus found it difficult to know whether he should dare to look forward to nature's grey-white slumber or whether he would—as usual—simply clamber straight into a winter depression where he would remain.

He got the map out of the glove compartment and anxiously checked the address. The care home was at the Åkersberga shopping centre, so he would have no trouble finding it. It was the task that made him uneasy.

He shook his head, as if he was shaking off the thought of how Gunvor would react to the news of the death, then he got out his mobile and called home.

'Hi darling.' Linn's voice sounded thin.

'How are things?'

'Monica is going to buy groceries for us.'

'Why?'

'Well, because the kids and I are sick and it's impossible for me to drag two kids with fever around the shops. For starters.' Linn had something of a sharp tone in her voice. 'I'm really struggling here. Isn't it good that she offered?'

His bad conscience stung like the bite of a horsefly, but since there was nothing he could do he mostly felt irritated. It didn't feel right to need your neighbours to pitch in and help out. They'd always got by on their own.

There had never been any grandparents standing up to be counted. Magnus's mum lived in a nursing home and his dad was long dead. To begin with it had been difficult without support, but now they had got so used to it that they even dealt with the difficulties as part of their routine.

Linn had no contact with her parents. Somewhere along the way, she had reached the point where she felt so bad meeting them that the kids had started to be affected, at which point she made the decision to break contact with them. It had been tough for her—and it still was—but it had been worse before. He wasn't sure exactly when he had got sick of his trying in-laws himself. Perhaps it had been when his father-in-law had driven the kids to the zoo while drunk, or maybe it was when he and Linn had been obliged to drive him to casualty after he had mixed his spirits and sleeping pills. It no longer mattered: his parents-in-law were a closed chapter.

'Hello! Magnus, are you still there?' Linn shouted down the phone.

'Yes, sorry, was just thinking. It's great that Monica offered to help.'

'Yes, I think so too.'

'I'm in Åkersberga and have to deal with something, but I'll be home as soon as I can after I'm done.'

'Okay.' Linn's voice sounded distant at the other end.

'Will you be all right?'

'Yes ... although I reckon this is the crappiest illness the kids have had. But Moa has at least slept for a bit now. How are things with you?'

'The usual.'

'Murder? Perhaps we can have a glass of wine and watch a film this evening?' Linn regained her vitality.

'That would be lovely, I'll shop on the way home.'

Magnus hung up. It had begun to rain and the road turned slippery and shiny. He turned on the news on the radio.

A lorry honked persistently. The Åkersberga shopping centre—or rather, an enormous, brown car park—was visible before him. Magnus took a sharp turn across the railway and continued along Åker's canal. On the other side of the water he glimpsed a red brick building through the pounding rain. It adhered to the norms of old people's homes in every way. Big, worn out, ugly. Soon the news of the death would be delivered. Somehow, there was never a good way to do it. It was a baptism of fire and the only thing you knew for sure was that it would be unpleasant—even for him.

It was just before four o'clock when he parked outside the doors of the nursing home and got out of the car.

The buzzer crackled before a man's voice became audible:

'Hello?'

'Hello. My name is Magnus Kalo and I'm from the county CID ... '

There was a brief beep and the door opened automatically. The hospital-like environment and odour of linoleum reminded him of the transience of everything and he felt his heart sink a little in his chest.

A young woman, her hair dyed blonde, with a slightly ruddy

face, appeared in the foyer. Her hair was short and she was wearing a wine red blazer in a style he hadn't seen since the eighties. He stretched out his hand.

'Hi, Lise Evertzon. I'm the HR Manager. I heard you're from the police?'

'Yes, I have sad news for Gunvor Berggren. Unfortunately, her son has died.'

Lise's face seemed to get a little redder, but she quickly collected herself.

'What a shame.'

'Yes.'

'Gunvor is up on the second floor watching TV in her room. It's worth you knowing that she has dementia, so she may not understand ...' Lise stopped for a moment, as if taking a run up at a difficult question. 'Is it really necessary to tell her this? She probably doesn't have long left, you know.'

Magnus grimaced apologetically.

'Regrettably, the family must be informed.'

Lise's face fell.

'That's a pity,' she said briefly.

'Yes, it is.'

'She's in room fourteen. Come down and let me know when you're done. She may need someone to help her afterwards.'

'Of course, I'll do that.' Magnus was already halfway into the lift, he wanted to get it all over with as quickly as possible.

Gunvor's room was at the other end of the corridor on the second floor. Magnus knocked timidly, but there was no reply so he nudged the door ajar.

'Hello—Gunvor?' he said cautiously.

No response. Magnus opened the door and stepped in. The sour scent of old, dusty furniture and urine struck him, strangely supported by the sickly sweet sterile smell of care institutions that he so deeply despised. He tried to hold his breath. The blinds were down and apart from the flickering blue light from the TV—where an advert for some skin product was being shown—the room was dark. A pair of feet in support stockings was sticking out from behind the armchair that was facing away from him.

For a brief moment, he thought Gunvor Berggren was dead too—but then he heard her give a low wheeze. He took a few steps forward.

'Hello, Gunvor. My name is Magnus Kalo and I'm from the county C … ' He stopped abruptly. He couldn't comprehend what he was seeing.

The woman staring back at him expressionlessly had spatters of blood on her face, and the lower part of her body was a maelstrom of red flesh. She was looking at him in confusion. Her eyes expressed no pain—they were shiny and questioning.

Magnus could feel his stomach wanting to flip. He picked up Gunvor Berggren's frail body in his arms and shouted. His voice was hoarse and pitiful, but help came.

6

'MUM!'

Moa screamed loudly from her bed. She wouldn't stop until the first mouthfuls of breakfast were calmly resting in her tummy. By that point, the rest of the family had usually given up any hope of sleep.

As Linn laboriously rolled over on the other side of the bed, she gave Magnus a hard push.

'Go,' she mumbled. 'I've been up four times tonight.'

' ... but I got up yesterday,' said Magnus.

Linn turned round and pulled the duvet over her head.

'MMUUUUUUUMMM!'

Magnus rolled out of bed. They shared out the nights, but Linn almost always had to get up eventually. Neither Moa nor Elin wanted him to appear when they shouted into the night, and if he tried, it would often end with them screaming like mad until Linn turned up.

Moa sat bolt upright in bed when Magnus came in, looking at him angrily.

'I want mum to come. JUST MUM!'

Magnus furrowed his brow deeply and sighed. The tingling in his legs had kept him awake half the night and he felt infinitely tired. The sensation of thousands of ants patrolling inside his skin was driving him crazy, but he still hadn't told Linn anything. This was because he knew exactly what would happen. She would immediately get on the computer and find a range of mystical illnesses that matched his symptoms, and would then nag him incessantly until he made a doctor's appointment. No, it was better to keep quiet—he wasn't all that worried anyway. He was only thirty-five and in good shape. Whatever it was, it would probably sort itself out.

'Mum is asleep, she needs to sleep,' he said, expecting another round of yelling, but instead the door opened and Elin, wearing her green pyjamas, tiptoed in.

'I don't want to sleep,' she said with an unwavering expression.

Magnus looked at his daughters in resignation—they had already cast themselves at each other and were tumbling around the bed.

'Let's get up. It's the morning,' he said.

7

There was a slightly rotten odour when Magnus entered Roger's office a couple of hours later. His colleague's desk was—as usual—covered in papers, coke cans and half-eaten croissants. Magnus was sweating. The sleep deprivation during the night and yesterday's visit to the nursing home had taken their toll on him and it felt as if the room was swaying. He sank onto a chair and rubbed his hands across his face. The image of Gunvor, bleeding, replayed itself repeatedly in his mind. There had been something about her eyes, something so ... astonished.

Roger leaned over the desk.

'Are you all right?'

'Yes, just a little tired.'

'It must have been pretty unpleasant ... '

Magnus gave a quick nod. He had already described most of the events at the care home and felt no need to do so again.

Roger dropped the subject immediately. He knew there was

no point in putting his colleague under pressure. Sometimes he thought Magnus was like a man from another age, a world where you needed a couple of shots of vodka and a long stint in the sauna before you could talk about your feelings.

'I talked to accident and emergency at Danderyd Hospital,' he said, instead. 'They've admitted the lady to the intensive care ward. Given the circumstances, she's doing okay and doesn't seem to have realized what happened to her. Possibly the only upside of dementia?'

Magnus gave a jaunty smile.

'The doctors say she was under the influence of something when she was admitted,' Roger continued.

'What?' Magnus raised his eyebrows in surprise.

'A high dose of some pain killer—probably to keep her quiet while she was being tortured.'

'How does it look?' Magnus said flatly.

Roger suddenly looked older than his forty-five years. He lowered his voice.

'The genitals have been burnt with boiling water, more or less like the son—third degree burns. The pan was still on the stove—it had boiled dry.'

Magnus nodded in distress. He had already seen it all.

'A senile woman, it's ... ' He fell silent and clenched his jaw. 'Why do you think she was allowed to live?'

Roger shrugged his shoulders.

'The attacker was probably interrupted ... perhaps by you? I've interviewed the staff at the home, but no one seems to have seen anything. Apart from an orderly who saw a woman leaving the care home a little after you arrived.'

'What did the woman look like?' Magnus's senses sharpened. Gunvor, with her huge eyes, was etched permanently in his memory. It was disgraceful. The last thing an elderly person experienced on this earth shouldn't be insane evil. He was overwhelmed by a strong desire to punch someone in the face—anyone.

'Wearing a shawl on her head, dark clothing, not much of a description.'

'Do we have an exact time for when this was?'

'So-so, she left around ten minutes after you arrived.'

'Well, that might make sense in that case.' Magnus looked at Roger thoughtfully. 'Can we talk to Gunvor yet?'

'No, she seems to be completely out of it. The only thing she is saying is that there was a big, horrid fly in the room. She's said it over and over.'

Roger pulled up his shoulders and his short, set body looked more compact than ever.

'Sofie and I will go and re-interview the staff. In particular, I'll talk to that orderly who saw the woman leaving the building.'

'Mm ... by the way, how did it go with the neighbour at the allotments? The pensioner, Wingedahl?' asked Magnus.

'Unfortunately, I didn't get anything else out of him.' Roger picked up his leather jacket from the chair. 'I'm going for a bite to eat now. Let's meet at quarter past four.'

'Sure,' Magnus replied absently.

8

Moa and Elin were glued to an animated film on TV, so Linn took the chance to take a shower. Water streamed down over her blonde hair, turning it a lifeless brown. A few days with sick kids had taken its toll and it felt like she was waking up out of a mist as the warm water gushed over her. She was normally a fighter in most situations, but right now she was feeling more than a little befuddled. She sat down in the bath. The new case that Magnus had told her about fascinated her and she hadn't been able to help asking him about every last detail. There was something remarkably chilly about the course of action. Very few people managed to perpetuate protracted violence in the way Magnus had described. Why hadn't the perpetrator just used a knife or something? Why boiling water in particular?

She reached for the soap. Perhaps it was an occupational injury from working as a therapist, but she simply couldn't help poking around in the worst of human excesses, even when they affected her badly.

She sank into the warm water gathering at the bottom of the tub and absent-mindedly shaved her legs while thinking about the murderer.

Were you angry? Frightened? Perhaps excited? What did you do after? Did you stay and watch Erik Berggren after you were done? And why did you attack his poor, old, defenceless mum? Was she meant to die too?

Linn held the razor under the tap and the light strands of hair swirled down the drain as if they were in a hurry to vanish. Then she put the razor down on the edge of the bathtub.

The crime in the allotment hut had demanded extraordinary self-control—and you needed a special personality for that. This was no careless, sloppy murder by a nervous sadist. This was far more elaborate.

A shrill cry interrupted her thoughts. Moa and Elin were fighting loudly in the living room. Linn got up abruptly and got out of the bathtub. There was one thing she did know for certain—a parent of young children would never have had the time to think through the details in such an advanced scenario. She quickly reached for her towel.

9

The room, kitted out with an enormous beech conference table and beige curtains with embroidered tulips, had a worn and slightly seventies feel. The carpet that had once made the room cosy was now a breeding ground for mites that could kill a dust allergy sufferer. Magnus balanced on his chair between his colleagues and impatiently drummed the edge of the table with his pen. By the time everyone had a cup of coffee, Sofie looked as though she was going to burst. She had obviously come up with something. Without taking any notice of her excited face, Arne Norman stood up at the front and wrote the names Erik and Gunvor on the whiteboard. Then he turned round.

'Well, who wants to start?'

'Me.' Sofie craned her neck, her voice literally vibrating with excitement. She was reminiscent of one of the clever girls in class who eagerly wanted to give the right answer to the teacher's question. Magnus and Roger exchanged an amused glance that fortunately she missed.

'I've come up with a couple of things,' she began. 'Both Erik Berggren and his mother have been burnt, so naturally I searched for similar cases in the records ... I didn't find any matches, but do you know what I found instead?' Sofie paused and looked at the others in satisfaction before carrying on:

'Gunvor Berggren reported a case of animal cruelty more than thirty years ago when she lived on a farm in Flaxenvik, outside of Åkersberga.'

'And?' Roger looked at her in confusion.

Sofie thrust her lower jaw forward triumphantly.

'It was their dog. It had been burnt and beaten to death.'

There was silence and Sofie scratched the corner of her eye in an attempt to disguise her delight.

'It was found in the barn,' she continued. 'The perpetrator was never apprehended, but the son—Erik Berggren—was under suspicion.'

'Why?'

'Mostly because he seemed a little odd, I think. But there was no evidence. Nothing at all.'

Arne smiled.

'Good work. The burning is of course very interesting. The only problem is that Erik is dead. Were there any other names in the picture during the investigation?'

Sofie shook her head.

'I can't imagine they bothered with a full investigation for a dead dog.'

'Obviously. But look into this as much as possible. Perhaps some old neighbours might remember something?'

'Of course.'

Arne pinched the bridge of his nose.

'Well, that's all good. How do things look for the rest of you? Have you found out anything?'

Magnus leaned back on his chair.

'Yes, I spoke with Gunvor's niece, Annika Wirén, by phone. She might be able to tell us about Gunvor and Erik, but she's at a conference in Skåne for a few days at the moment. She works for a tarpaulin company. I'm planning to meet her as soon as she's back.'

'Ask her about the dog as well. Does she know what happened?'

'No, I'll ask about it when we meet. All I said was that the family had come up in the investigation and I asked for a few quick details. She probably thought it was a little strange that I wanted to talk to her, but she didn't say anything.'

Arne nodded.

'What information did you find out?'

'Well, apparently Gunvor and her husband, Gösta, moved to the farm Sofie mentioned at the start of the fifties. They had Erik, who of course was slightly disabled, late in life. Annika said that he functioned mentally at the level of a ten-year-old, but that it could vary a bit.'

Roger looked at Magnus in concern.

'Vary?'

'Yes, sometimes he seemed a bit older in manner, and sometimes younger. I guess it can be like that. Anyway, Gunvor worked on the payroll at the sawmill in Åkersberga. Erik also worked there for a while.'

'What about Gösta Berggren?'

'All I know is that he died of cancer in the early nineties. Then Gunvor moved to an apartment on Södermalm. Soon after she got her allotment.

'Where the son was found?'

'Yes.'

Arne coughed gently.

'And Erik Berggren—what did he do with his life?'

Sofie perked up again.

'I know. I talked to his former boss at the sawmill this morning, Mark Martikainen, eighty-two years old, but his mind is still sharp as anything. He could clearly remember Erik as he had been forced to fire him. It was apparently uncomfortable afterward since he worked so closely with Erik's mother.'

'Why did he get sacked?'

'Well, according to Mark, Erik would spread disquiet wherever he went. Other employees felt uneasy when he was there. He stared too much, he said.'

Roger laughed drily. 'Ha, I wonder what the union would say if we started sacking people for staring ... '

'Hmmm ... well, after that job he didn't do much of anything,' Sofie continued. 'He lived as a recluse, drank booze, but didn't use anything harder—that we know of. Retired on health grounds.'

Arne Norman sat down at the big, beech table and looked encouragingly at Roger, who was stubbornly drawing stickmen in his notepad.

'Did your visit to the care home turn up anything?'

Roger lifted his gaze.

'No, not much. No one had seen or heard anything whatsoever. The orderly who saw the woman at the entrance couldn't provide a better description than before, but she seemed certain she had seen her just after Magnus arrived. At about ten past four.'

'How does she know that?'

'Because she normally meets another orderly sneaking a smoke at the back of the building every day at four on the dot, and they had just finished their smokes and were about to head back in when they saw the woman pass.'

Arne grimaced and shrugged his shoulders.

'It could have been anyone. Women are rarely that violent.'

He unconsciously allowed his gaze to fall on Sofie, who was shyly looking down at the table.

'Well, we're done for today, I think.' Arne pushed out his chair and stood up. Sofie accompanied him out of the room.

Magnus looked at Roger.

'What do you say we go and check out the old family farm at Flaxenvik?'

Roger nodded.

10

Linn switched on the coffee maker—she didn't like the taste and rarely drank more than a couple of mouthfuls—but she liked the sound the machine made. It was soothing to hear it spluttering and rattling, and it smelled delicious. Funnily enough, the same smell had made her want to throw up when she had been pregnant. They were both asleep now, breathing heavily through their colds in their respective bedrooms.

Linn sat down at the computer and relaxed. While Googling

for therapist jobs, she carefully sipped the hot drink. Granted, she already had a job as a cognitive therapist at Huddinge Hospital, but it was too difficult working full time with two three-year-olds. She was exhausted and frankly a little sick of all the depressed patients crying and feeling bad. It was impossible to deny that a lot of them had no more than shitty little problems that they could quite easily deal with without her help. The worst kind was the over-achiever—they would cry because they didn't have time to make apple sauce with fruit from their garden in the autumn or because they didn't have time to make clothes for their kids by hand. It drove her mad.

Both she and Magnus wanted nothing more than to be at home together, but their everyday lives were constantly being propelled forward at speed. When she thought about how little time they had off with the kids and each other, her mood sank like stone.

She sipped the bitter contents of the mug and her thoughts returned to the macabre case Magnus was investigating.

Why had the murderer burnt their victims? She wished she could look at the material pertaining to the investigation, check out the photographs. It might make the bizarre slightly more comprehensible to her. Magnus had told her lots, of course, but pictures could tell a great deal more. There was one thing she was sure of: whoever had done it had a special relationship with boiling water. The burning was no coincidence. She leaned over her coffee mug and murmured to herself:

'Burning ... removing gender.'

Is it their sexuality you want to get at? Is that what needs to be destroyed? But why an old lady and her son with learning difficulties? It doesn't make sense ...

The angry sound of her mobile phone interrupted her. *Where was the headset?* She got up and rooted through the cupboard in the kitchen filled with wires in confusion. She didn't want to get brain cancer—but her headphones were never to be found when she needed them. When she spotted that it was Magnus calling she answered anyway.

'Hi.'

'Hi, it's just me. How are things?'

'Good. Moa and Elin are taking a nap.'

'I was just calling to say that I'll be home a little late today. Roger and I have to go out to Åkersberga again.'

She pulled a disappointed expression and was glad he couldn't see it.

'What are you going to do there?' she said.

'We're going to check out an abandoned farm a little bit outside of town.'

'When will you be home?'

'Seven, half past at the latest, so I can help put Moa and Elin to bed.'

'Good. Bye.'

'Kisses.'

Linn looked out of the kitchen window. She knew that Magnus did what he could to get home early, but right now while the kids were ill it was really hard.

For some reason she began to think about when they had met for the first time. It had been at the hospital, back when she had been on placement. She had been sitting with her lunch tray in the canteen and there he had been standing—an enormous being with a slightly arched back. 'Is this space taken?' he had asked, and for a brief second she had gazed into the most fantastically green eyes she had ever seen. In the same moment, she had known that she would spend the rest of her life with him. His eyes were so fascinating that it had taken her almost ten minutes to notice that his hand was bandaged. The result of a cut from an especially rough match while playing for the police bandy team.

The day after he had rung her doorbell and a couple of minutes later they had been lying naked, intertwined in amongst muddy boots and old trainers. There was passion and there was no doubt.

It took a couple of months for them to move in together. It still felt good after three years of small children and no sleep. It might not be as passionate as in the beginning, but she loved him deeply even though she sometimes got annoyed because he was a bit slow. Then she would fantasize about leaving altogether. Doing what she had once dreamed of doing—travelling around India with a worn leather strap round her wrist or working with lions in Africa. Of course she could have ended up more or less anywhere in life, but she had chosen safety and she'd done it because deep down she needed it.

11

'Isn't it idyllic?' Roger nodded toward a pair of brown Icelandic ponies placidly grazing in a paddock. The green hillocks rolled toward the surrounding forest and in the soft evening sunlight the landscape looked like it had come straight out of a saga. Their white Toyota had just turned off Margretelundsvägen and was now driving toward Flaxenvik.

Extended holiday cottages and new builds were scattered here and there among the trees, but their plots were often so undisturbed that you could dance outside naked if you wanted to.

'I could never live this far away from it all,' said Magnus.

'I could—but not alone.' Roger paused. His greatest dream was to have a family of his own, but he was ever so slowly giving up on the idea. Having just turned forty-five, there was little sign of a relationship on the horizon, let alone children.

Magnus said nothing. He put some *snus* inside his lip and

turned up the radio. They ought to be there soon.

At the same moment he had the thought, Roger pointed toward a barn and a red farmhouse on a hill ahead of them.

'Could that be Berggren's old farm?'

'It must be—it was supposed to be by the cove.'

'What a location!' Roger exclaimed with a tinge of jealousy.

'The plot must be worth a lot—odd that they haven't sold the lot if they're hardly ever here.'

'Who owns the place again?'

'Eva and Per Boström, both dentists in Vaxholm. I spoke to the woman. She said no one has been here for several years. They were going to do the place up, but apparently never got round to it.'

The car's wheels skidded in the gravel as they drove up the hill.

The farmhouse was well built but in a sad state of disrepair. The transomed and mullioned windows were broken and the green front door was banging in the gentle sea breeze.

Roger shook his head in shock.

'It's got incredible potential—why do they just leave it alone?'

'No idea. Eva Boström said they work a lot. I suppose they've simply not had time.'

'Idiots,' Roger muttered acidly, as he opened the car door and got out.

As Magnus got out, he wondered what point there was in visiting. It was many years since the dog had been tortured—albeit here and in many ways similar to the way Erik Berggren had been—but there would be nothing in the way of worthwhile evidence here and now. Anyone could understand that. The house had also been owned by a different family for many years.

Roger, on the other hand, seemed to be completely enchanted by the house's potential. He pushed his pocketknife into one of the window frames.

'Hmm, yes—you can't get hold of timber like this any longer.'

'Shall we start inside the barn before it gets completely dark?' Magnus said.

'Yes, of course.' Roger reluctantly allowed himself to be torn away from his real-estate dreams and they walked across the gravel to the barn. Thin strands of light penetrated into the building, revealing a pair of dilapidated stalls in which there were things hung up that they assumed were horse accessories. They took a couple of steps into the darkness. The building had a dirt floor and along the walls were one or two steel buckets and a dirty old kitchen chair. In the corner there was a huge pile of old hay.

Roger lowered his voice:

'Have you got a torch? It's so damn dark.'

Magnus shook his head.

'No, hang on—I've got one on my mobile ... '

He pulled his phone clumsily out of his pocket, but when he lit the torch the phone gave a distorted beep and died.

'Sorry, the battery ran out.'

'Never mind, we've probably seen everything there is to see, let's check out the farmhouse.' Roger was keen to leave the dark, damp building, but just as they turned round to leave they heard a slight rustle from behind them.

'What was that?' Roger turned round to face the hayloft.

'What?'

'Pah, I guess it was just a rat—you normally find them in hay.'

Magnus bent slowly to the floor and picked up a stone that he threw forcefully toward the wall of the barn behind the mound of hay.

As expected, the thud smoked out a rat that quickly ran away along the wall before vanishing behind one of the buckets.

Roger laughed in embarrassment.

'Fuck, Kalo—I was almost scared. I thought there might be someone lying in the hay or something like that.

Magnus grinned.

'Just a disgusting little rat.'

When they returned to the courtyard it was almost completely dark, but they were both eager to make sure they had time to search the house before leaving so they made haste toward the building. Neither of them noticed the figure slowly rising out of the hay behind them, nor did they notice the hate-filled eyes that followed them carefully through a crack in the barn wall.

Magnus ran his hand over the old wood stove. The rusty contraption was the only thing indicating that the house had once been a home. Apart from the stove, there was not a single furnishing. Somehow, the house reminded him of where he had lived as a child, but this one was rather less pleasant.

He glanced at Roger, who was thoughtfully wandering around the creaking wooden floor. There was a kitchen and another small room. The wallpaper was peeling off the walls and it was obvious that nothing had been done to the place since the Berggren family had moved out in the nineties.

Magnus turned to the door.

'Come on, let's go. There's nothing to see here.'

It was nearly seven o'clock and Linn shouldn't be forced to put the kids to bed by herself. At the very least he wanted to be there to give them their medicine before they went to sleep.

'Wait, there's something pretty bloody strange here.' Roger cast his eyes around the room again.

Magnus looked at him quizzically.

'What? I can't see anything.'

'Check out the crap on the floor, Magnus. Someone's been here.'

'Yes, us,' Magnus replied impatiently.

Roger quietly bit his lip and cracked his neck.

'Yes, perhaps.'

On the way home Magnus drove exactly six kilometres over the speed limit. He had once heard that car manufacturers set speedometers a little on the low side so that drivers would drive at the legal speed. Astonished at the car industry's conscience, he had tested this himself by driving back and forth past a speed checker and it had turned out to be true. So he now always drove extra fast to even things out.

Once they were well onto the motorway back to town, he turned to Roger.

'We may have to work a little tomorrow if we're going to get anywhere.'

Roger looked a little upset.

'It's a Saturday.'

'I know, but we can't let this go cold. There's a lot we need to go through. Witness statements, the forensics. The person who did this to Erik and Gunvor won't take the weekend off.'

Roger nodded self-consciously.

'True, but can't we start after lunch? I've got something important to do in the morning.'

Magnus raised an eyebrow in surprise, but his colleague stared straight ahead at the dark road, as if the subject was resolved.

A little while later he dropped Roger off at his apartment on Sankt Paulsgatan on Södermalm and headed to Aspudden.

When he got home the lights were off. Even though it was only a couple of minutes past eight, Linn and the girls were already in bed asleep. Magnus was filled with a strong sense of tenderness. He spread out some pillows on either side of the bed so that Moa and Elin wouldn't fall onto the floor, and then he curled up on the sofa in the living room. His legs felt like they were filled with fizzy drinks. It would be another sleepless night.

PART 2

12

The day that Carlos Fernandez was pulled out of his car at work and beaten to the ground had started like any other. He had drunk coffee, eaten bread and ham, kissed his wife on the cheek and wondered what to wear. Blissfully, he was still unaware that his life was about to take a grim turn.

It wasn't especially warm outside, but despite this he had the car window rolled down and the fresh breeze tickled his face when he turned on the ignition. His cheeks were newly shaven and the faint scent of cologne blended with the smell of wet tarmac. The kiosk owner further down the street was pulling out sack after sack filled with cigarette butts and ice cream wrappers, some children in school uniforms were chattering noisily and a lorry driver was unloading heavy boxes filled with meat outside the butcher's. Everything was as normal—even the stray dogs seemed to be following their predetermined route around his neighbourhood.

Together with his brother, Carlos owned a bookstand in Plaza Dorrego—one of the most charming squares in central Buenos Aires. They had started the company as students, but had soon realized that they could in fact make a living from it. It had been a great relief for them, and just as great a disappointment for their parents who had reacted with anger. But over time, their parents' irritated talking-tos had given way to resigned sighs. Now the days seemed to chug along like bubbles in a coffee machine for the two brothers. In their little nook behind the stacks of books they would drink tea and discuss politics, read books and search for exciting new releases for their customers. When they returned home to their expectant wives late in the evening, it was with the knowledge that life was good.

There were several stands around the square selling handicrafts, including silver goods and embroidered cloths. There was also a circular stage surrounded by large flowerpots. Every Saturday there was tango dancing on the stage. There would be on this day too—but Carlos Fernandez wouldn't experience it. His brother had rather inconsiderately told one of his acquaintances that Carlos didn't like the military junta.

When Carlos saw his wife again, almost two years had passed. He weighed fifty-eight kilos and was suffering from serious dehydration. His body was covered in scars, broken bones had healed wrongly and his right arm was broken. But the worst injuries were on the inside. He was a wounded man, who had lost part of his soul and all the joy in his life.

Naturally he tried to make a fresh start. But the memories from the junta's dungeons whirred around inside him like lost rings of Saturn. He would increasingly stay in bed until late in the afternoon. When he eventually got up he would listlessly wander around the apartment. There was no logic to what he had been subjected to, no solution. His body was free but his soul was a prisoner. The simplest of chores took days to accomplish. A mean comment might lead to a breakdown. His wife struggled on, but eventually she couldn't carry her depressed husband any further. It felt as if he was pulling her down, revelling in an eternal darkness. With a heavy heart, she left him—even she had been affected by what had happened.

That was when Carlos made a decision. The military wouldn't break him, he would move to a new country and make a new life for himself. There would be no more torture or any of the other things he had gone through. He would repress it so deeply within himself that it would eventually disappear.

Karina Sunfors was completely unaware of what Carlos had gone through when she met him almost twenty years later. She saw a man who was different from every other man she had ever met. A man with a sorrowful gaze and long, dark eyelashes. She was forty-two years old, but he made her feel like a recently smitten teenager. In turn, Carlos smiled for the first time in years. Karina made him forget and he decided to never tell anyone what had happened to him. Of course, she wondered why his body was scarred and why he sometimes winced when she stroked him, but he explained it away saying he had been in a car accident back home in Argentina. Karina didn't believe him. She would be woken by his tortured, heart-rending cries at night, and she could see the pain in his eyes. But she said nothing. It was as if she was waiting for him to say something—something that explained everything. She so desperately wanted him to come to her and confide his grief in her, but he didn't.

Not until the day they went to Elgiganten in Arninge to buy a new toaster. That was when it happened—but it didn't turn out the way she had expected.

13

Carlos had slept badly. His night had been nightmare-ridden and it had been awful, showing him once again what it had been like in the military junta's basement more than thirty years before. In the dream he was beaten bloody with an electrical cable and his arm crushed by the pounding of the baton.

'How about one of those red toasters? They're kind of cool.'

Karina's voice cut through the mist. He looked at her gratefully. Everyday activities were his salvation. He filled every minute with something commonplace to prevent his thoughts from dwelling on the past.

'What if we change the colour of the kitchen? Then it won't work ... ' he smiled.

Karina shrugged her shoulders.

49

'We've just repainted. Toasters don't last forever, surely?' she said in a tone indicating that she truly wanted to toast bread in a red machine.

Carlos considered the options and concluded it wasn't worth arguing over.

'Then let's get a red one,' he said cheerfully.

It was at the till that it happened. As Karina was signing the receipt, Carlos allowed his gaze to sweep across the electric razors on a shelf a little further into the store. At first he saw the man diagonally from the side and moved on, but then he felt the knot in his stomach. He looked at the man again—he was twisting and turning a shaver. Granted he was furrowed and grey, but it was without a doubt him.

Carlos felt himself turn to ice. He had seen Pedro Estrabou's face in his dreams a thousand times and he had sworn revenge just as many times. Now there he was—Pedro Estrabou was just five metres away from him at Elgiganten in Arninge, and he felt completely paralysed.

Karina turned around and put her hand on his shoulder.

'Time to go?'

He winced.

'Yes.' He took Karina's hand and quickly walked toward the car. His facial expression had changed, he looked pale and sweaty.

Karina looked at him in concern.

'Are you all right?'

Carlos looked over his shoulder. Pedro Estrabou was still standing there, examining razors. When they got out into the car park, he said:

'Get in the car Karina.'

'What?'

'Get in the car.'

Karina's eyes widened in astonishment. She had never seen him like this.

'What is it?'

Carlos held the car door open.

'I'll tell you later. Get in.'

It was impossible to mistake the desperation in his voice.

Karina got in in silence and a second later so did Carlos. His eyes were wide open, locked on the entrance to Elgiganten.

'Listen—a man is going to come out of there soon. We're going to follow him and see where he goes.'

'Are you kidding?' Karina laughed nervously, but one look at Carlos made her stop.

'Who is it?'

For a brief moment Carlos felt stupid. Why hadn't he told Karina? Why had he held back such a large part of his life from her?

But he knew why. If she had known what had happened to him in Argentina they wouldn't have been able to live a carefree life together. The memories of torture would have resurfaced all the time and destroyed their relationship in the same way they had ended his marriage back home. He had dwelled and dwelled until his wife had had enough and left him. He didn't blame her—it had been too much and she had become his psychologist rather than his lover. No, it was better this way. The things Pedro Estrabou and his pals had subjected him to were not going to devour the rest of his life—which was why he continued to serve up his half-baked lie.

'It's the man who injured me.'

'You mean it was him you had your crash with?'

The opening she offered was too good to ignore.

'Yes, exactly. He got away, he has to be stopped.'

Karina nodded. She didn't know what to think, but didn't have long to do it because suddenly Carlos hissed between clenched teeth:

'That's him.'

Karina looked at the man who had just come out into the car park. He looked like anyone else. Around fifty-five years old, thin with a furrowed face and small chin. It was not apparent that he had South American ancestry because his skin was pale and his eyes also looked bright. She guessed they were blue.

'He's driving off. He's leaving.' Carlos spat the words out and turned on the engine.

There wasn't much traffic at the shopping centre, so they had no problems following. Pedro Estrabou drove onto the motorway. Carlos was glued behind him.

Karina glanced at Carlos. Why did she get the feeling he wasn't telling the truth?

'What are we going to do after?' she asked cautiously.

He was quiet. He hadn't thought that far yet.

'Don't know,' he replied tersely.

'Are you going to report him to the police?'

'I said I don't know.'

The red car took a right toward Mörby centrum shopping mall. It drove past the ugly seventies shopping centre and took another right.

They were in a residential area and Carlos increased the distance between the cars to avoid discovery.

Suddenly, Pedro Estrabou pulled up onto the drive of a fifties detached house with beige render.

'What do we do now?' said Karina.

Carlos parked the car by the pavement. He was breathing worryingly hard—panting.

Karina looked at him in concern.

'Are you okay?'

He grimaced in pain and grabbed hold of his left arm.

'I can't brea ... I think ... having a heart attack.'

Karina couldn't quite recall what happened when she got him to the hospital. All she knew was that she had driven faster than she had ever done before and that she had done it well.

'Are you Carlos's wife?'

The nurse gave her a friendly look.

'No, his partner.' Karina gulped.

'All the same. He's going to be okay,' the nurse smiled.

Karina could feel the tears inside her. All her energy was gone—all her will. Carlos was not allowed to leave her. Tears began to run down her cheeks.

'Go in and see him if you like.'

She quickly dried her face with her sleeve. Her legs were shaky when she got up from the old sagging sofa in the waiting room.

The nurse looked deep into her eyes and repeated in a calm voice:

'He's going to get better. Trust me.'

Carlos was sleeping deeply with his hand on his forehead. Karina looked at him. His soft grey locks framed his lively, wrinkled face that was a witness to everything he had done and everything that he was.

What was he hiding from her? And why? She loved him so much she was almost breaking apart.

Finally, he opened his eyes and saw her. They looked at each other for a long time, whirling around and finding closeness. Eventually he whispered to her:

'If I tell you something, do you promise not to leave me?'

'I love you.' Her voice trembled.

'Yes, but do you promise to stay?'

'I've been looking for you my whole life. I could have married and had kids like everyone else, but I was looking for something else. When I found you, I knew what it was. Do you really think I would leave you?'

Carlos closed his eyes, absorbing her words. They were relieving and comforting.

'I was ... was tortured by the military junta in their basement,' he began, uncertainly. 'The man we were following was the worst of the lot. He kept on beating and beating. I thought he would kill me. It was more than forty degrees, unbearable ... I couldn't breathe'.

He fell silent—couldn't bring himself to say more. Karina squeezed his hand. Then she said cautiously, her eyes filled with tears:

'What do we do now? Do we report him to the police?'

'I don't know. I want him to die.'

PART 3

14

Roger took down his wet umbrella and came into Magnus's office. He was elated. There was a big plaster on his cheek and his hands were covered in pieces of medical tape.

Magnus set his glass of water down so heavily that the contents splashed over his notes.

'What's happened to you?'

'Ferret.'

Roger sounded like he was suffering.

'Yes—I bought a ferret this morning. I'm a lonely man, what else can I say? But never mind that. I came across something—last night I couldn't sleep so I came back here. I wanted to go through a few things and see what I could find out about the Berggrens.'

'And what did you find out?'

'Well, I started by checking out Erik Berggren's dad Gösta a bit more, and it turned out that he worked in Argentina at the end of the fifties.'

'Oh?' Magnus looked drowsy. Roger continued:

'Yes. Gösta apparently worked on some railway project in a town called La Rioja. But what's interesting is the reason he came back home.' Roger paused for effect before saying:

'He was accused of rape.'

Magnus whistled.

'You don't ... '

'Yep. Gösta was suspected of having raped a fourteen-year-old girl from an upper-class family. If she hadn't been rich the rape probably wouldn't have become a police matter at the time, but there was a report made.'

Magnus gazed in wonder.

'Was he convicted?'

'No, he fled back to Sweden. The Argentinian police tried to extradite him once, but there was some kind of foul-up and since there was no particularly strong interest from their side, nothing more happened. I found it all in our own records, but there's no detailed information. Not even the name of the girl.'

They looked at each other. Magnus broke the silence.

'You don't have any further details?'

'No, but it sounds as if we ought to look into this more closely doesn't it? Perhaps it's got nothing to do with the violence against Erik and Gunvor, but you never know.' Magnus ran his hands through his hair so that it stood on end.

Roger nodded.

'In any case, it's an unusually high number of brutal incidents in the same family. There's only one problem. Gösta is dead.'

Magnus shrugged his shoulders.

'I guess we'll have to start by finding the girl from La Rioja ... she must be ... ' Magnus thought for moment. ' ... around seventy by now, if she's even still alive. We can call the police in Argentina right away. Do you speak any Spanish?'

Roger grimaced.

'Did you think I might? We'll have to try English, or get hold of an interpreter.'

Within a short space of time they managed to find the phone number of the La Rioja police. While Magnus was dialling the long number, he wondered how he should phrase things. He had never been one for speaking.

'Policía de la provincia de La Rioja, Claudio Marcelo Revuelta hablo,' said a soft man's voice when the phone was picked up.

'Hello, I'm calling from the Swedish police. We need your help in a murder case.'

There was silence for a moment at the other end, then he heard the man's voice again.

'Excuse me for a minute,' the man said in perfect English.

Magnus felt like an idiot.

A hum of chatter was audible in the background and then a new male voice came onto the line.

'Hello, I'm Osvaldo Ortiz, Jeje del Comando Superior. How can I help you?'

Stumbling, Magnus explained what he wanted. Somehow, it felt like he was groping in the dark. How could a suspected rape in Argentina in the fifties have anything to do with the murder of Erik Berggren? Despite this, he wanted to get hold of the woman, if only to rule her out of the inquiry.

'Oh, that rape happened a long time ago,' said Ortiz hesitantly.

'Yes, but it is very important for us to know more about this woman.' Magnus emphasized each and every word to ensure the Argentinian police would understand how serious a matter it was.

'We'll see what we can do. I'll call you back.'

Magnus hung up and leaned back into his chair. He looked at Roger who was sitting on the other side of the desk.

'Well, now all we can do is wait and see. They're going to try and find her for us. How about a quick review and then we'll wrap up? Moa and Elin are getting better, so we thought we'd do something today.'

'Let's do the review on Monday. It's already four o'clock so let's go home,' Roger said decisively. It was obvious that he was being drawn back to his ferret.

15

The autumn sun cast its golden rays onto the façades of the houses as an elated Magnus drove between the functionalist homes on Torsten Alms gata. The Argentinian line of inquiry was definitely interesting. He cast his gaze over the beige buildings. All the same but in slightly differing hues of beige and brown. Three storeys, sometimes four, but never more. Front doors with round wooden handles, balconies made from green corrugated steel. Their own building wasn't quite as charming. It was a gigantic thing from the eighties set slightly back from the other houses.

A pile of rubbish had gathered on their garden patio. Toys, sledges and old cardboard boxes that didn't fit inside or that were waiting to be thrown away fought for space in an area just a couple of metres square. He could see the detritus peeking above the top of the rail as he approached.

They had been living in their three-bed apartment in Aspudden for almost five years and Magnus was sick of it. Both he and Linn had thought it was great to live so close to the city centre before they had children, but now they just wanted to get away from there. Preferably to somewhere that the children could run around in the garden and where the neighbours made nice small talk about the weather when they popped out for their morning papers. The more he thought about it, the more he hated living here. Someone had stolen fuel from their car on several occasions and as if that wasn't enough, a middle-aged man a few floors up appeared to be dealing. Youths would be knocking on the man's door at all hours and they never seemed to stay longer than a couple of minutes.

The same amount of time it took to exchange cash for drugs, Magnus reflected bitterly.

If someone had suggested to him a few years earlier that

a house in the suburbs would be his dream, he would have laughed himself hoarse. He might even have emitted a patronising comment including the words 'bourgeois' and 'splendid', but he now found his thoughts would increasingly often drift off to houses and lush areas of greenery. Now he wanted to live in the same fashion he had as a child, in a house with lilacs and apple trees. It would be good for everyone. In addition, he and Linn would have more time if the kids could run around and play in the garden. He might even get an old boat to mess around with—he had always dreamed of doing it. Perhaps an aft cabin boat? The idea put him in a better mood.

The rest of the day was just as calm as he had hoped, even if he couldn't completely stop thinking about the Berggren family. There was such brutality in the acts of violence—a real chill.

They grilled sausages on a disposable barbecue in the Vinterviken Park, just five minutes from home. The kids were in a great mood and were cheerfully jumping around among the tussocks while Lake Mälaren glittered like a mass of diamonds in the sunshine. The leafy trees formed an autumn red ceiling canopy above them and rays of sunshine trickled through the foliage onto the frosty ground, as if they wanted to warm them up.

16

Magnus entered the surgical ward at Danderyd Hospital and looked around. Gunvor Berggren had been moved from the emergency ward and he assumed that her condition was more stable. Outside her room was the officer on guard, Astrid Flodin, who was reading a book. Her glasses had slipped a long way down her crooked nose. When she caught sight of Magnus her face lit up and she gave him a friendly smile.

'Hi Astrid. Everything okay here?'

'Absolutely. Gunvor has been a little worried, but that's probably no surprise after what she's been through. Otherwise everything has been fine to be honest. But she doesn't seem to like big people—as soon as a nurse of greater stature enters the room she hisses that they are ugly fat flies, screams and acts up. You're unlikely to get much sense out of her.'

Magnus opened the door and stepped inside. Gunvor Berggren was sitting in a reclining position in bed with a yellow woollen hospital blanket covering her. She had bruises under both her eyes. Magnus was struck by how small and slight she was, like a bird famished by winter. A drip was attached to her thin wrist with a substantial bandage. When she saw Magnus her eyes immediately began to cast daggers.

'I don't want any food!' she hissed.

'I'm called Magnus and I'm a policeman. Can I have a word?' he said with a smile.

'Yes, talk away.' Gunvor glared at him.

'Someone has been unkind to you—can you tell me about it?'
Magnus sat down on a chair beside the bed and smiled again.
The old woman looked confused and Magnus tried again.

'Someone has done harm to you, Gunvor ... '

'It hurts,' she whimpered, and her hand moved awkwardly to
her head.

'Yes, I understand. Do you know who did this to you, Gunvor?'

'Can I have soup? I like that.' Gunvor looked at Magnus
expectantly, who in turn tried a stricter tone of voice.

'Who hurt you, Gunvor?'

'You're stupid. Where's my mum? She's kind.'

Gunvor cast an innocent and quizzical glance at Magnus,
who sighed in resignation.

'I don't know, Gunvor. But thanks for letting me speak to you.'

He took her hand and held it in his. She gently squeezed back
and grinned broadly.

'You're sweet, you are.'

'You too, Gunvor. Take care now.'

He picked up his jacket from the chair by the door, said
goodbye to Astrid and walked away along the corridor.

He was about to open the lift doors when someone put a
hand on his shoulder. When he turned round he saw a stylish
woman of around forty wearing her dark hair up and dressed in
a white doctor's coat.

'Sorry if I frightened you. I'm Cia Herdik, Gunvor's doctor.
Can I have a moment?'

' ... of course.'

'Astrid told me who you were and I had something I wanted
to ... ' She looked around anxiously. 'Come with me, we can talk
in my office.'

They entered a typical consultation room further down the
corridor. Magnus sat down on the green couch, taking care not
to wrinkle the protective layer of paper. Cia Herdik sat down on

a chair, her hands clasped in her lap.

'Yes, I've examined Gunvor further and I thought you might be interested to hear what I've concluded.'

'Naturally. I thought one of my colleagues had already spoken to you. We must have dropped the ball somewhere.'

'Yes, maybe. Anyway, we've previously noted that Gunvor was under the influence of some sort of painkiller when she was admitted here. I think she was given a mixture of sedatives and painkillers, perhaps a blend of morphine and midazolam ... or maybe diazepam, the effect is more or less the same.'

'Why a mixture?'

'To keep her awake during the act itself—that's my bet.'

'Isn't it hard to get the dose right?'

'Not if you've got medical knowledge.'

Magnus nodded thoughtfully.

'Do you have to be a doctor?'

'No, it's often nurses who administer these things—even orderlies sometimes.'

The crease between Magnus's eyebrows deepened.

'So our murderer may work in healthcare?'

'Yes, but you can learn this stuff too.'

Magnus sighed.

'Of course. What about the injuries—can you tell me anything about them?'

'Well, she's been a bit unlucky.' Herdik curled her lips as if she had said something distasteful. 'To get third degree burns—which she has—the water must have been poured over her slowly. Typically you only get second-degree burns from boiling water. Third degree burns are normally down to other causes—hot toffee or something like that.'

'It looked very bad ... is she going to survive?'

Cia Herdik held out her hands.

'At her age, tiny things can be critical. She feels well at the moment, but it could just as easily turn and be the beginning of the end.'

Magnus got up dejectedly and said farewell to the doctor, but after just a couple of steps he turned round.

'Sorry, just another question ... a completely personal matter. I've had a strange sensation in my legs—it feels as if ants are walking around in them. What do you think it might be?'

Cia Herdik raised her eyebrows.

'It could be all manner of things. You should get checked out.'

'I know, but you've no idea what it might be?'

She shrugged her shoulders.

'Perhaps it's something completely harmless or maybe it's nerve damage, MS, well, it could be anything. You should make an appointment with your GP.'

Magnus nodded in disappointment. Typical doctor being so diffuse.

'Thanks—it's tough finding the time.'

'Just don't leave it too long.' She gave him a serious look before disappearing into her office.

Magnus stayed where he was for a couple of seconds, before twitching his head and brushing away the thoughts. Nerve damage? That was too much to deal with right now.

17

On the way to the CID, Magnus stopped at the Pressbyrån by the university. He bought a large coffee and a cheese sandwich on rye. When he returned to the car, thoughts were whirring around inside his head. Moa and Elin had woken up a total of seven times during the night and he could feel an aching pressure point between his eyes. He gave a wide yawn, took a large gulp of coffee out of the paper cup and forced his thoughts back to the investigation.

Demented Gunvor had been tortured with boiling hot water—exactly like Erik with his learning difficulties—and the attacker would probably have killed her too if Magnus hadn't tramped into her room at that moment. But the question was why? The old lady was hardly a threat to anyone.

Of course, another dilemma was Gösta. The fact that he had raped a girl in Argentina in the fifties didn't have to be significant. But at the same time, there might be some kind of revenge motive at play.

He took a bite out of his sandwich. He couldn't put it together—and to top it all there was the complication of a thirty-year-old report of a dog burnt and killed.

He pinched the bridge of his nose. He needed to find out more about the Berggren family. He sincerely hoped that Erik's cousin Annika would be able to help him when she returned from her business trip.

A little later when he turned off toward the CID car park, Gunvor reappeared in his thoughts and at the very moment he was keying in the door code it came to him—the staff at the casualty department had said straight after the assault that Gunvor had been talking about a big, disgusting fly in the room non-stop. At the time, he had barely registered it, but now their words echoed in his mind with renewed significance. Astrid Flodin had also said that Gunvor had been babbling about big, fat flies as soon as any of the bigger nurses came into her room, hadn't she? What if Gunvor meant big women whenever she was talking about fat flies? And what if it was a woman he had interrupted when he entered Gunvor's room?

Suddenly it felt like the pieces were falling into place. A woman in dark clothing had also been seen leaving the care home just after he had arrived. Of course, this was all circumstantial, but Magnus felt convinced that the murderer was a woman—a woman who had trained as a nurse.

18

The copper door at CID was so heavy that it could easily crush a person if it fell out of its frame. But it didn't—instead it sat there, as if on a throne—acting as a wall between those within and those outside. The strong fittings and the heavy rivets meant it stood out compared with the other doors on the street. For anyone who took the time to stop and look at the gleaming door, all they saw was weight and stability—but behind the closed doors there was currently only restlessness and worry, at least in the homicide unit. Almost everyone there could sense the unpleasant atmosphere.

Roger looked even more mangled than he had done on Saturday, if that was possible. His hands and forearms were covered in plasters and scratch marks. Sofie raised her eyebrows in concern.

'You've had a tetanus shot I take it? You know you can get tetanus from ferret bites?'

'Perhaps I should.' His face contorted into a pained grimace.

'You have to. Where did you get the ferret?'

'An advert online. It'll sort itself out, it's just not used to me yet.'

Sofie nodded sympathetically. Magnus interrupted with a laugh.

'What's the terror called?'

'Oskar.'

'Oh really—that's an intere...'

Arne Norman interrupted their conversation by loudly and demonstratively blowing his nose. He put his handkerchief back in the pocket of his white jacket and pushed the pad of paper across the table in front of him as if to signal that the time for nonsense was over.

'I've read what you've come up with and it's not good enough.

Not one bit. We have a highly unpleasant murder and a violent attack on our hands. The press have begun to show interest.' He paused to let his words sink in before continuing:

'Magnus, if you think the murderer is a woman, make sure you get hold of better evidence to support that.' He spread his hands as he looked at the group.

'And this girl who was raped in Argentina—is she really relevant to the investigation? Is it even certain she was raped? It feels like you're barking up the wrong tree. Don't you have any firmer leads to follow up on?'

Roger hesitated for a moment, then he said slowly:

'We think the girl is important... '

Magnus interrupted: 'Yes, because if this Argentinian girl has been subjected to sexual violence then she has that in common with Erik and Gunvor. And all of them are connected to Gösta. Okay, perhaps the rape has nothing to do with the crime, but we still have to check.'

Magnus looked at Arne with a serious expression and the latter turned away.

'So find her then. What sort of contact have you made with them out there? Should I call and find out if anything is being done?'

Magnus feared that Arne's demanding manner might in fact have the opposite effect on the courteous Ortiz, so quickly countered, 'We've got good contacts down there—I'll call them after the meeting.'

Arne ran his hand over the tabletop. He looked dogged.

'Okay, let's do that. By the way, I got the results from the forensic examination of the cabin. There were fingerprints on a saucepan that probably contained the boiling water the victim was burnt with. The prints don't belong to Erik Berggren, so we're probably dealing with a careless attacker or someone who wants to be caught. Unfortunately they don't match anything in our database, so the perpetrator presumably has a clean record.'

Magnus furrowed his brow. It seemed strange to have made such an obvious mistake. The murderer seemed to have an agenda—would he or she really be so careless about easy things like fingerprints? Or was it just a madman they were dealing with after all? He had real trouble believing that.

Magnus didn't need to call Ortiz. A few minutes later when he sat down at his Mac, he saw he had already received an email from him.

He quickly glanced through the message. Ortiz had found out the name of the girl who was raped—she was called Domenique Estrabou and they knew which village to search for her in.

Magnus gave a start and felt joyfully restless. For a moment, he wanted to throw himself at the phone and call to offer his thanks, but he calmed down and decided to let the Argentinian police do their jobs in peace and quiet.

Ortiz had proven to be bloody efficient.

He sent an email instead, offering a simple thank you. He wrote that he was looking forward to receiving whatever they turned up.

19

A few hours later, Magnus stepped out of the building onto Kungsholmsgatan. The buildings looked even more grey than usual in the rainy weather, but not as grey and insipid as the people passing by.

When the door had closed behind him, he stopped and put a pouch of *snus* tobacco under his upper lip. He had given *snus* up when the kids had come along, but whenever he felt heated he would still buy a pack.

It began to drizzle. He quickly headed to the car park, pulling his mobile phone out of his back pocket and calling Linn. She answered after three rings. In the background he could hear the delighted cries of Moa and Elin.

'Hi, I'm on my way home now. Do you need me to get anything?'

'Err ... no, I don't think so. Actually, some formula—we don't have any left.'

'Nothing else?'

Linn thought for a moment.

'Wait ... bread, juice, milk, lactose-free milk for me and jam.'

'Raspberry?'

'Yes. When do you think you'll be back?'

'Around quarter past five. See you later.'

Magnus put his phone away. He had suddenly felt like someone was watching him. He turned round and looked at the car park—but there was no one there, just a tall woman going through a door further down the street. Magnus got into the car and turned on the engine.

20

Moa and Elin came running and their feet pounded the parquet floor like drumrolls.

'Hi Dad!' they shouted in unison.

Magnus put the shopping bags down on the floor and crouched. Both kids jumped neatly into his lap.

'Can you read *Bamse* to us, Dad?' said Elin.

Magnus grinned.

'Yes, of course. I just have to say hi to Mum first.'

'She's in the kitchen.'

Moa nodded sagely and said with satisfaction:

'She's actually making pancakes.'

The kids ran off into Moa's room where they were in the middle of a major construction project. All the books from the bookcase had been turned into a garage in the middle of the floor.

When Magnus came into the kitchen, Linn had her back to him and was laying the table.

'Hi darling,' she said cheerfully.

'Hi—how have things been here?'

'Good. Guess what—a girl who sometimes does cover at day care might be able to babysit for us sometimes.'

'Oh really—who's that?'

'A young girl called Amanda. I talked to her today—she seems nice. Then we could have some time to ourselves occasionally ... ' Linn looked at him meaningfully.

Magnus smiled broadly.

'Then we'll call her during the week so that she can come and visit.' He bent down and got the raspberry jam out of the bag.

Linn sat down at the table and watched him put the shopping into the fridge.

'How was work?'

'Okay, I think. But this case is so bloody strange Linn. This torture stuff feels so elaborate and then there's a whole bunch of stuff that I'm not even sure is related to the case.'

She looked curious.

' ... like what?'

'Well, like the dad in the family. Gösta. He seems to have been a real arse. He was suspected of raping a fourteen-year-old girl in Argentina at the end of the fifties.'

'Fuck,' Linn exclaimed in disgust. 'But it's so long ago—can it really have anything to do with the case? Is this dad even alive?'

Magnus shook his head. 'No, but Erik had no friends or even enemies so far as we can tell, so we'll have to dig into what we've got.'

Magnus looked at her and continued: 'And then there's a dog that was also burnt and killed in roughly the same way as Erik.'

'In the cabin at the allotment?' Linn looked surprised.

'No, no—it was found thirty years ago on their farm. You can see it's all very confusing.'

Linn put the pancakes on the table.

Elin had crept up behind Magnus and violently tugged his top.

'Dad, can you read to us now?'

'Yes, but first we should eat. Can you fetch Moa?'

Elin vanished and Magnus turned back to Linn. 'Let's talk more once the kids have gone to bed.'

She nodded.

Moa held on until ten o'clock and then fell asleep in protest at the foot of Elin's bed. Magnus and Linn sank into the sofa and Linn put her feet in Magnus's lap.

'Tell me more about Erik and his family.'

'We don't know much about them yet. It appears they lived a pretty isolated life. The neighbours we've got hold of—the people who lived close to them in Flaxenvik—don't seem to have had much to do with them.'

'And what about after they moved to town?'

'Same thing—people barely seem to remember them. They're a bit like shadows.'

Linn looked concerned. Magnus got up. 'I'm just going to put Moa in bed.'

He went into the sleeping girls' room. They were breathing calmly and almost seemed completely well. Magnus carried Moa to her own room and wedged a few books between the mattress and the edge of the bed.

It was a long time since either of the children had fallen out of bed, but he wanted to be certain. When he was done he looked at her with a smile. Then he slouched into the kitchen and turned on the kettle.

Linn was still on the sofa and was in the middle of frantically jotting something on the back of a newspaper when he returned with mugs of tea. When she was done, she leaned back and stretched.

'I've been giving some thought to your case … At first one might have assumed it was a sexual sadist, but given the victims are relatives I don't think that any longer. Sexual sadists' preferences for victims are normally similar—different genders and ages like in this case are not their thing. There's probably another motive.'

Magnus leaned forward, interested. Linn continued.

'The violence is related to sex, but doesn't necessarily have to turn the attacker on—that's what I'm getting at.'

'There are no signs of sexual assault, either,' Magnus added.

'No, exactly, because this is something else.'

'Revenge?'

'Perhaps, and that makes this Gösta guy's rape history more interesting, doesn't it?'

Magnus thought for a while about what she had said.

'But Gösta is long gone—so are you suggesting it's some kind of blood revenge?'

Linn shrugged. 'Whatever it is, I think there's some kind of trauma at the bottom of it all.'

'Yes, probably,' said Magnus. 'But the funny thing is that the murderer hasn't tried to hide the crimes. It's as if we're meant to see what's been done and appreciate the details.'

Linn gazed into her steaming cup of tea.

'Yes … but you can probably count on it being someone who can appear quite normal as well.'

'What do you mean?'

'I mean that if he has sufficient self-control to calmly carry out a crime like this, he can probably keep his everyday life in check as well. It's probably someone who most people don't even notice.'

'Most people?'

'Yes, he's probably learned how to behave over the years to make sure his problem remains invisible. If he has a job, then he probably doesn't work very closely with anyone else.'

'What do you mean?'

'Well, they're definitely not a team player, put it like that.'

'Is there a diagnosis?'

'Mad. Absolutely raving mad.' Linn laughed loudly.

'Stop it.'

'Okay, if I was going to speculate on the basis of this flimsy evidence, I would guess he might have narcissistic psychopathic tendencies. That might explain the almost sacrificial ceremony surrounding the murder of Erik—he might have wanted to show off.'

Magnus rubbed his face. 'You mean a straightforward, normal murder isn't enough?'

'More or less.'

'Do you think our murderer has spent time in psychiatric care?'

'Maybe. You should look for men who have sought help from open psychiatric clinics. When he's been down, it's not impossible that he might have looked for help.'

Magnus grimaced in disappointment. 'It's practically impossible to check this kind of thing if we don't have a suspect. By the way, why do you keep saying "him" all the time—does it have to be a man?'

Now it was Linn's turn to look puzzled. 'Yes, do you think otherwise?'

'Don't know.'

'Yes, you do!' Linn grinned teasingly.

'Okay, I think it's a woman,' he replied reluctantly.

'I'm betting it's a man, probably in his prime. This has demanded physical strength. I would probably struggle to get a big bloke up onto a table.' Linn wiggled her toes to encourage Magnus to massage her feet.

'But do you think it is someone who lives alone?'

'I don't know, but if he or she has a partner then it's a complete disaster for them.'

'How so?'

'Well, people like this generally need complete adulation from their partner, and if they don't get it then they can easily become threatening. His girlfriend could end up in real trouble ...'

'Would he be violent?'

'Not necessarily, but he might punish her somehow—probably severely.'

'Has he taken it out on her before?'

'Probably.'

'Why would anyone stay with someone like that?'

Linn yawned and replied, her voice filled with irony: 'Well, you know, the classic "He says he loves me and would do anything for me, it was me who was stupid and deserved what I got, it wasn't his fault, blah blah blah ... "'

Linn pulled up her legs and sipped her tea while she looked at her husband over the edge of the blue mug.

He smacked his lips sceptically. 'What you're saying might be right, but I think it's a woman.'

Linn laughed. 'Well then, what do you need my theories for? You might of course be right—it might be a woman with gigantic biceps ... and a moustache,' she mumbled sarcastically while getting up. 'I'm going to bed.'

'Coming soon. I was just going to watch some TV—I need to think about something different.'

Magnus zapped from channel to channel and chose a music

gala for the starving in Africa. He stretched out on the sofa and fell asleep in exactly four minutes.

21

Linn opened her eyes; had she heard something? A thud? Her body and legs felt heavy. She listened again. It was probably nothing. She reached out for Magnus with her hand and groped under the duvet, but he wasn't there.

He must have fallen asleep on the sofa, she thought, at the same time as she pulled the duvet more tightly round her and tried to fall back asleep.

But there was the sound again, as if something was moving around the apartment. It was a faint crackling sound that she didn't recognize.

Her voice was barely audible when she whispered.

'Magnus?'

No reply. Silently, she pulled off the duvet and put her feet down on the cold parquet floor. She wished she hadn't been sleeping naked. It made her feel exposed and vulnerable. She could hear Magnus snoring in the living room now, but between him and her there was the hall—an impassable ocean. If she went into the hall she would be visible from every room.

She imagined a stoned burglar stabbing her in wild panic and shuddered.

A low hissing sound from the kitchen interrupted her runaway imagination. Why wasn't Magnus waking up?

She stayed where she was, sitting on the edge of the bed, unable to bring herself to do anything. She listened.

The kids! Suddenly it felt as if cold hands were squeezing her throat and making it hard for her to breathe.

She took a deep breath to calm down and crept off the bed. She carefully opened the bedroom door a couple of centimetres. Through the crack in the door she could see that the doors to Moa and Elin's bedrooms were still shut. She sighed in relief and hoped they wouldn't wake up and come running out.

The living-room door was open and she could see Magnus sleeping deeply on the sofa. Perhaps she just had the heebie-jeebies? She let her shoulders relax a little and took another couple of steps forward. There was a light on in the kitchen—she could see through the crack above the door. Hadn't she turned it off before bed?

The crackling sound was audible once again. She ground to a halt as if she was nailed to the floor. There was someone in the apartment, she was quite certain. She looked around desperately—what should she do? Magnus had borrowed her phone the evening before as his had run out of battery and now he had both their phones in the back pocket of his jeans. She couldn't call for help and if she called for him then he would wake up completely unprepared. She was shaking. Imagine if the thief was looking for valuables in the flat, imagine if he came out of the kitchen soon to go into the kids' rooms?

Linn made up her mind. She was going to show herself and frighten him off. That was normally what happened when burglars were discovered, or so she had read. *Just as long as it isn't a stoned madman, because then anything might happen.* Disturbed by the thought, she pushed the door wide open. She took a couple of uncertain steps into the hall and then coughed loudly to make the person in the kitchen aware of her presence. She waited. There was silence. Ominous silence.

'Who's there?' Her voice was weak.

What happened next she couldn't possibly have envisaged. At first she barely noticed the thin haze of smoke, emerging from under the door in spirals and slowly caressing the walls on the way up to the ceiling. But she saw the thicker smoke that followed—it coiled up the kitchen like toxic grey ringlets, forming a dark cloud beneath the ceiling.

Fire—there's a fire, she thought as she opened her mouth to shout.

'Fire! Magnus—there's a fire!'

She could now hear the flames raging and crackling with full force in the kitchen. She rushed across the hall to Elin's room and tore open the door. There was already a dense layer of smoke, but she could still pass under the poisonous smoke blanketing the room by crouching.

'Elin! Moa!' she screamed. Elin's small, three-year-old body was limp and heavy. Linn clasped her hard in her arms and ran on to Moa's room. She was alternating between sobbing and screaming.

Now Moa was sitting up in bed and crying. Linn tried to pick her up with her spare arm, but she fought back.

'Come on! There's a fire—we have to get out!'

'Stupid!' Moa shouted, half asleep, angry at being woken so abruptly. Finally, Magnus came, his strong arms lifting the screaming Moa out of bed and together they ran, bent double, into the hall to avoid the toxic smoke. Linn coughed violently.

'Down! You have to crawl!' Magnus shouted, pulling her arm hard. When they opened the front door, the kitchen door behind them exploded and the fire advanced forward like a raging monster. The flames licked the walls and ceiling. They ran like they had never run before and somehow managed to get up the stairs and out into the yard. Linn's legs buckled.

She sat naked, cross-legged, with Elin on her lap and rocked back and forth, tears running down her cheeks. Elin had woken up, but was dazed and coughing violently. Magnus swallowed. Shocked and confused, he clutched Moa in his arms. She had quietened down and mostly looked frightened.

Magnus slowly took off his T-shirt and put it awkwardly over Linn's bare skin.

Soon the neighbours began to appear and together they watched in silence as the fire crackled and roared in their home. Then they heard the sirens.

22

Just before ten in the morning, Arne Norman knocked timidly on Roger's office door.

'Come in,' Roger mumbled.

'Am I interrupting?'

'Not at all.' Roger cracked his neck.

'Have you heard there was a fire at Magnus's?'

Roger stood up rapidly, but Arne raised his hand soothingly as if to stop him.

'The whole family is fine. They're in hospital resting up. One of the daughters inhaled too much smoke, so she'll have to stay in for a few days. I've told Magnus to take some time and stay with his family until they're all better.'

'My God! This is terrible ... ' Roger looked shaken.

'Hmm ... yes, the fire spread very quickly. They had probably forgotten to turn off some electrical appliance—but just to be sure I thought I'd send over the forensic specialist Elias Vadasc.'

'The American—he's good.' Roger's voice trembled.

'Not that I think the fire was arson ... but still,' Arne said, looking at Roger seriously. 'You've not been threatened, have you?'

Roger shook his head in confusion.

'Good. I hope you're okay taking over Magnus's assignments until further notice?'

'Yes, of course.'

'You'll have to talk to Magnus so that he knows.'

Roger nodded dumbly.

'I'll call him straight away,' he murmured.

Arne Norman hadn't even left the room before Roger picked up the phone.

23

Magnus was holding Elin's hand—she looked so incredibly small lying there in the hospital bed, so innocent and vulnerable. Magnus felt his chest tighten. He looked pleadingly at Linn and she put her hand on his arm to soothe him.

'She'll be fine.' Her voice almost sounded strict, as if she not only wanted to persuade him but also herself.

'I know, but where will we go? We've got nothing ... ' His voice sounded alien to him—hoarse and broken.

'We have each other ... ' Linn was interrupted by the sound of Magnus's mobile phone. She took a step back but kept hold of his arm.

He put the mobile to his ear.

'I can reject it ... it's Roger.'

'No, pick it up ... ' Linn let go of him, her blonde bangs falling over her eyes and concealing her irritation. How could he even contemplate answering the phone at a time like this?

He heard Roger's voice at the other end of the line, soft and worried.

'Hi, how are you?'

'Wait a second, I'm just going into the corridor so I don't wake Elin. Right ... yes, we're okay given the circumstances.' His voice revealed that he was far from all right.

'I don't believe that—how are you really?'

'We're coughing a lot. Elin is being given oxygen on and off, but she's sleeping now. Moa is too.'

Magnus looked out of the window, his faced reflecting a mixture of fear, confusion and anger. He followed a parking warden with his gaze as they moved among the cars below.

'Roger, the fire was deliberate. Send over forensics. There's not a chance in hell we would have started that fire ourselves, we were asleep.'

'Perhaps it was an electrical fault?'

'I don't think so.'

'Arne's already sent over Elias. He wondered whether you had been threatened.'

' ... no.' Magnus stopped, as if thinking. ' ... but there is one thing I've been thinking about. I was the one who interrupted the murderer at Gunvor's,' he said slowly. 'That's all I can think of right now.'

'So you think the fire might be connected to our investigation into the murder of Erik Berggren?'

'I don't know, I can't think clearly right now.'

'I understand. Rest up. By the way, where are you going to stay when you leave the hospital?'

'I haven't thought about that yet.'

'You can stay with me if you like. I can move in with my mum for a few days.'

Roger sounded as if he was shuddering with unease as he made the suggestion. He avoided his mother as much as he could and Magnus discerned a sigh of relief when he declined the proposal.

'Thanks, but no need for you to shack up with your mum. I'm going to talk to Arne and see whether we can borrow that safe apartment they have in Bergshamra—I think it's empty. Thanks all the same.'

'You know you just have to say the word.'

'Roger ... '

Magnus stopped. He had been going to say that he couldn't

cope with the job, that enough was enough, but he didn't have the strength to have that conversation yet.

'I'm taking over your assignments,' Roger said. 'Was there anything in particular you were going to do next?'

'Yes, can you check my emails and stay in touch with the Argentinian police. And it would be great if you could go and meet the last person alive in the Berggren family—Erik's cousin Annika, she should be back from her business trip now.'

Magnus looked out of the window again. The parking warden had disappeared and the only things moving outside were some brown autumn leaves swirling on the ground. The area outside looked harsh and unwelcoming. He ended the call.

'Roger, we'll have to talk later. I need to go now.'

'Tell Linn I'm thinking of her and the kids,' Roger grunted, a little embarrassed.

Magnus stayed where he was for a while before returning to their room. His eyes were dark. For the first time he felt the dread. The fire had almost taken their lives and anger and horror washed over him in massive, sickening waves. It felt like he was drowning.

24

The dark lay across the road like a black blanket as Roger drove toward Annika Wirén's home just outside of Norrtälje. Large hailstones pattered against the windscreen and despite the streetlights it was difficult to see more than ten or so metres ahead.

He watched the verge attentively, constantly prepared for a deer or another wild animal to appear in front of the car. He kept on thinking he could see dark figures and shadows reaching out to him, and he regretted choosing the old Åkersbergavägen route instead of the motorway. He had been meaning to see if there were any charming, red cottages for him to dream about, but he had got away too late and now it was too dark to see anything. He sighed in resignation.

It was just after half past six by the time he was standing outside Annika Wirén's house, a well-tended, yellow wooden house located in a clearing in the woods. His breath formed a cloud in the chill air as he pressed the doorbell.

He heard a brief, surprised shout from behind the door. Shortly after, someone approached with shuffling steps and pulled a security chain off.

The woman who opened the door looked at him in astonishment. Her dark hair was in a loose bun and she was pretty and petite. Roger thought she looked like a ballerina.

'Yes ... ?' She looked at him quizzically.

'Hello. I'm Roger Ekman from CID. Are you Annika Wirén?' She nodded.

'I wonder if I could come in for a few minutes?' Roger said.

Annika glanced anxiously over her shoulder.

'Is it okay if we talk here. My boyfriend has been working nights. He's sleeping and doesn't want to be disturbed.'

'I'd rather come in, if it's all the same—it's a sensitive matter concerning your cousin Erik and his mother Gunvor. I don't think we should discuss it out here.' Roger gave her a friendly smile.

Annika looked at him, evaluating him from top to bottom. Reluctantly, she took a step back to let him into the hall.

'Can we sit down somewhere?' Roger looked around the dark hall.

'We can go the kitchen if you like. I'm just going to close the bedroom door so that we don't wake my boyfriend.'

Roger sat down on what he assumed must be some kind of designer chair by the kitchen table. Everything was incredibly clean, apart from a few cookbooks carelessly piled onto a shelf.

He wondered whether she actually used them, or if they were just there for decoration.

The kitchen looked completely unused, like it was in a catalogue. Once he might have thought it attractive. Now he mostly thought it was tragically impersonal.

'Would you like something—a cup of tea?' Annika seemed to have relaxed a little.

'No thanks. I'm sorry to have to inform you that Erik Berggren is dead—murdered—and that his mother, Gunvor, has been the subject of a murder attempt.'

Annika stared at him and it looked like she was holding her breath. All the colour vanished rapidly from her face and she succumbed to a bout of severe shivering. It was always difficult giving this kind of news. It was impossible to get used to it, Roger reflected, while putting a soothing hand on her shoulder.

Annika shut her beautifully made-up eyes, breathing hard and quick.

'What happened? The other policeman who called didn't say anything about ... '

'I'm afraid I can't go into the details of an ongoing investigation.'

She nodded and held the palms of her hands against her cheeks, as if to calm herself.

'How often did you meet the Berggren family?' Roger asked, pulling out his notebook.

'I haven't seen any of them since I was a teenager,' she said blankly.

Roger's head dropped in disappointment.

'I was there during the summers when I was little, but since then we've not been in contact.'

'Why not?'

Annika shrugged her shoulders.

'I don't know, people develop in different directions and so on. Life, you know.'

'I understand—but what was your perception of them then?'

'They were okay.' Annika got up and began to empty the dishwasher.

'Can you tell me more? Did you like them?'

'Don't know, it was so long ago.'

'Do you know if there was anyone who ... had a grudge against them?'

'Had a grudge? I don't know, I was so young. I don't remember.' She sounded annoyed. She suddenly turned round violently.

'Why are you asking me this? I don't remember anything—I told you!'

Roger looked at her agitated face in surprise, but before he could say anything she waved her hands in an apologetic gesture.

'Sorry, this is so hard for me ... '

'I quite understand.'

Annika looked down at the floor. 'It's all been a bit much for me lately,' she said nodding toward the bedroom. ' ... barely have time to see each other. Meet at the door, you know. And now it seems like he might lose his job too.'

'I'm sorry, there are a lot of redundancies these days.'

Annika looked at him for a moment in confusion, then lowered her voice and said in a serious tone.

'I really hope you find the person who did this, but I don't know anything that ... '

'Did you know that Gösta Berggren was accused of rape in Argentina?'

Annika turned her back to Roger and put a mug into a cupboard. 'No,' she replied curtly.

Roger realized he was defeated. He would find nothing

here—that was obvious. He pushed back his chair and got up.

'Thank you for your help. Call us if you think of anything to do with the family that you think might be important.'

'Of course.'

Annika fired off an unexpected smile that hit Roger in the midriff—perhaps even lower.

As he left, he felt off balance. He had thought she was beautiful and attractive, but he hadn't managed to place her into any category. A little reluctantly, he acknowledged that this had piqued his interest. But she already had a boyfriend. Disappointed, he got back into the car and went home to his ferret, Oskar.

PART 4

25

Among the harsh red-brown mountains of northern Argentina lies La Rioja. By Argentinian standards, it is a medium-sized town. There are few trees there other than those planted in the town's many parks. The buildings are low—just a few are three storeys tall. This was where Domenique Estrabou had grown up in a middle class family. Her father had been an engineer and her mother a housewife. She had also had two brothers. Now only the younger of the two, Augusto, was still alive.

Augusto was standing in the yard outside his small house surrounded by a white wall three metres high. The neighbour's Doberman was barking furiously on the other side—it always did. He would like to poison that dog—throw a steak over filled with rat poison so that the damn thing would shut up.

When he had worked as an archaeologist at the Patrimonio del Cultural, he hadn't been at home enough to get worked up about it, but since his retirement the noise was driving him crazy. He looked at his wife, Hulda, hanging up the whites to dry on a line suspended between the walls. Slowly, she hung up the clothing with clothes pegs. She found it difficult to move since being diagnosed with Parkinson's. Augusto wondered how things would work out. She had always stood by him. She had been loyal as a dog—even when he had slipped up.

He had always seen it as a weakness in her—she forgave everything—that he could make her do anything. Now he knew that he was even weaker. He was struck by an odd mixture of tenderness and irritation.

Hulda hung up his underpants and looked at him. Her hand swept away the grey hair that had fallen onto her forehead.

'Is everything okay?'

'Yes.'

'That policeman who was here earlier—the one who asked about your sister—he called again this morning.'

Augusto stiffened.

'You didn't say anything, did you?'

'Of course not.'

'What did he want?'

'He just wondered if we had remembered anything else. If anything had occurred to us.'

Augusto gave her a warning look.

'You know that we have to keep quiet about this. It happened a long time ago and can't possibly have anything to do with Sweden. The man who did it is probably long since dead and I don't want people to start talking again. It was an awful incident, but she brought it upon herself. She has to take responsibility.'

Hulda protruded her lower jaw and locked her eyes on her husband.

'She was just a child. You know that. It wasn't her fault at all.'

'You weren't there. She was a whore. Domenique was no innocent little virgin, that's for sure.'

In that moment, Hulda hated her husband. She was too old, too tired. She had spent her whole life fighting to keep him. He had been her God, beautiful, exciting, and interesting—but sometimes he had been incomprehensibly cruel, like when he had told her about his infidelities just to see her reaction. When the kids had been small, she had considered leaving him, but he had threatened to kill himself—said that she meant the world to him. She had cried every night after she had put her little boys

89

to bed, then she had taken him back, licking her wounds like a downtrodden dog. After that, Augusto had got more careful—keeping his affairs more discreet, and she had looked the other way.

Now he was impotent, she thought with satisfaction. Perhaps that was why she had got tired of him. He was hers now, whether he wanted it or not. There was no sport left.

Hulda bent down and picked up the washing basket. She carried it inside, changed shoes and went back out.

'I'm going shopping,' she said.

Her husband nodded.

'Buy the morning paper while you're out, please.'

Hulda Estrabou got into the yellow Opel and drove onto the dusty street. She drove straight to the chief of police, Osvaldo Ortiz, at his office.

26

Despite Magnus having sat up and watched over Elin for most of the night, he didn't feel tired. The anger had begun to grow inside him and was now so raging that his body ached with tension. Someone had attacked his family. His kids.

He clenched his jaw and stared angrily out of the hospital window. It was time to be the person he had been before the arrival of Elin and Moa into this world. It was time to focus.

He turned round and looked at Linn and the girls—they were sleeping deeply. With a couple of rapid steps, he went into the bathroom and pulled a blue fisherman's jersey over his head. When he carefully shut the door of the hospital room, he had already punched the dialling code for Argentina into his phone.

27

Roger Ekman was asleep with Oskar on his tummy when the phone rang. He grunted with displeasure and sat up. Once he had managed to find the phone with his fumbling hands, he heard Magnus's sharp, reproachful voice.

'Are you still asleep this late?'

Roger twisted a little, unsure of how to respond, but Magnus wasn't waiting for an explanation.

'I called Ortiz.'

'Sorry, I was going to call but I went straight home after seeing Annika yesterday,' Roger said, trying to sound awake.

'It doesn't matter. He's found the address of the rape victim, Domenique Estrabou. I'm coming over.'

'But ... ' Roger tried to interject. It was too late. Magnus had already hung up.

Roger looked around the messy apartment. Bloody typical—couldn't we have met at work instead, he mumbled sleepily as he wandered into the bathroom to root through his laundry basket for a passably clean T-shirt. For a moment he considered cleaning up, but he quickly realized it was pointless.

Instead, he opened the freezer and pulled out a bag of croissants. Glad to have found something to offer to a visitor, he went back into the bathroom for a piss. A rustling sound from the kitchen made him hurry up.

'Bloody hell, Oskar ... ' he exclaimed as he surveyed the devastation on the kitchen table. The ferret ran away like a lightning bolt, squeezing under the sofa while Roger cleaned up the chewed chunks of croissant and plastic from a wide blast zone. The two croissants that had come through most unscathed were put back on the table.

A quarter of an hour later, Magnus and Roger were in the kitchen, a cup of coffee each in front of them.

Magnus looked suspiciously at the croissant that Oskar had taken a couple of bites out of, but said nothing. Instead, Roger spoke.

'Tell me what Ortiz said.'

'He's got an address for Domenique Estrabou. She lives in Chuquis, which is close to La Rioja. He's going there to meet her on our behalf. He was already in the car when we spoke.'

'How did they find her?'

'Ortiz apparently talked to her brother's wife. They received a letter from Domenique several years ago in which she explained where she lived, but the brother threw it away. He didn't want any contact with a *whore*, which is apparently what he called her.'

Roger sighed in resignation.

'So the brother's wife squealed. Why did she do that?'

'No idea, but what does it matter? She probably had her reasons. Now we at least know that the woman is alive and where she lives. Ortiz will call once he's been there.'

'Good. Finally we're moving forward. There's actually something else that has happened,' Roger said cheerfully.

'What?' Magnus' eyes widened.

'Eva Zimmer, the forensic pathologist, called me yesterday. She had done tests using various sharp objects and concluded that Erik Berggren was probably stabbed to death with one of those two-pronged fondue forks.'

'One of those ones that looks like a small corn holder?'

'Yes, exactly. But longer. Not something you normally carry around in your pockets. At least I don't.'

'And they haven't found one like it in the cabin?'

'No, but forensics did find something else.' Roger's eyes lit up.

'There were bicycle tracks in the garden inside a hedge.

Someone had recently put their bike there.'

'Did Erik have a bike?'

'No. It appears not.'

Magnus's eyes narrowed.

'I can interview the allotment holders again—perhaps someone noticed a cyclist. By the way, did the interview with Annika Wirén generate any leads?

Roger grinned broadly.

'No, not much really. She hadn't been in contact with the Berggrens for years—but Jesus she was fit.'

Magnus hesitantly took a bite from his croissant. The fondue fork, he thought. There was something tragicomic about the whole thing.

An hour or so after lunch, Magnus had got hold of the gardening enthusiasts who had been in their allotments around the time of the murder. Most people in the allotment association had finished their garden chores for the season, but a few hardy ones had held on. There were six of them in total, and he booked them in over the afternoon at twenty-minute intervals. None of them had objected to coming to the office for a chat. Quite the opposite—most of them had been pretty keen to discuss something as serious as a murder at their allotments.

Some of them had sounded a little too excited, Magnus had thought. One of them was Maud Rydberg. She had already made herself comfortable in the interview room when Magnus opened the door. Her henna-coloured hair cascaded around her very wrinkled face and the contrast between the powerful red of her hair and her pale skin made her look strange. She shook Magnus's hand firmly.

'You'll want to know whether I saw anything, of course,' she said hoarsely. Her eyes sparkled with pure desire for sensationalism.

Magnus disguised his disgust by sipping some Ramlösa mineral water, before slowly replying.

'Yes. Did you?'

Maud Rydberg ignored the question, instead leaning forward and whispering: 'He was a strange chap was Erik Berggren. Disturbed, somehow. I thought we should terminate his mum's contract to get rid of him, but there were some people who felt sorry for him so nothing came of it. And look at what's happened now—a murder in the association.'

Maud looked Magnus in the eyes with a triumphant gaze. 'He drank and acted up, you know.'

'What do you mean by acted up?'

'Well, he didn't look after the garden. Let all manner of weeds thrive and spread to the rest of us. The cheek of it.'

'Was there anyone particularly bothered by him?'

'No, not so much so that they would beat him to death—that's what happened to him, I take it?'

Maud's eyes considered Magnus curiously. Somehow, she reminded him of a hungry dog begging for food at the table. She was just as annoying.

'Unfortunately I can't say anything about that,' he replied drily.

Maud's eyes dimmed just as suddenly as the lights in a power cut.

'Oh, right,' she said acidly.

'But did you see anything around the time that might help us?' Magnus doubted this. She seemed more interested in *obtaining* information than giving it.

'Perhaps,' she said deceptively. 'Was he beaten up or what?'

Magnus sighed heavily.

'If you know anything then it's your duty to tell us.'

Maud jutted out her jaw and seemed to consider her options.

'I might not remember anything,' she snapped sharply.

If Magnus was going to get anything out of her, he would have to make a fuss. He hoped the information was worth it.

'I can tell you're a sharp one. I can tell you that this is a murder enquiry—not manslaughter.'

Maud smiled with satisfaction.

'Now I remember. I saw a tall person outside the gate to Erik's allotment. Then they cycled away.'

'We're dealing with a murder investigation—why didn't you tell us this when you were interviewed the first time?' Magnus looked sternly at the woman before him.

'I didn't think it was important—I didn't have time to describe everything at length. I was on my way to the hairdressers.'

Magnus breathed heavily to calm down. *Stupid, stupid, idiotic woman*, he thought, while forcing himself to sound calm.

'Did you recognize the person? Could it have been Erik Berggren himself?'

'No, it wasn't him. Erik was overweight with thin hair. This was a slender person, but I only saw their back—I was standing fifty metres away on my door step.'

'Was it a man or a woman? What were they wearing?'

'I don't know, it was so far away.'

'But was there anything distinctive you noticed at all?'

Maud creased her forehead.

'They got onto the bike. I thought he or she had been on the allotment and done something, and then I saw there was a bag on his doorstep—but I don't know what it was. Looked like one of those purple bottle bags from Systembolaget.'

'How old was the person? Did you get any impression of that?'

'Not as old as me. I don't jump onto a bike with such ... how can I describe it—with such a spring.'

Maud's eyes now looked more tired than greedy. She pulled a handkerchief out of her handbag and blew her nose.

'Was that everything?'

'Yes, for now. Do you remember what time you saw this person?'

'Absolutely. It was in the morning—almost exactly at half past five.'

'How do you know that?'

'I sometimes eat breakfast in the cabin before going to the Meeting Place and I always come to my allotment at that time. That means I've got time to do some work in the garden before going there. But at this time of year it's mostly gathering the apples.'

'What's the Meeting Place?'

'It's a place for old folks like me to meet friends. You'll notice that people you think are your friends aren't. There aren't many left when it really matters. You've really only got yourself.' Maud smiled. It was obvious she found something about teaching this young policeman about the real world deeply satisfying.

Magnus was relieved when she left. He took a quick break to wash away the bitterness permeating the room like a haze, wondering what had shaped Maud Rydberg. Which events had made her so unpleasant. But he didn't have long, because the next gardening enthusiast was already knocking on the door.

28

The dust stirring up from the road was like thick fog as Osvaldo Ortiz thundered past stray dogs barking like mad in his police car. He drove straight through the mountain village of Chuquis. The air here was cooler than at home in La Rioja. The village was right at the foot of the Andes and the white houses looked like small pieces of torn up paper against the gigantic reddish mountains.

Ortiz looked at the time. He hadn't wasted a moment. Just

ten minutes after Hulda Estrabou's unexpected visit he had got in the car.

It had been a perplexing meeting initiated by Hulda determinedly throwing open his office door.

'My husband is a liar,' she had exclaimed in a highly dramatic voice.

A small vein had been hammering at full throttle in her right temple as she had made her confession in the same tone. Ortiz tried to remember her words as he drove up the mountain.

'My husband told you that he didn't know where Domenique was, but he does know. He's ashamed of her. He thinks that she is light-footed and that what happened all those years ago was her own fault.' Hulda's face had clouded.

'He's like that, you know. Unforgiving and tough. Domenique sent us her address in a letter years ago. She wanted to rekindle contact.'

Ortiz had asked if she still had the letter, but Hulda had merely shaken her head.

After her confession, she had collapsed and looked as vulnerable as an abandoned kitten. Her voice had changed and become sad.

'It's just as well, because my husband is an idiot.'

Then she had taken Ortiz's hand in hers and squeezed it long and hard.

'Do what you can to find Domenique. She's had a tough time.'

29

Domenique Estrabou knew nothing of her sister-in-law's visit to Ortiz. She was lying in a hammock, squinting at the blue sky above. She was holding her hand over her forehead to protect herself from the scorching rays of the sun. The hand was scarred; full of furrows and lines that showed the hard life she had lived. But right now, in this moment, it felt like most things were going her way. Her cupboards were filled with food and there was money in the bank.

Perhaps everyone is given good and bad cards when they are born, and it all depends on how you play your hand, she thought. The idea that people could somehow influence their own lives cheered her up—but her own journey had been painful. The past would still make itself known to her several times a day. Normally at quite the wrong moment, like now, when everything was calm and pleasant. It was as if she couldn't allow herself enjoyment—or perhaps she simply didn't dare relax.

She closed her eyes. Remembered even though it hurt. She had been sitting in the austere parlour when her father came home with the two Swedish men. One of them was short and grey, while the other, Gösta, was conspicuously good-looking, with blond hair and blue eyes. He had blushed when he saw her.

During the dinner that followed, the excitement was so intense she thought she might burst. The grey man had explained that a large part of the railway that they had laid had been stolen and that the thieves had probably sold the materials on—but she hadn't been listening, she had been far too excited, concentrating on the other man.

The day after she had put on her school uniform, *forgotten* to button the top two buttons and secretly borrowed some of her mother's rouge. The air had been vibrating with heat when she met her friend Maria in the square. The two girls had giggled like mad as they crossed the road and continued past the whitewashed buildings on the other side.

They had quickly gone round the houses and carried on across the expansive field. Domenique remembered exactly how the dry grass and cracked mud had felt under her soles, but above all else she remembered the smell. The musty odour that made her want to throw up. The residents used the field as an ad hoc tip and the wind had dispersed plastic bags and other rubbish everywhere, right up to the sporadic cardboard houses and debris that flanked the field.

The area was unsafe and poverty made people desperate. Many of the houses were missing a wall and it wasn't unusual for hens to be pecking around inside the buildings, which in due course gave rise to biting beetles that caused heart disease.

The girls had been an unusual sight here in their neat school uniforms and they would surely have been in trouble if their parents had found out where they were—but they didn't.

Domenique turned onto her side in the hammock, trying to shake off the image of Gösta whom they had met on the embankment. His satisfied smile when they appeared, the innocent meetings that had followed the note he had pressed into her hand—a drawing depicting a red heart with her name in it. She had been so certain then. He loved her. And of course, she had loved him—with all of her fourteen-year-old heart. *But that was before.*

Domenique opened her eyes and laboriously got out of the hammock. She hadn't known then—how could she have?

30

'I found a timer, probably from an old video machine that was cut up.' Forensic scientist Elias Vadasc looked straight at Magnus, unsure of whether his colleague really understood the meaning of his words.

Magnus lurched. It felt like he was going to throw up. He sank down at the desk, his hands on his forehead. The voice was barely audible.

'So the fire *was* deliberate?'

'Without a doubt. You were lucky.'

'What was it?'

'Some kind of small petrol bomb.'

'What does that mean?' Magnus could hear his heart pounding.

'Nothing, absolutely nothing. Anyone could put one of these together. All you have to do is read a tutorial online and use a few normal things from your garage, petrol and some soldering wire. Nothing out of the ordinary. It's the combination that's dangerous.'

'Did you find anything else?' Magnus said, tonelessly.

'Yes, an old paint can. It was under the sink along with the timer. You should move into a safe house—this is a sick bastard.'

' ... but Elin can't leave hospital yet.'

'I've spoken to Arne,' Elias said, 'and he said you'll receive protection while you're there.'

Magnus shook his head and tried to erase the image of the fire raging around his family, flames licking up the walls and the insidious smoke coiling into every corner.

Someone knew his identity and someone didn't care whether his children and family lived or died. His throat tightened uncomfortably. He had put a lot of people behind bars, but he couldn't think of anyone who currently had any reason to take him out.

In his head, he totted up all the cases he had been involved in, but finally it felt like listening to a broken record. Some were capable and had the opportunity, but however much he searched through his memory bank he couldn't think of a single person who would do something like this. The only one he could possibly think of was Erik Berggren's murderer. He or she was still walking the streets free. Free to make petrol bombs. Free to kill. But why? Magnus hadn't even been close to catching him or her—or had he? Had the murderer seen him when he went to visit Gunvor, as he suspected?

His head spun.

Elias looked at him, concerned.

'One more thing. I think the attacker came in through the balcony door in the kitchen. The door was open.'

Magnus sat down heavily on the desk. Had the murderer been watching them from out there in the dark? Seen them getting ready for bed?

'Can you check the clump of trees beyond the balcony?'

'I had already thought of that, but there was nothing there. I'll let you know if I find anything else.' He looked at Magnus sympathetically. 'You should take a few days off,' he said, before leaving the office.

Magnus picked up the phone and rang Linn. She had to know, although naturally she would be angry. Angry first, then frightened—and with good reason. She hated his job and he increasingly felt that she was justified.

It rang seven times—perhaps eight—but there was no answer. Swearing quietly, he hung up.

Then he pushed back his chair to rest his head on the wall behind. He wanted to pull the perpetrator apart, but there was still no face to direct his hatred at. Not a single suspect had turned up and the days were passing by, ticking on ceaselessly like the clock on the wall.

He wrote a few brief notes on a piece of paper.

Someone had burnt a dog thirty years ago and now Erik Berggren and his mother Gunvor had been injured in the same way. Then there was the father's rape story, but did it even have anything to do with the case? If it wasn't for the fact that Gösta had died of cancer decades ago, he would have been a natural suspect—but now there was no reasonable pattern. Or was it just him who was failing to see things clearly? Perhaps it was like Elias said—he should take a few days off. But how could he do that?

Magnus got up and went to the door. He had to come up

with something now. He couldn't simply stand by and watch as someone tried to kill the people he loved.

31

Osvaldo Ortiz had driven some way past the high street and the white chapel in the middle of the village when he glimpsed Domenique's house. It was old and frayed. The whitewash had gone and the roof tiles were cracked. Yet it felt like an orderly and pleasant home. Purple bougainvillea was clinging to the façade entwined with vines, and on each side of the battered blue door were urns filled with herbs and spices.

There was no fence round the garden, so he drove up the edge of the lawn and parked the car. His blue shirt had large patches of sweat under the arms and his breathing was heaving and laboured. He was well past sixty and had never taken care of himself. Fatty food, smoking and booze had left their marks and now his health was beginning to fail.

Ortiz stroked the gilded silver cross round his neck and pulled a pack of Camels out of the glove compartment. He hesitated for a brief moment, but then he leaned back in the car seat and lit a cigarette. The first puff was incredible—it always was.

He hadn't had time to prepare for his meeting with Domenique Estrabou and now he went through what he wanted to get out of the visit. He hadn't even had time to think that thought when a crooked old woman in black clothes and a white cardigan came hobbling toward him. Domenique Estrabou's face looked quizzical when he opened the car door.

32

Roger was behind his desk, looking grim. The bull neck had sunk down between his shoulders and he was drumming the desk with his pen. Magnus understood why as soon as he came in. Arne Norman was occupying a seat at the other end of the room. He also looked morose.

'So,' he said with resignation when he caught sight of Magnus. 'You couldn't stay away? You were supposed to take a few days off. You'll perform better if you're stable and you definitely aren't right now.'

Magnus stuck out his chin. 'I feel fine. We're short-staffed and I think I'm needed.'

Arne looked hesitant, then he shook himself lightly, as if to dismiss the doubts he felt. 'Okay then. There aren't enough of us whatever the case.'

Roger glanced at Magnus. There was no doubt about it— Magnus was heading for a complete breakdown. Roger didn't have a family of his own, but could guess how it felt if everything you loved was threatened. Beneath Magnus's responsible and controlled exterior were unimaginable tidal waves and the person who had set them in motion ought to be frightened, he thought.

Arne stood up. 'The media doesn't know any of the details and that's how it's going to stay. There have only been a couple of short articles about a body being found—that's all. I've spoken to Sofie too, so now you all know that you're gagged on this one. Refer anyone who tries calling you to me.'

Magnus nodded.

'Are we getting more personnel?'

'Unfortunately not, it appears. You'll have to keep doing the best you can. We can meet for a situation report tomorrow. I'm at the dentist this afternoon, but call me if anything spectacular happens.'

Arne turned on his heel and vanished out of the room. Magnus took his seat and pulled it up to the messy desk so that he was directly opposite Roger.

'You know what I want to do with the person who set the fire,' he said, his voice trembling a little.

'I know. But you won't do it, will you?' Roger replied, a challenge in his voice.

The words lingered in the air. Magnus raised his shoulders, as if to protect himself.

'Let's go over everything again,' he mumbled through his clenched jaw.

33

Osvaldo Ortiz pulled his police badge out of his pocket.

Domenique Estrabou shook her head and gave a wry smile.

'You don't need to show me that. I know a policeman when I see one. I've been involved with the police before.'

Ortiz didn't quite know how to react to this information.

'Thank you,' he said, waiting.

Domenique was on her guard. Her green eyes looked him over.

'What do you want?'

'I want to talk about the rape.' Ortiz tried to smile sympathetically.

Domenique closed her eyes and for a couple of seconds he thought she might faint. He quickly put his hand on her arm.

'How do you feel?'

'I need to sit down—help me inside please.'

A few minutes later, Ortiz was sitting beside Domenique on a flowery, pink sofa. She looked at him in resignation.

'Why are you tormenting me like this? It was all so long ago. I told the police everything when it happened.'

'We don't have a report in the office.'

Domenique shrugged her shoulders.

'They might have thrown it away—it probably wasn't very

important at the time. I kissed voluntarily, you see.'

Ortiz raised his eyebrows in surprise.

'Gösta Berggren?'

'Yes, I was in love with him. But why do you want to know all this now?'

'The Swedish police have contacted me. Gösta's son has been murdered and his wife tortured.'

Domenique suddenly looked very old and frail. She sighed.

'Yes, he was probably capable of that ... '

'No, it wasn't him who did it. Gösta has been dead for many years. They're looking for someone else, but their police obviously want to know everything about him and his family.'

Domenique's senses sharpened. Her voice sounded tense.

'Is he dead?'

'Yes, he died long ago.'

Domenique allowed the answer to sink in, before leaning forward with her head between her knees. He was dead. Her tormentor was gone. Once again, she was back in the past at the railway barracks. Back when she hung on to his arm, laughing, back when her breast had been filled with desire.

She looked up at Ortiz.

'Do you want me to tell you what happened?'

He nodded slowly and the words suddenly flowed out of her. For the first time since the rape, she felt her burden ease. It was as if she had been holding her breath for all these years and only now could she fill her lungs with air.

The tears began to flow. She cried about all the years she had felt guilty and the relief that Gösta Berggren was dead. It was as if the words wouldn't end.

The angular and roughly hewn policeman sitting next to her inspired confidence and for a while she allowed herself to be the fourteen-year-old girl she had once been. Over and over she felt her voice choking, but she wanted him to understand, so she tried again.

'Gösta had his friend with him at the railway barracks. At first I was surprised, then I was frightened. He was a changed man and they were grinning so unpleasantly at each other, as if they had some kind of secret pact. Gösta asked if I wanted some tea, but I said no. I wanted to leave, but then he pushed me in the back and made me fall over. He grabbed my feet and the other one held my arms ... they tied me to the table and tore off my clothes.'

Domenique leaned heavily back on the sofa. She was breathing harshly.

'I cried, begged them to stop, to leave me alone, but they laughed as if it was a game. I can't forget it. You ... I tried to get away but they hit me on the mouth—here—with a belt.' Domenique pointed at a scar that ran from her upper lip to her nose.

Ortiz had a dull feeling in his stomach. He had thought she was hare-lipped.

'There were two of them?'

'Yes, but Gösta was worse. The other one mostly watched.'

Domenique paused before speaking again.

'They kept going for so long. It hurt. And then I couldn't feel anything any more. I just switched off. Fell silent. They shouted at me telling me I was a whore, that I loved what they were doing to me ... they ra-- Finally I threw up, and Gösta said I had to get clean. At first I thought he meant I would be set free to wash ... but that wasn't what he meant.'

'What did he mean?'

Domenique swallowed.

'They poured boiling water on me, here.' She made a sweeping gesture toward her genitals and the tears ran down her furrowed cheeks.

Ortiz wanted to brush away the tears, but he didn't for fear that Domenique would stop talking.

'Then what happened?'

'They left me lying there. They didn't let me go until it was dark. I didn't have any clothes, I was shaking, could barely walk. I went to Maria's house and she helped me get to a doctor. It still hurts when I move.'

'What help did you receive?'

Domenique shrugged.

'I'm deformed—when my skin stretches ... well, I need morphine.'

'They took a lot from you.' Ortiz sensed how inadequate his words sounded and was ashamed.

Domenique laid her hand on his and looked him in the eyes with a tender gaze. She was smiling.

'I was given something too.'

'What?'

'A son.'

34

Linn sat on a bench in the hospital corridor, staring at Magnus, her face bright red with indignation.

'Do you seriously mean that you're going to carry on in the police despite what has happened? You must surely understand that the kids and I can't go on like this? What are you waiting for? Something worse to happen to us?'

'Stop it, Linn. I have to carry on, don't you see? We won't be safe just because I quit. And I have to catch this bastard. What happens afterwards is another matter. We can cross that bridge when we come to it.'

The panic grew in Linn. Whatever they did it felt like they were stuck in a vice. Without thinking, she got up and gave Magnus a resounding slap.

'Idiot!' she shouted in desperation.

Magnus felt tears come to his eyes. A mixed feeling of sorrow and surprise.

Linn looked at him in confusion, then she began to cry. Magnus put his arms round her and held her tight against his chest. When she relaxed, they held each other as if they never wanted to let go.

Linn was the first to say something. The sobs made the words stick in her throat and she sniffed.

'Do you understand what you've got us into? We might die— do you understand?'

Magnus knew she was right and it hurt more than he could

deal with. His guilty conscience made his insides writhe like a snake's nest. Regardless of whether he was right that it was Erik's murderer who had them in their sights or not, he was certain about one thing. It was through his work that he had come into contact with the person who had burnt down their home.

He pushed her away so that he could meet her anxious gaze and tried to calm her by saying, 'Nothing is going to happen. I'll take this person down.'

'You don't know shit about what's going to happen!' she screamed, tearing herself out of his grasp.

'Sorry.' Magnus didn't know what to say. She was right—truth be told they knew nothing.

Linn had sunk back onto the bench. Ashamed, he sat down next to her and took her hand.

'I'm doing what I can, you know that.'

Linn dried the tears away with the back of her hand. 'I know. Sorry. I just can't wait. I want to see the material from the investigation so I can help out. This is about me, Moa and Elin too.'

Linn's tear-stained face looked determined. Magnus felt uncertain. 'You know I can't.'

' ... but you'll do it, right?'

Magnus sighed. He didn't have much to oppose Linn with when she had set her mind on something. He stepped uncertainly from one foot to the other.

'Yes, okay then. But you have to promise not to leak it to anyone. I might lose my job.'

Linn looked at him tenderly and smiled weakly.

'As if that would be the worst thing that could happen.'

35

When Magnus returned to his office on Kungsholmsgatan in the afternoon, there was a note on his messy desk.

Call the Argentinian police chief Ortiz immediately.

Magnus sought out the phone number in his diary.

A quarter of an hour later he put down the receiver with a crash. Finally, something not dissimilar to a major breakthrough.

He put his hands behind his neck and stretched. The line had been crackly and Magnus had only caught every other word, but as he understood it, Domenique had been burnt during the rape in exactly the same way as Erik, Gunvor and the dog. This meant that what had once happened in Argentina and had now happened in Sweden were connected. It felt almost unreal.

But the most surprising information Ortiz had provided was that there had been two rapists. Gösta Berggren had had an accomplice—an engineer called Josef Lidhman.

The news made him vibrate inside. There was another perpetrator.

He spent a brief period gathering his thoughts before reaching for his Mac. He pretty quickly established that Josef Lidhman was about seventy-five years old and lived in (so far as he could tell) prosperity in an apartment on Tysta gatan by Karlaplan. He had never been married and according to the tax office, he didn't have any children.

Magnus set off for Roger's office, and within a couple of minutes they were in the car together. The drizzle pattered on the window and the faint creaking of the windscreen wipers emitted small whining noises. Roger glanced at Magnus.

'But don't you think we should interview him at the office instead—after we've done a bit more to prepare? It's hardly likely he's the murderer, Magnus. Be honest—how many pensioners do you know who can tie up a big guy like Erik?'

Magnus looked straight ahead as he turned onto the street. He grunted almost inaudibly: 'Erik was drunk, perhaps blind drunk, when he ended up on the table. Anyway, I want to talk to

Lidhman and we've got no time to sit around waiting.'

'Yes, he might have been helped I suppose. But are we going to storm in without working out what we're going to ask?' There was a touch of acid in Roger's voice.

'I know what I want to know.'

Roger became sulky.

'So is this a one-man race? Why are you so damn pissed?'

Magnus continued to look straight ahead. He understood full well that he couldn't storm into Josef Lidhman's like some kind of angry rhino—but inside he was snorting like a raging beast.

Roger continued in the same tone:

'Are you trying to muck up the whole investigation? What use do you think this is to your family?'

At the same moment as the word family crossed his lips, he realized he had crossed the line. Magnus turned toward him— he was positively boiling over.

'Can you shut up!' he bellowed.

Roger retreated reluctantly.

'Sorry, it's not my thing—but you understand what I mean, I think.'

Magnus clenched his jaws and let his eyes follow the road. He pulled over suddenly between parked cars, turned off the engine and turned round to face Roger. He was still angry, but had calmed down sufficiently to control his volume.

'Okay, I think Lidhman has something to do with this murder and I think my family is being stalked because of this bloody case.'

Roger looked at him incredulously.

'How can you be certain that it's Erik's murderer who is after you?'

'I've gone through every case I've ever had, and all of Linn's half-mad patients. And there's no one—no one—that would do anything like this. It's so fucking twisted Roger. It's all completely sick.'

'But why right now? Why not me—surely I'm just as involved in this as you are?'

'I don't know, but I think that he or she saw me at Gunvor's and thinks I'm in the way.'

Roger looked doubtful, so Magnus carried on.

'But that's just a suspicion and you need to keep bloody quiet about it. I don't want to get suspended because I'm a victim in an ongoing investigation.'

Roger waved his hand.

'I won't say anything. By the way, it's just a feeling you have—there's no evidence that the fire at your place has anything to do with the case whatsoever ... even if I believe you,' he added.

Magnus's aggressive expression softened slightly.

'But what do you think we should do with Josef Lidhman?'

'Kid gloves. We're interviewing him as an old colleague of Gösta Berggren, then we'll see what the lie of the land is. We've got nothing on him and the statute of limitations on the rape of Domenique Estrabou expired long ago.'

Magnus groaned in frustration.

'But if we can crack him then we do it.'

Roger gave a sardonic grin.

'Naturally.'

36

The anticipation of what would happen made both Magnus and Roger focus in silence.

One of them trying to subdue his anger, the other wondering how to handle the situation if the former didn't succeed.

They could see the high-rises looming above the leadless poplars on Tysta gatan through the windscreen. It almost felt like the buildings were steeling themselves for the incipient winter chill.

This was one of the best addresses in Stockholm. In front of the buildings was a well-tended avenue and in the summer there were neat flowerbeds. Karlaplan metro station was just a few metres away. Magnus wondered how much an apartment here might cost—probably the equivalent of two houses in the suburbs. There weren't any people on benefits living here, and hardly even anyone from his own salary band.

Roger nodded toward one of the buildings. 'So, the rapist lives here.' He pulled the leather jacket more tightly round himself. 'He'll be dead soon and won't have suffered one bit for what he's done.'

Magnus bit his lower lip.

'Yes, that remains to be seen. Let's go inside.'

Beyond the stout outer door of darkened oak was a marble staircase covered in a long, red carpet with gold edging. The carpet led right up to a richly ornamented lift gate made from iron. Time had stood still here. The only things that showed the passing of years were discreet indentations in the steps.

Roger looked at Magnus thoughtfully.

'If you can't keep calm, let me talk.'

Magnus suddenly felt embarrassed.

'It'll be okay,' he replied curtly.

Josef Lidhman lived on the second floor. He had a fresh wreath of rowanberries on the door. Roger rang the doorbell and the door opened almost immediately. Josef was short. His face was finely chiselled and his grey hair carefully combed. He was wearing a blue-and-white striped shirt in combination with black suit trousers, and had a somewhat pretentious air. A faint smell of perfume surrounded him.

When he saw the men outside the door, a look of surprise

flickered across his face—but he quickly regained his composure and assumed a condescending grimace instead. His voice had a challenging tone.

'Yes?'

Magnus and Roger quickly flashed their badges and Roger smiled politely.

'We're from the CID. Are you Josef Lidhman?'

The man looked at the two men before him in confusion. Then he gathered himself and his thin lips bent into a scornful smile.

'It's probably best you come in.'

With a sweeping arm gesture he showed Magnus and Roger into the flat. If the entrance to the building had come off as grand, then Josef's home was extravagant, not to mention pompous. Every nook was stuffed with antiquities, the walls covered in oil paintings with gold frames and the floor bedecked with oriental rugs. Magnus and Roger were led into the library.

Roger cleared his throat.

'We have a few questions about your stay in Argentina during the fifties that we'd like you to answer.'

Josef raised his eyebrows, then his face returned to its neutral expressions.

'Wait here. I'm just going to put on some coffee for us.' He disappeared, taking quick steps. Roger rolled his eyes at the man's back before he and Magnus sat down in a velvet yellow lion armchair each.

37

Josef Lidhman stood at the counter. His hands shook as he put the filter paper into the coffee maker and it was not due to his old age. The police were here. Shadows from the past had caught up with him. Argentina. The railway. It had been so important back then to show he was one of the guys—to show he liked *cunts*. And now he was suffering for it again. The old feelings of hurt that he had gathered around him as a stale protective layer piled up now like a safe but stifling wall. *It wasn't his fault!*

Slowly, he picked coffee cups out of the cupboard and put them on the tray he had inherited from his mother. He breathed deeply. Perhaps he would be forced to lie, but it couldn't be helped. It was at least something he was good at—he had been lying to himself for his entire life.

The coffee was ready, but when he poured it into the cups it looked far too black. He watered it down using the hot water tap.

38

Five minutes later the old man sank down into a leather armchair opposite Magnus and Roger. He leaned forward across the coffee table, as if encouraging them to begin. His face revealed nothing. Only a twitch in his right eye showed there was anything going on inside.

Magnus felt a shiver of discomfort and was convinced that Roger felt the same way.

'So, what's on your mind?' Josef said in an overly cheery tone.

'We're investigating the murder of Erik Berggren and the attempted murder of his mother, Gunvor Berggren. We know you worked with her husband Gösta in Argentina many years ago,' said Roger.

The man showed no reaction. He carefully placed a spoon of sugar into his coffee and leaned back with the cup in his hand.

'Yes?'

'Gösta was accused of the rape and assault of a young woman—a child. Domenique Estrabou.'

The man immediately looked pale.

'Yes, I remember that. But the investigation was dropped. He was found innocent.'

Magnus felt the anger welling up inside him again. His voice turned bitter.

'And? We've spoken to Domenique Estrabou. She says you were there. That you and Gösta Berggren raped her together for several hours and poured boiling water over her. She still suffers incredible pain. We're talking about a lifetime of suffering.'

The old man's eyes wandered nervously. His voice suddenly sounded fragile.

'I wasn't charged with anything. What is this? Didn't you come here to talk about a death?'

Magnus looked at him, examining him for a long time with his head at an angle. Then he spoke.

'The statute of limitations on your possible crime against Domenique Estrabou has expired. But we want to know what your relationship with the Berggren family was. If you know of anyone who has cause to get rid of Erik and Gunvor.'

Josef sat motionless.

'No, sorry. I don't know anything. I haven't seen Gösta or anyone from the Berggren family for several decades.'

'And what are your thoughts on the fact that there are major similarities between the rape of Domenique and the murder of Erik?'

Josef looked stiff.

'Well, I couldn't know anything about that, could I? I was never involved in that business.'

Roger sighed in resignation and met Magnus's eyes. As if in silent agreement, they stood up.

'Very well—we won't disturb you any longer.'

' ... but don't you want to finish your coffee?'

'Thanks but no thanks. We need to go—but please come to

Kungsholmsgatan 37 tomorrow morning at ten so we can continue our conversation.'

'Why?'

'It's just procedure.'

When the door slammed behind the police, a quiet sigh escaped Magnus's lips. He looked thoughtfully at the trees waving in the rain. A change was coming and he could almost hear the wind whipping it up.

39

Magnus and Roger jogged to the car as the rain continued to pour down, forming small rivers in the gutters. The car windscreen had been covered in sticky, brown leaves. They jumped into the car, frozen. Magnus turned up the fan and turned on the windscreen wipers.

'He wanted to say something, did you notice? Tomorrow he might talk. I can crack him. He trusts me. I could feel it.'

'Do you think he's the murderer?' Roger said doubtfully.

'No, it's probably like you said. I don't think he's physically capable of murder. But he seems to be loaded enough to pay someone else to do it.'

'Yes, but why?'

Magnus ran his hand through his hair in thought.

'Yes, why? Gunvor and Erik might have known more about the rape than Lidhman wanted them to.'

'Yes, but if they hadn't blown his cover previously then there was no reason they would do so now—and Gunvor is completely demented and Erik would probably not have been considered a reliable witness as such. He was hammered.'

'No, and the statute of limitations has expired,' Magnus sighed.

Roger pulled down the corners of his mouth.

'It might be his reputation that he is protecting, of course. But it seems a little over the top to say the least to pour boiling water on their genitals if he just needs to get rid of them'

'Yes, but I still think Josef knows more than he's saying.'

Magnus turned onto the street. His face reflected the worry he felt for Linn and the kids. It was as if a soft, suffocating weight was covering him—but the feeling was also mixed with rage. The latter was good. It meant he was more decisive.

'I'll make him sing tomorrow,' he said darkly.

40

Josef Lidhman remained at the window watching the police drive away in the rain. He was sweating profusely. Should he tell them about the letters? No, he couldn't. He would have to explain his complicated love for Gösta, about how he had wanted to appear strong and manly in his presence, about the feelings of regret that sometimes came over him and perhaps even about the times when he had thought back to what had happened with excitement.

His blood was pumping, with a surprising amount of force in his trousers. He quickly turned on his heel and headed toward the bedroom. On his way he glanced into the library and saw something black on the table. The dark-haired policeman's mobile phone. He left it there. He could take it to the police station tomorrow instead. He got comfortable under the sheets and began to fantasize. His hand was already in his trousers and it knew what to do.

41

Where was his mobile? Magnus searched his jacket pockets. The lack of sleep was beginning to feel like a blanket round his skull and he wanted to go to the hospital. He was just going to call Linn and ask if he should buy some Thai food on the way. He pushed the stacks of paper on the desk around impatiently, but his mobile wasn't there either.

When had he last had it? It took a while before he remembered he had put it down on Josef Lidhman's coffee table. He had wanted to be sure he would hear it ringing if Linn wanted to reach him.

'Shit!' he exclaimed. For a moment, he considered calling Josef Lidhman and asking him to bring the mobile in tomorrow—but he quickly realized how idiotic that was. He needed the phone back straight away. There was nothing to be done but to go back to Tysta gatan. Just the thought of his mobile being at Lidhman's was unpleasant.

Magnus had just shut his office door when he remembered that he had promised Sofie Eriksson that he would look in before leaving. With an annoyed groan he put his keys in his pocket and went to her office.

Sofie stuck her head out from behind her computer. She was the same age as him—about thirty-five—he thought. Her eyes were deep-set and her powerful chin made her look saucy. Magnus thought she radiated respectability, as if she would tell someone off for jaywalking or committing another pointless violation of the rules. In other words, he suspected she was both narrow-minded and dull, but he hadn't worked with her for long enough to have his suspicions confirmed.

'Hi—good thing you came,' she said. 'Sit down. I've got a couple of things to discuss with you. Mostly how we're going to deal with the witness statements. We've interviewed almost two hundred people and it's starting to get messy—despite the computer system.'

Magnus reluctantly sat down. The clock on the wall showed it was already quarter past six. If Lidhman had wanted to, he could already have gone through the mobile several times over.

While Sofie spoke, he considered whether he had sent any important text messages about the case to colleagues but couldn't remember doing so. He dropped his shoulders slightly—there was no point worrying.

Not long afterwards, Magnus got into the car and shut the door. He still hadn't called Linn to say he would be late, but he was too tired to go back up to the office—he would have to hurry home after retrieving his mobile.

42

The doorbell made Josef jump and he awkwardly pulled up his trousers. It must be that policeman, come back for his mobile phone.

He quickly threw the soiled towel under the bed and sat up on the edge of the bed.

A faint metallic snap could be heard from the front door. Were the police already trying the handle? Josef hurried into the bathroom and looked in the mirror. He sprayed a little perfume inside his shirt and noted with satisfaction that he looked just as well turned out as he had done earlier. Then he walked through the library toward the hall with a wide smile.

43

It didn't take long to drive to Karlaplan, but as usual it was impossible to find anywhere to park. Magnus eventually parked outside a garage door. Despite the fact that cars were parked everywhere, the street was deserted. Not a soul appeared to be outside in the foul weather and he could understand why.

Tysta gatan was very quiet. Light autumn mist slowly swirled past him, brushing his cheek like a damp caress. He hurried into the building and pressed the button to call the lift.

Nothing happened. A couple of seconds passed and then the sound of someone pulling the gate shut was audible from a few storeys up. Magnus started to walk instead. Halfway up the stairs he met the slow lift on its way down in the narrow lift shaft—he caught a faint glimpse of someone behind the coloured glass.

On the second floor he found Josef Lidhman's rowanberry wreath on the floor and the front door ajar.

Magnus froze. Something was wrong.

Instinctively, he stood with his back against the wall and turned off the safety on his service weapon. His heart was beating faster—he held his breath. Far below he heard the sound of someone walking through the street door and he prayed no one would come up. The last thing he wanted was for some uncomprehending neighbour to get in the way.

He glanced at the stairs in concern while carefully nudging the apartment door with his left arm. He had quietly taken off his trainers and he slid along the wall of Lidhman's hall past the toilet in just his socks. He was almost at the library when he lowered his weapon a little and let his shoulders fall.

'Hello? Josef—are you there?'

Complete silence. But then he noticed that his feet were wet—he looked down.

It was blood! His white socks had turned red and he was standing in a pool of blood. In the same moment that the visual impression reached his brain, he heard a faint gurgling sound from further inside the apartment. His heart was galloping as he breathlessly took two steps into the library—far enough to determine that the room was empty and that his mobile wasn't on the table. After a couple of seconds he spotted bloody drag marks on the genuine rugs—the trail led straight to Lidhman's bedroom. He followed it slowly with his eyes and what he saw made his stomach turn. Josef's naked, mutilated body was splayed across the bed. Blood was running from his neck onto the pillow and bed sheets. His trousers were pulled down and the skin around his genitals was mangled.

Magnus staggered backward against the wall. Then he rushed across the slippery floor. Josef was already dead. His eyes were staring vacantly up at the stucco like a pair of soulless water pearls. With his weapon still drawn, Magnus bent forward, his hands on his knees, breathing slowly to calm down. That was when he heard the ringtone coming from the hall—from a mobile phone—his mobile phone.

Magnus felt the horror exploding inside him and his grip on the pistol tightened. He stood stock still for a couple of seconds, then he heard the front door to the apartment being opened with a bang and someone running down the stairs.

Magnus rushed after, lost his balance on the stairs, slipped in his wet and bloody socks, and then regained his footing again. He heard the street door being opened below, increased his pace and was soon outside in the bewildering sharp illumination of the streetlights.

Where? He screamed internally. He glimpsed a running silhouette in the darkness at the corner of Valhallavägen. Magnus ran so hard his lungs wanted to burst, there was the taste of blood in his mouth, the thunder of blood in his temples. Then the shadow was gone.

He stopped and looked around desperately. It was as if the figure had vanished from the face of the earth.

The metro. The murderer must have run into the metro station!

His feet skidded on the cold ground, gravel penetrating into the soles of his feet. Everything was going so fast. No time to think. Magnus headed down toward the platform.

Catch him. Must catch him. The thought pounded inside his head like a bongo drum.

44

Arne Norman was raging. He paced back and forth in the meeting room and his eyes shone with disgust. He turned to Magnus and hissed:

'What the hell were you thinking? Why didn't you call for backup? We've got a team here. You, me, Roger and Sofie. But you seem to think you can do it all!'

'I didn't have a phone—I told you. The murderer took it.'

'You could have used Lidhman's phone!' Arne roared.

'Then I would have missed him.'

'But for Christ's sake ... you did anyway. It was a lethal situation.'

Arne ran a hot-tempered hand through his light hair as if he wanted to pull it out.

'We can't risk lives. You and your family have already been through enough, surely?'

'Have you rung the murderer?' Sofie interrupted.

Magnus nodded.

'No answer?'

'No, of course not. And now it's switched off.'

Silence fell and Magnus cast his eyes down in anger. He was embarrassed about the fact that the others thought he had gone rogue—but the reprimands were also making him so indignant that he had no intention of apologising. Sofie broke the deadlock.

'I wonder what we should do about the press now? They've

called five times—and that's just today. If they hear about another murder then ... '

Arne waved his arm deprecatingly and forced his voice to include a warmer tone.

'I'll deal with it.' He turned toward Magnus who had crumpled onto the table where he had been resting his face in his hands.

'Did you see the person? Was it a man or a woman?'

'Don't know,' Magnus looked exhausted.

'Did you really see nothing?' said Roger in surprise.

'It was dark—there was fog too.'

'Were they tall or short? You must have seen something?'

'I saw them from behind from a distance of thirty metres. I might recognize the pattern of movement. There was something tense about their back.'

'Did you see their hair?'

'No, they might have been wearing a hat—I don't know. Don't you think I would tell you if I had anything to offer?'

Roger cocked his head.

'This is the second time you've got in the murderer's way—has that occurred to you?'

Magnus put his palms in front of his eyes.

'Yes, of course it has. He must really love me now,' he groaned.

'We'll get him,' Roger said calmingly. 'Have you called home yet? Linn must be very worried about you by now.'

Magnus felt confused. Surely he had called home? No, he had been so busy sorting out the emergency meeting and getting the scene of crime team to Lidhman's apartment.

He got up abruptly with his eyes on Arne.

'I'm going to call now. We're done for this evening, I take it?'

Arne gave a tired nod.

'Yes, let's call it a night. We probably all need to get some sleep.'

Magnus rushed into his office and picked up the phone. Linn would be beside herself with worry. It rang four times, but he got no answer. Perhaps she was sleeping—it was really quite late. Magnus called again, but gave up after five rings. With a tinge of worry, he took his black jacket off his desk chair and headed for the door. She usually always answered—was she really sleeping that heavily?

He stopped at the threshold, turned on his heel and went back. It took a while to find the number for the on-duty police officer assigned to sit outside their hospital room.

It was an unusually dark man's voice that answered.

'Jonas Orling.'

'Hi, it's Magnus. I just tried calling Linn but got no reply. I just wanted to check everything was okay.'

'Everything's fine, but she's not here right now. I'm looking after the kids.'

Magnus felt himself tense.

'What do you mean?'

'Well, she went out a while ago. You were supposed to be meeting her.'

Magnus's voice sounded dangerously shrill when he replied.

'Meet?!'

'Yes, she said you wanted her to come and get you.'

Magnus roared like an animal in distress.

'Where? Where was she coming to get me?'

Jonas stammered nervously.

'She said you sent a text message saying she should come and get you from Gärdet because your car had broken down or something like that.'

Magnus threw down the phone, grabbed a mobile phone and began running.

45

Linn had the car stereo on top volume. She was listening to jazz and despite the time she felt quite chirpy as she drove past the massive concrete walls of Radiohuset. Of course she was disappointed that Magnus hadn't been in touch all evening, but it wasn't the first time. He often forgot the time, particularly when he was working on a case. What was strange was that he wanted her to collect him from Gärdet rather than in front of the office like she usually did. But there was a restaurant out there—perhaps they had been there? It was in any case somewhere around there that he wanted to be picked up. As Linn drove in under the trees she pulled out her phone. She had a couple of missed calls from a withheld number that she probably hadn't heard because of the music—but nothing from Magnus. She tried to call him again. It went straight to voicemail. *Was his phone off?* She put down the phone. Gärdet's grassy areas lay around her dark and silent. *Imagine there being such a deserted place in the city* she thought, feeling a certain sense of relief that she was sitting in the car where the damp darkness couldn't reach her. She switched on her full beam headlights and sang aloud to keep any anxiety at bay. It sounded shrill and false—she laughed quietly to herself.

46

Gärdet would soon be crawling with police cars. Magnus had already reported their white Saab 900 and he was now driving for his life. Could Linn really believe that he wanted to be picked up from Gärdet so late at night?

He shuddered—of course she could. She'd received the message from his mobile. Linn would even think it was good to be able to help out.

Small beads of sweat began to cover his forehead. He was terrified. Thoughts tore through his mind. Linn smiling, Linn sounding concerned and asking him to quit the police, Elin and Moa—and the pictures permanently etched onto his retinas: Gunvor Berggren, defiled in her armchair, Josef Lidhman's decimated body.

... *Oh God please, please leave her be.*

He clung to the steering wheel and his hand shook as he called the other units.

'Is anyone there? Has anyone got there?'

47

Linn slowed down. Magnus had sent a text message saying he would be standing near the Kaknäs tower, but she couldn't see him. She peered between the trees by the edge of the road again—*he ought to be here somewhere.* Linn turned her headlights on to full beam to see better. And it was then she saw it. The dog was standing completely immobile in the middle of the road and its eyes reflected the light from the headlamps like two torches.

Linn floored the brakes. The brakes screamed for a split second and she was thrown at the wheel like a limp rag doll. The pain as her forehead hit the solid plastic was indescribable. She gasped for breath. She sat still with her head leaning forward for a minute or so, dazed by the blazing pain in her head. Then she leaned back and put her hand to her mouth, panting.

She looked through the windscreen in confusion. *The dog— where had it gone?* It was gone. There was nothing other than rain trickling across the tarmac to be seen outside. Was it under the car? Her heart raced and she could feel the tears coming.

With all her might, Linn opened the door and climbed out of the car while trembling. The dog was lying on its side, illuminated by the sharp headlights. A little black terrier by the front right-hand wheel. She crouched beside it in shame. Her head ached.

Slowly, she put her hand on the animal's ribcage that was rising and falling heavily. One of the legs was twisted into an absurd position, but the animal was still alive. Perhaps it could still be saved? She spoke to it in the kindest voice she could, while stroking its damp coat. Only now did she think to look for the dog's owner, but the woods around her were desolate and silent. She carefully slid her hands under the dog's wet body without worrying about her knuckles scraping the hard tarmac, but when she picked it up the leash strained—it was stuck under the car. She pulled at the loop but it wouldn't come off. She carefully put the dog back down and lay down on her stomach in front of the car to see better. Her eyes widened. She stared at the arrangement for a couple of seconds without understanding what she was looking at, then she felt the fear creeping in and she quickly withdrew on all fours. The leash was attached to a large rock.

She never saw the shadow that appeared behind her. The blow made her head feel like it was going to explode into atom-sized pieces and when her nose was crushed on the tarmac a second later she barely noticed. Everything was black. The sound of police sirens was audible in the distance. *Too late*, she thought sorrowfully.

48

Magnus lay with his head on his wife's stomach and cried quietly. His eyes were swollen and his head was throbbing. The world was collapsing around him. He brushed away the tears with the back of his hand. She shouldn't have to wake up and see him like this. Now, more than ever, he had to be strong.

A serious concussion and broken nose. She looked frail and broken lying there in the hospital bed with a bandage across her face and around her head.

He still hadn't told the kids and he honestly didn't know how he would. How do you tell two three-year-olds that someone tried to kill their mother?

He picked up Linn's limp hand and brushed it against his unshaven cheek like a bird moving its dead mate to see whether it might come back to life.

But Linn wasn't dead. It had been close, but they had arrived in time. They didn't know what injuries she had sustained. She had been found on her belly in the mud.

Magnus shivered and squeezed her hand. What would have happened if the whole of Gärdet hadn't been filled with the sound of police sirens?

Fear filled his throat with a faint taste of iron. He was quite certain now—it was Erik's murderer who was after them. This monster had—seemingly unaffected by what he had subjected Lidhman to—stolen the mobile and on sudden impulse decided to trick Linn into going to Gärdet. There was something so evil and cunning about the whole thing that Magnus felt sick.

Josef Lidhman could have been a suspect in the murders of Erik and Gunvor, but he was dead now. The only person left with a motive—so far as Magnus could tell—was Domenique Estrabou in Argentina. She had every reason to want Lidhman dead, but why would she attack Erik and Gunvor? And why would she wait almost fifty-five years before taking her revenge? Furthermore, it was surely rather unlikely that a contract killer would take on his family. He didn't understand.

Magnus hugged Linn's hand.

49

Josef Lidhman's apartment had been illuminated all night by powerful lamps. The forensics team had been hunting among the rugs and antiquities searching for revealing evidence. They had moved like silent shadows in the blinding light and only occasionally had a 'look' or 'check again' been audible among the deadly serious faces. Not before the sun began to rise again were they done. Magnus, Roger, and Sofie arrived just in time to see the team gathering up their equipment.

A rotund and bearded forensic specialist of around fifty that Magnus knew was called Ulf Kerne approached them in the hall. He pulled off his thin latex gloves and smiled.

'We've taken all the photos, done all the tests, and so on—we're going home to sleep. You can take a look around if you like.'

He turned round to leave but Magnus put a hand on his shoulder and stopped him.

'Did you find anything?'

'We'll see—a towel covered in what we think is dried sperm was found under the bed, but that might be Lidhman's. I'm taking samples to the lab, but we didn't find a murder weapon or anything like that I'm afraid. Forensic medicine is already looking at the body.'

Ulf Kerne and his three colleagues disappeared through the door.

Magnus looked around, his gaze unwillingly turning toward the bedroom. There was hardly any trace of what had previously happened apart from the blood spatters on the wall by the head of the bed and the big, dark patch on the sprung mattress.

Roger broke the silence.

'Well, gloves on and we'll get started. I'll take the bathroom.'

Sofie looked at Magnus with a pitying look.

'I can take the bedroom if you like.'

Magnus smiled gratefully at her.

The library's walls were covered in books and he decided to start from the top. He stepped onto Josef Lidhman's library ladder and pulled out two copies of Bonniers encyclopaedia. Should he be so thorough that he went through the books or should he merely shake them? He decided the latter.

Roger wasn't having much more fun in the bathroom. Razors, shaving foam, anti-dandruff shampoo, a bottle of Prada after-shave, a black comb. Nothing that revealed anything unusual about Lidhman except that he was vain.

Sofie looked painstakingly around the bedroom, but forensics had done a good job, there was little else to do. The desk drawers had already been thoroughly examined, so she headed instead for the wardrobe. Naturally, it had also been checked through, but Sofie still hoped the contents might say something about Josef Lidhman as a person. The clothes make the man, she thought with a small grin at her own cliché.

The classic wardrobe was made from oak. Lidhman seemed to have invested in several expensive suits from labels like Armani and Boss. They were hanging neatly on hangers and were sorted by colour. The only items enjoying a wilder life were socks and underwear, which were stuffed carelessly into a basket inside the wardrobe door. Sofie was reluctantly rummaging through the underwear with her hand when something hard touched her fingertips. Her first thought was that she had reached the bottom of the basket, but to be sure she pushed aside the underwear and looked. It was a DVD without a case.

With a surprised expression, she pulled out her find and stared at it—then she put the disk into an evidence bag.

Roger was helping Magnus in the library when she came in.

'What's that?' he said when he saw the bag in her hand.

Sofie shrugged her shoulders.

'Might be nothing, but isn't it a bit odd to keep DVDs with your underwear?'

The others looked at the bag in interest.

Magnus nodded at the television.

'He's got a DVD player there—let's take a look.'

All three of them felt expectant as they sat down in Josef Lidhman's velvet armchairs and started the film. The opening credits rolled. A short while later they realized that there were far more sex positions than they had thought and that Lidhman was presumably homosexual.

'I can only conclude that their imagination is impressive,' Sofie said tartly, pursing her mouth.

Roger laughed.

'Yes, life always provides little surprises. I never thought I would watch gay porn.'

Magnus creased his forehead and tried to focus.

'Perhaps he is ... or was homosexual then. But he was involved in the rape of a girl. How does that work?'

'Perhaps he was bisexual,' Roger suggested.

'Yes ... ' Magnus replied thoughtfully.

'No matter what, he seems to have been sadistically inclined,' Sofie said.

Magnus turned in his armchair.

'Hmm ... well I don't know. But Lidhman was injured around his genitals so there's no doubt at least that the murder is connected with the others.'

Sofie turned off the DVD and they continued going through Josef Lidhman's possessions in silence.

50

After much nagging of the nurses, Linn had been trundled into Moa and Elin's room. She had nausea and the room felt like it was rocking. But she was with her kids and she was happy to be alive.

Moa and Elin were sitting next to her on the edge of the bed, their small faces looking serious and concerned. In the background was Jonas Orling, acting more as a child-minder than a policeman now.

Elin was almost completely better following the fire, but still had a persistent dry cough. She leaned over Linn and fixed her big blue eyes on her from just a couple of centimetres away.

'Hi Mum.'

Linn's voice sounded like a hoarse hiss as she replied.

'Hi my darlings.'

Elin looked shyly at her with her head cocked to one side.

'You've got paper on your face.'

Linn smiled weakly.

'Yes—does it look strange?'

Both Moa and Elin nodded.

'I've hurt myself, but I'll get better soon.'

Moa looked at her quizzically.

'Did you fall over, Mum?'

Linn nodded. She pulled Moa and Elin close and hugged them hard. Emotions welled up inside her like a tidal wave and suddenly tears were gushing down her cheeks.

Jonas Orling gave her a napkin. Despite being only twenty or so, he possessed a strange sense of calm. Some would have called him slow, but right now he was exactly what Linn needed. She blew her nose loudly and felt a sharp pain from her broken nose.

Moa and Elin jumped off the bed. A sense of inner

gratefulness struck Linn when Jonas pulled two new toy cars out of his pocket and distracted them on the floor. She was exhausted. Her eyelids were twitching and sleep hit her like a train.

The kids were taking their afternoon nap in the next bed when Linn woke up—their breaths sounded calm and harmonic. She looked around the room to get her bearings. Jonas wasn't visible. He had probably returned to his post on the wooden chair outside the door.

She switched on the small night light next to her while still partly lying down.

'Jonas.' Her voice was quiet enough not to wake the children, but loud enough for the man outside the door to hear it. Jonas opened the door straight away.

'Do you want something?' he said.

'Yes, could you give me the folder that's in my bag please?'

Jonas did as he was told and crept back toward the door.

'Just say if there's anything else.'

'Of course. Thank you.'

Linn didn't think she'd need anything else for a good while. She put on her reading glasses that she had left on the bedside table and let them slide a little way down her plastered nose. It was time to confront reality and it was high time that they regained control. She opened the folder and began to read.

51

Magnus pulled a final book out of the bookcase and shook it. His forehead was covered in deep creases—something was missing—where were the photo albums, the phone book, the personal things? Josef Lidhman's apartment was infested with strange antiques, but apart from the porn film there was nothing that told them anything about Josef Lidhman the person. They had at least been able to take one step forward by concluding that he had probably been gay, but that wasn't enough. Magnus felt perplexed. The investigations at Erik and Gunvor Berggren's hadn't offered them much—witness statements were vague, not even the sex of the murderer was clear. It all felt too much. Tomorrow he would try to restructure everything.

He had been given a new mobile by Arne that he now pulled out of his pocket. There were two missed calls—the first was Sofie Eriksson, who had managed to track down the owner of the stolen terrier, the second from Elias Vadasc, the forensic specialist. His voice sounded exalted in the message he had left. 'Call me as soon as you get this. I've found something here in the ditch. Something big.'

Magnus rang him immediately.

'What's happened?'

Elias spoke with a low but intense voice.

'Well, I'm sitting in the car with Ulf Kerne at Gärdet. We examined the area where Linn was attacked yesterday.'

'Yeees ...?'

'We've been here a couple of hours and at first I thought that the rain had washed away anything of interest. It rained rather a lot last night.' Elias paused for effect before continuing.

'But I found a weapon. An iron post—the kind road signs are mounted on.'

Magnus snorted.

'Are you sure?'

'There's blood on it—and obviously we'll check it, but that's not all.'

Magnus held his breath. Fingerprints. Could he have been that stupid again? It would connect the assault to the murder of Erik, if the fingerprints on the saucepan belonged to the murderer anyway. His hopeful thoughts were interrupted before he had time to daydream any further.

'Fibres—there was lint on the iron post. He probably carried it against his clothing or something because it's got stuck to the rough, rusty bits.'

'What can you get out of that?'

'A great deal. The fibres come from a knitted garment that was blue and black. I'm betting it's a jumper. Did Linn have one like it?'

Magnus thought for a moment.

'No, she was wearing a green jacket.'

'Okay, I'll analyse the fibres tomorrow to see exactly what kind of material it is.'

'Will it be usable as evidence in a trial?'

'That's up to you—I just check things. But if you find a blue and black jumper stick it in one of your little plastic bags.'

52

'I would put away those papers if I were you. You've taken a real blow to the head and it's best you rest.'

Linn reluctantly put the investigation to one side on the bedside table.

' ... and I'm afraid you'll probably be here for another couple of days,' Dr Åsa Romem added. Her voice had a tone of sympathy with a hint of warning. She had learned a lot in her forty or so years as a physician and one of the most important things was to spot the people who wanted to go home too soon.

Linn groaned demonstratively. Every cell in her body wanted to leave. Yes, her head might be thudding so much she was being driven mad, but she hated the hospital. The narrow beds, the bad food and the constant interruptions to private life that the visits of nurses involved. Intending to protest, she opened her mouth, but a look from the doctor made her realize there was no point.

The woman appeared to be made of iron.

'The CT scan we took earlier shows there's been a little bleeding in your brain.'

Linn raised her eyebrows anxiously.

'Is it serious?'

'It doesn't have to cause any symptoms at all—but I want you here a little longer just to be sure.'

Linn nodded.

Åsa Romem smiled maternally and patted her on the shoulder. When the doctor left the room her grey pageboy haircut bobbed in time with her determined steps.

Magnus had taken the kids to the hospital cafeteria since they were literally climbing up the walls and Linn was grateful for the peace and quiet. She picked up the investigation folder again and propped the heavy bundle against her raised knees. She was about to begin reading when there was a knock on the door. It was Jonas Orling with some coffee and a slice of sponge cake.

'I thought you might like some *fika*,' he said tactfully and a cheerful smile spread across his broad face. His red cheeks made him look like little more than a boy—Linn doubted whether he had ever had to shave. She caught herself thinking that he could have done anything—petrol pump attendant, insurance call centre or even postman. In all likelihood he liked the outdoor life, hiking and jigging for herring.

She put the cup to her lips and carefully sipped the hot coffee. While there was nothing she wanted to do except read Magnus's folder, she couldn't turn down Jonas's well-meaning gesture. He was sitting on a chair in the corner taking large gulps out of his mug, seemingly unconcerned by the beverage being piping hot. The steam veiled his rosy face in a mist and it was easy to imagine what he might look like during his *fika* break on a frozen lake on a cold winter's day.

Linn felt very distant from youthful alertness and freshness, lying there in a hospital bed with two black eyes and a large dressing on her nose. Well, at least she could console herself with the fact that the doctor had said her nose would be straighter than before because they had straightened it up. She looked at Jonas curiously.

'Why exactly did you become a policeman?'

Jonas took the cup of coffee from his mouth and looked at her.

'Both my Dad and bruv are police back home in Borlänge—it was just expected.'

Linn smiled encouragingly.

'Was it a good choice?'

He shrugged his shoulders.

'It's totally okay. Just a job like any other. But guard duty isn't much fun to be honest ... ' He stopped himself and smiled at Linn in embarrassment.

'It's okay, I understand.'

Jonas looked relieved. He sat in silence for a moment, then continued. 'I like being outdoors in nature. It would be great to work like that—but I don't know what I'd do. Maybe a fishing instructor or adventure guide?' He seemed to be posing the question more to himself than Linn, but she nodded.

'Yes, that sounds fun. You'll have to look into it—do some research.'

He took a big bite out of his bun.

'Yes, maybe I will.' The smile exposed the soggy, chewed up bun in his mouth.

Linn let her eyes travel down to the folder on her lap again. She had been right about Jonas's outdoor interests—would she be able to assess the murderer quite so accurately?

Rage and fear welled up inside her as she passed her hand over the folder. This was someone who didn't care about life, someone who ruthlessly removed anyone who got in the way of his mission. But what was his mission? Was it just revenge for Domenique? Could it be that stupidly simple? Someone being avenged? But why Magnus? Why them?

Linn screwed her eyes shut and the wrinkle between them deepened.

You wanted to kill me to get to Magnus, she thought. *You knew he would be crushed if I disappeared. And that's what you want. Because he represents something to you—doesn't he? Something you hate.*

53

Astonishment spread across Linn's face an hour later when she looked up to see the huge bouquet of flowers that Jonas Orling was holding.

'They're for you.' He saw her confused expression and quickly added:

'Well, they're not from me. I was given them by the nurse outside.'

'Are they from Magnus?' Linn looked doubtful. Magnus rarely gave her flowers—or rather, he had only ever done so once, when he had proposed.

Jonas nodded encouragingly to her.

'Check the card.'

'There isn't one.'

'Then they're probably from your husband.'

Linn smiled. It was so nice of him to think of flowers at a time like this when everything else was such a whirlwind.

'Can you put them in some water? I was going to rest for a bit.'

Jonas disappeared into the corridor and returned with the flowers in a vase before going back to his chair in the corridor.

Linn suspected he was reading, but she couldn't be sure.

She turned onto her side and stared at the white hospital wall. Images of the murders towered before her, photos from the scenes of crime, witness statements, forensic reports. She tried to create a structure internally—a map to follow, but the contours were still unclear.

The murderer's emotions must be completely absent. Her own youth with an abusive father had amputated her emotions for many years and she imagined that the murderer had a similar trauma in their background. As a child she had chosen to turn off her emotions since they did nothing to change anything and it probably hadn't been until Magnus had come into the picture that she had begun to rediscover them.

Linn sighed. Was the murderer just a twisted version of herself? Someone who had lived in a hopeless situation and tried to find a new, viable way to live? He might simply have chosen a different way out? She closed her eyes. There had to be some sort of justification. But where was the justice in her lying here? The kids needing a guard outside their door?

Bitter tears burnt her eyes. Everything she had built up was collapsing. The strong feeling of hate welling up in her made her hug the yellow municipal blanket so hard that her knuckles turned white.

PART 5

54

Ortiz was standing in his office looking down at the street through the open window. A couple of guys on mopeds were having a loud conversation about something or other to do with engines. They were gesticulating wildly with their arms as if their lives depended on it, but as if by magic the heated conversation was suddenly over and they went their separate ways. The mopeds kicked up a cloud of dust and Ortiz quickly shut the window. He sat back down at the desk. He drummed his fingers restlessly. It felt as if he had forgotten something. He opened the top desk drawer that housed a simple system of two piles: one was for open cases and the other for closed cases. He pulled out Domenique Estrabou's file.

It didn't take long to glance through the notes from their previous conversation, and when he was finished he leaned back with a groan.

It had sort of fallen by the wayside that Domenique had given birth to a son as a result of the rape. But he had been sleeping when Magnus Kalo had called. Well, he could check out the son straight away and then call Sweden if the guy turned out to be of interest.

Ortiz wiped the sweat from his brow with a handkerchief. It wasn't always easy to have your wits about you when you were woken up in the middle of the night—especially not after a nice evening with a few glasses of wine, he reflected.

Anyway, it probably wasn't important to the Swedish investigation.

55

A world away, Magnus was cutting up a cinnamon cake in the CID coffee room. He felt anything but balanced. He had sensed that Arne wanted him to take leave, but he had no intention of giving his boss the chance to bring up the subject. All he had to do was bite the bullet and drink coffee as if everything in the world was as it should be.

He sat down in front Arne, Sofie and Roger and sipped his drink. It was an enforced group *fika* break, and he could see that Sofie was desperately looking for something else to talk about, so he resolved to rescue her.

'Erik Berggren's funeral is the day after tomorrow. One of us ought to go.'

A glimmer of embarrassment flickered through Sofie's eyes and she forcefully stirred her coffee.

'I can't, unfortunately. I'm meeting someone in the afternoon,' she mumbled while a red flush began to expand up from her throat to her cheeks.

'My mum is coming tomorrow and staying for a few days, but of course I can ... ' Roger held out his hands.

Magnus smiled.

'I can go. Take care of Mum instead.'

'Yes ... thanks.' Roger looked mildly amused and Magnus suspected he would have happily told his mother he was needed at work.

Sofie looked at Roger in astonishment.

'Aren't you happy your mother is coming?' she said, as if good parental relations were a given.

'Of course. It's always a joy to be visited by my old mum,' Roger replied. The irony in his voice was unmistakable, but Sofie didn't notice it.

Magnus smiled. He had met Roger's mother on several

occasions. She was a small woman with a perm and glasses. Like her son, she was happy to talk about most things, but unlike Roger she did so in a particularly irritating manner. There was not a single subject she did not have an opinion on and she was always cocksure, whether it pertained to ferret care or murder investigations. The only redeeming characteristic Magnus could see in her was that her absurd self-confidence was quite funny.

Roger changed the subject.

'Someone ought to go to Argentina and meet Domenique Estrabou. She might be at the heart of the matter.'

Magnus looked uncertain.

'What would we get out of it? Surely what Ortiz has come up with is good enough? Gösta and Josef don't seem to have been angels—isn't it possible they did something else to someone else here in Sweden?'

'Well, perhaps,' Roger said neutrally.

Arne, who had been quiet for a while, shrugged his shoulders.

'Well, unless we have more to go on, we won't be paying for any travel like that. I think we'll stick to Sweden for now. It's almost always a close relative who is guil--'

Roger interrupted him.

'It feels like the murderer is laughing at us. The other day, a guy walked past me in the street and stared me straight in the eye. I was scared shitless.' He turned toward Magnus. 'This person has found out where you lived, Magnus, as well as your name—and he didn't hesitate for a moment before attacking your family.'

' ... and next time he might come for you ... ' Magnus looked at him, tired.

Roger's face turned serious.

'Stop it. This is so bloody unpleasant. It's gone way beyond normal.'

Arne nodded in agreement and his face changed into a concerned expression.

'Yes, you really do have to be very careful. Extremely careful.'

56

Erik Berggren's funeral took place in Österåker Church—an old stone church surrounded by beautiful, rolling fields, thick forests, and a red cottage here and there. The graceful haze of frost from the night before was still covering the grass, but it was warm in the small chapel. Magnus wasn't surprised to be the only person in attendance. Erik didn't seem to have been in contact with anyone apart from his mother during recent years and there was a sadly empty echo when Magnus sat down on one of the grey pews.

Deep inside he had harboured hope that the attacker would be there to reflect upon their crime, just like murderers sometimes do in films, but of course that was naïve. The only company for Magnus in the chapel was Erik himself, resting in a coffin in the middle of the room. His final resting place was covered in an unassuming green cloth and a red rose.

Magnus felt ill at ease. The situation made him think of his own father's funeral many years before. He had only been fifteen when the car accident had happened, but the memories were still there. He even remembered the knocks on the front door the second before he opened it. Two short discreet taps. When the policeman was in the hall, Magnus knew straight away what had happened. He could hear his mother's voice echoing in his head: drive carefully darling—it's icy out there! And the door closed behind his father. When the policeman began to talk he sank onto the hall rug like a wet puddle. His mother later said he had emitted a bottomless roar, but he didn't remember it himself.

Magnus shook himself. He didn't want to think about this. Instead, he allowed his gaze to wander around the room. The coffin looked big under the green cover. He wondered what the minister would say about this alcoholic with minor learning difficulties. There were no relatives to tell nice anecdotes about what Erik had been like alive and Magnus was struck by the thought that not even he knew much about him. One thing was for certain—he had been a victim in more than one way. His unhappy life had ended in the most tragic fashion and he had always been an outsider due to his disability. People had considered him strange and frightening.

Magnus tried to imagine what it would feel like. Which emotions would it awaken? Anger, sorrow, or pure hate? Probably all of them. And now Erik was going to be buried, missed by no one. Not even his mum could grieve for him and perhaps that was for the best. Grief had no intrinsic value.

The minister stepped up to the altar. He had short blond hair in a pulled back style that made him look like he normally loitered in the pubs around Stureplan. Magnus noticed that he had his wedding ring on a necklace. He wondered why—had he put on weight? Or was it some obscure sign that he was considering divorce? He looked down at his own hands. It had nothing to do with him—but oughtn't priests to try harder than everyone else? After all, they had promised eternal love before a God they truly believed in.

He bit his lip. At the same moment, the organ started up with great force and the protracted notes made him feel depressed. It was when he got up to thank the minister that his gaze fell on the small envelope attached to the red rose. Magnus excused himself and stepped up to the coffin. The message on the card confused him. It said *forgiven*.

Magnus turned rapidly toward the priest who jumped in surprise.

'Where did the flower come from?'

'I think it was delivered by a florist this morning. Why?'

'Which florist?'

'She came from the florists in Åkersberga shopping centre. I don't remember the name. Actually ... Berga Flowers. That was the name, I think.'

'Thanks.' Magnus's voice echoed right to the back of the church. Even before he had reached the car he had got hold of Roger on the phone and asked him to find out who had ordered the rose.

What did the card mean? Who had forgiven Erik and what for?

He left. The car swept forward through the grey, wet woods. They looked rather bleak now that the colours of the leaves had ebbed away. Everything felt awful: the fire, Elin's hospital stay, the attack on Linn. Magnus came to a stop at the edge of the road and buried his face in his hands. Despite wanting to cry, he was too tired to produce any tears. He kept his face in his hands. It was not the time for a breakdown. The kids needed him. Linn needed him.

The card he had found might lead somewhere. But he wasn't hopeful.

He blinked and looked out of the window. Right now he wanted someone he could call. Someone who understood what he was going through—but there was no one. Linn had enough on her plate—she didn't need to worry about him too.

A bird of prey flew past and landed on a telephone pole a little distance away. It sat still for a while, as if considering something, before stretching out its wings and slowly gliding away above the lifeless landscape. Magnus followed it with his eyes until it vanished into a tiny speck in the distance.

57

Roger Ekman knocked on Sofie Eriksson's door timidly. She was bent over her desk writing something when the door opened. Her office was meticulously arranged. Apart from the papers in front of her there were no disorganized heaps—even her pens were carefully sorted into boxes, as if they had never been used. The contrast with his own hovel was marked.

He cleared his throat to get her full attention—apparently quite unnecessarily since she was already looking at him curiously.

'I've checked the card from the florists,' he said, sitting down on the edge of her desk.

'Yes, and ... '

'The staff don't remember who bought the rose, but they still had the delivery details. Only one rose was sent to Österåker church yesterday and it was paid for by Visa, so it won't be any trouble to find out who sent it.'

'Good, I'll make sure we get the details.' Sofie smiled.

'Call and let me and Magnus know when you do—no rush with Arne.'

Sofie turned in the chair, concerned.

'Of course,' she said curtly. 'Where is Arne anyway?'

'Fuck knows. My bet is a tanning salon somewhere.'

Sofie dropped the pen she was holding.

'What's your problem with him?' she spat out.

Roger shrugged his shoulders. He should have taken more

care not to say too much in front of Sofie. She seemed nice, but she was probably one of those tedious conscientious types who thought work was holy and their boss was god.

He spread out his hands in a dismissive gesture and grinned disarmingly at her.

'Oh, I'm just kidding. I've got a few things to do, but let me know what you find out,' he concluded, before heading for the door. Sofie remained in her seat, confused.

58

Once the morphine had spread throughout her body she felt better. It was so tempting to take more than the doctor had prescribed, but the drug burnt holes in her veins. When she died, her insides would be like a sieve. The embalming fluid would probably leak out of her. She knew it. Only when it was at its worst—at its very worst—was she allowed to take the medicine.

Domenique put on her coat. There was a parade on the high street today. The mayor was going to give a speech in the square, a brass band was going to play a fanfare and the kids were going to demonstrate traditional dances.

The street would be filled with balloons, champagne corks and lively shouts, but Domenique didn't care about that. She just wanted to post the letter to Sweden. Not that she didn't trust him, but it was still for the best to let him know.

59

Linn put down the book. Moa and Elin had wanted to hear the same story four times in a row and she was relieved that Magnus could take over for a while.

While he read the story for the fifth time, she lay on her side with her eyes shut. Even the hospital bed felt good after staying up until the evening.

'Thanks for the flowers I got, by the way. I forgot to thank you for them. It was really nice of you,' she murmured, drunk on sleep.

'What flowers?' Magnus looked up, confused.

The words made her wide awake as if someone had poured a bucket of ice cold water over her. She sat straight up and stared at her husband.

'The flowers I got a few days ago—weren't they from you?' she said tensely.

A crease appeared between Magnus's eyebrows.

'I haven't sent any flowers.'

Linn felt the blood rushing from her head down into her legs and grabbed hold of the edge of the bed with vice-like strength to avoid sliding onto the floor.

'I got flowers ... weren't they from you?' She nodded toward the flowers standing in a vase on the window sill—but she knew the answer at the same moment she asked the question.

She felt cold all over. Elin and Moa looked at her with curiosity and she made an effort to look calm.

Magnus shook his head and got up from the floor.

'Time for you to play on your own for a bit—I'll be back soon.' His eyes were dark when they met Linn's.

'I'm going to check where they came from. Wait here.'

'Where would I go?' Linn looked shaken.

Jonas Orling was on shift in the corridor. When Magnus pulled open the door, he pulled a cola can away from his mouth in fright.

'My wife received flowers a few days ago—who brought them?'

'Eeerrr ... the nurse.'

'Which one?'

151

'The blonde one. Mariette is her name, I think.'

Magnus rushed through the corridors and thundered into the staff room. Two nurses looked up from their lunchboxes at him in astonishment .

His face was as pale as paper as he struggled to avoid simply shouting.

'Where's Mariette?' he managed to say, but he understood his eyes must have given away his desperation, because the younger of the two nurses looked scared witless. It was the other nurse, a steady woman of around fifty, who replied.

'She's off sick today.'

'Where does she live? What's her phone number?'

The women exchanged uncertain glances.

'We can't divulge that kind of information.' The stout nurse tried to conjure up a determined voice that inspired confidence.

Magnus exploded.

'This is a police matter. Give me the information now!'

The nurse stood up, affronted, and growled in reply.

'We have to do our jobs properly you know.'

She wandered over to a bookcase and pulled out a file with a green spine.

'Let's see. She lives in Bredäng, south of town. Here's the address and phone number. Do you want me to write it down for you?'

'No, there's no time. Thank you.' Magnus snatched the folder and ran out of the room. The nurse's face contorted into a worried grimace.

A couple of minutes later he had Mariette the nurse on the phone.

'Hi, this is Inspector Magnus Kalo from the CID. My wife received some flowers from you a couple of days ago. Who gave them to you?' His voice sounded brusque and challenging.

'I, um . . . they were on the counter at reception. There was a note too, I think it had your wife's name on it.'

'Where's the note now?'

'I probably threw it away—it didn't say anything else on it.'

Magnus emitted an annoyed groan and hung up.

'We have to leave!' he said through clenched jaws, standing beside Linn's bed.

She brushed a tear out of the corner of her eye. Then she spoke in a low voice so the children couldn't hear.

'It's that nutter, right? It was him who sent the flowers? He's never going to let go of us.'

Magnus nodded.

Their presence at the hospital was no longer a secret.

PART 6

60

The bank clerk looked across the counter at her.

'Yes, the money's arrived. It's the usual amount.'

'Oh that's good.' Domenique smiled and fine wrinkles spread across her face.

'Sorry for asking, but who sends the money?'

'Why do you want to know?'

'I ... I don't know ... ' The young woman looked uncertain.

'It's a private matter.'

'I'm so very sorry madam. I was just curious.'

The drawn out corners of Domenique's mouth straightened slightly. 'It's warm today,' she said curtly.

The clerk looked relieved and attempted a smile. 'Yes, not long until those lucky enough to own a holiday cottage head up into the mountains.'

'I already live in Chuquis, so I don't have to.'

'Oh—lucky for you. It's so beautiful there and the air is cool. A really sweet little town.'

Domenique nodded, more relaxed now. 'Yes, although it's more of a village—there's no bank for instance. Barely anything else either.'

'But still, the scenery.' The clerk passed over the bundle of notes. 'Take care with all that money in your bag,' she winked.

'I always do. Until next time, Miss.'

With a polite smile, Domenique vanished through the bank's glass doors. Now she had enough to get by. It was a real stroke of luck that he was helping her out. What would her life have been like otherwise?

It was certainly a long time since she had been forced to sell her body for cash, but she hadn't forgotten the humiliation. Thank God for the military junta—it had saved both her and Pedro when, at the end of the seventies, they had given him a nice job at ESMA, the Navy Petty-Officers School of Mechanics.

She didn't believe for one moment the people who said ESMA was a torture centre and claimed that thirty thousand innocent people had vanished during the junta's regime. It was nonsense. Pure lies.

She looked down at her shoes, which were covered in rust-coloured dust. The sweat ran down her spine beneath her black dress as her thoughts wandered back in time.

She thought about all the claims people had made to her— out of context allegations that the junta had drugged people and thrown them into the sea, or that they had shot and killed people during staged escapes. No, she didn't believe a word of it. Not one.

Her own neighbour had even claimed that the military had kidnapped pregnant women and sold their children. It was simply frightful that they could think her Pedro would participate in something like that. He would never do anything like that. He was a father too.

Poor Pedro. They had called him a son of a whore right from the very beginning—had always fought with him. As a mother it had been painful to see. Her own contradictory feelings toward him had given way; it had helped that he looked so much like her. The same straight nose, the same almond-shaped eyes. Apart from the blue eyes, he shared no traits in common with his father and for that she was eternally grateful. It would have been far harder to take to Pedro if he had looked like Gösta.

Domenique increased her pace. The memories upset her so much that her cheeks became rosy.

The bus was already at the stop and she climbed up the high step with some effort.

The bus was nearly empty. At the very front was a man gabbling on about politics with the driver. Domenique stumbled down the aisle and sat down at the very back. She picked up one of the bags and looked inside. The fairy-tale figure in clay that she had collected from the potter's was wrapped in thin paper, but she unwrapped it and looked at the devil-like face in satisfaction.

Now only Pachamama was missing—goddess of earth—then her collection would be complete.

Pedro would be so happy when he was given them. The day he came home—then everything would be as it should have been.

Surely he couldn't live so far away from his family and be happy? Of course, he claimed he was, but she knew otherwise. She knew her son. The warmth was gone—it wasn't in the air or among the people. He was like a foreign bird, a reed in the wind. Lonely and rootless. The same feeling she had lived with her whole life.

She folded her hands together, prayed that he would soon have peace and prayed for him to return soon.

The bus began to struggle up toward the red mountains. Soon she would be home.

Outside, the balmy breeze continued to blow just as it had done on the day Pedro had disappeared.

61

Osvaldo Ortiz stared down at the old documents in front of him in shock. With a lump in his throat, he read the report on Paulo Mendez over and over again. Domenique Estrabou's son

Pedro had been involved in illegal adoptions.

His eyes stung and Ortiz pressed his sweaty palms against them. Thank God he had bothered to check the old paper archives.

'A fucking pig,' he muttered.

Domenique's son had grown up into a massive shit.

Ortiz felt sick.

It wasn't long before he had Paulo Mendez on the phone. Ortiz could hear a quiz show shouting on a TV in the background—it was a show he watched sometimes, if only to see the women dancing around in thongs and feathers in the background.

'I'm calling about your daughter, Laura,' Ortiz said after introducing himself.

The line fell silent, then he heard Paulo's voice again—it was slurred slightly, as if he was drunk.

'Have you found Pedro Estrabou?' he said.

'No, unfortunately not. I can't give you any details, but his mother's name has come up in a Swedish police investigation and we're looking into him too,' Ortiz said briefly.

'I don't know anything about that,' the man replied curtly, as if he wanted to get back to the television.

'I've read your report and gather that Pedro was involved in your daughter Laura's disappearance during the military junta regime,' Ortiz said.

The man sounded sorrowful and hiccupped.

'It was thirty years ago—but I can't stop thinking about it. I relive it every day, as if I might think of something that might change it—but that's impossible. It is what it is.'

'Can you tell me a little more about what happened?'

'Isn't it in the report? She was nineteen and pregnant—they took her, put her in one of their cells at ESMA. I've been there since. I know what it looked like in those damn cellars. Naked bulbs on the ceiling, a corridor ... '

Paulo Mendez wheezed, but Ortiz understood that he was trying to stop himself from crying.

'They took her new born child?'

'Yes, Pedro Estrabou took it—tore it from her womb and left her bleeding on the floor ... like ... like she was worthless. I don't know where the boy went, if he's even alive. I've never found him.'

He cleared his throat. 'She was nineteen years old. Nineteen!'

'I'm sorry. Did she die in the cell?'

'No, she was one of the ones that got out. But she couldn't deal with ... '

The man paused and Ortiz reflected that the cheerful noise of the television in the background was even more absurd than before.

' ... she hanged herself with a bed sheet in hospital,' said Paulo.

' ... was there anything else?'

'No, but thank you. I'm truly sorry.'

'Tell your colleagues to find Pedro Estrabou instead and give him the punishment he deserves,' said Paulo Mendez, distressed. 'I'm sitting here on my leather sofa and waiting for their call. I have been for years.'

Ortiz hung up, the parallel wrinkles between his eyes had furrowed deeper and when he opened the computer he felt awful.

A couple of hours later he had established what he needed to know from local records and the tax authorities.

Pedro Estrabou had married and had three children just after the fall of the junta in 1983. He had bought a vineyard outside of the university town of Córdoba and employed a number of people to take care of the hard work. Perhaps he had bought the vineyard with money earned selling children, Ortiz thought. At any rate, Pedro and his family had lived there until the new president, Néstor Kirchner, had removed the amnesty for those who had been mixed up in the junta's activities. Pedro had gone underground and left his family. Previous investigations suggested he had gone to Germany, but the trail went cold there. As far as Ortiz could tell, Pedro Estrabou could very well have gone on to Sweden since then.

Ortiz picked up the phone and dialled the number for his Swedish colleague Magnus Kalo. He had no idea what the time was in Sweden, but he suspected the Swedish policeman would want this information as soon as possible.

62

Magnus was sleeping when Ortiz called. He awoke from his anxious sleep with a jerk.

A couple of minutes later he was sitting in one of the waiting rooms of the desolate hospital, wide awake.

'What are you saying? That Domenique had a son as a result of the rape?' he said in rusty English.

'Yes, Pedro Estrabou. He should be just over fifty by now. I should have called you about it sooner, but I didn't know if it was relevant ... I wanted to check him out first.'

'But you now think he might be relevant to our investigation?'

'Well, perhaps. He doesn't seem to be here in Argentina at any rate. You may have heard about the trials of former war criminals going on here at the moment? Pedro Estrabou worked for the military junta and he'll be prosecuted when we find him.'

'So he's fled the country?'

'Yes, he hasn't been seen since 2003 when the amnesty was overturned. There's information to suggest he went to Germany then—but he has vanished.'

'Do you think he's in Sweden?'

'You'll have to find that out yourself. I'll contact you if anything else turns up.'

Magnus thanked the Argentinian chief of police, rubbed his eyes and dialled Arne Norman's number.

Arne answered immediately, as if he had been sitting by the phone waiting for a call.

'We've received new information. Domenique had a son as a result of the rape and he may be in Sweden ... we've finally got discernible motive.'

'I thought we were looking for a woman?' said Arne in confusion.

'I don't think so any more.'

'Oh right. Okay ... do we have enough to put out an alert on him?'

'Absolutely not. But we could start by contacting all Argentinian associations in Sweden.'

Arne sounded doubtful.

'But we need to get hold of him quickly,' he said. 'We can't dedicate time and resources on interviewing a bunch of association members. We could circulate a picture to the media saying that he was a witness to the murder of Josef Lidhman?'

'He's unlikely to get in touch.'

'No, but someone who saw him might do ... '

Magnus paced back and forth in the hospital corridor with his mobile pressed to his ear. He wondered how Pedro Estrabou would react if he saw his picture in the paper. Would he hide his tracks, react with wild panic, make a mess of it or simply give up?

Arne interrupted his train of thought.

'Hello? Are you still there?'

'Yes, I'm here. Arne ... give it some time before going to the press. He might just get scared and disappear.'

'Okay. But I'll ensure that every single police officer in Europe receives a copy of the picture.'

Magnus leaned against the wall with his hand.

'Good, do that. I don't want him to freak out if he is our man.'

Magnus stayed where he was, clutching his mobile. There was a suspect—a motive. A smile spread across his face from ear to ear.

He crept in and carefully lay down behind the sleeping Linn in the hospital bed.

Pedro Estrabou had worked for the Argentinian military junta. He had tortured before and now they had three more cases of torture. It was a big leap forward, even if he didn't yet understand why Pedro would attack Gösta Berggren's wife and son, let alone his own family.

He would tell Linn everything about Pedro. She might be able to make something of it.

He gave a tired sigh. When would their lives return to normal? When would they be able to talk about normal things?

Tomorrow they were moving to a safe house—an apartment owned by the police in Bergshamra. He couldn't help worrying about how Moa and Elin would take it. They had talked about 'home' so much—but there was no home to go to, no toys, no memories. They didn't even own a photograph of the family any longer.

63

Linn pushed her breakfast aside. The hospital food was beginning to get on her nerves.

'Oh, so you mean you've got him?'

'Probably. Pedro has strong motives.'

Magnus looked down at a piece of bread with a slice of sweaty cheese on top. He would need to eat pizza for months to regain the weight he had lost during the last few days.

Linn looked at him questioningly.

'Shouldn't you find out whether Pedro has even visited Sweden before drawing any conclusions?'

'Sofie and Roger are both on the task of finding him.'

'What are you going to do?'

'Someone knows you're here. I'm going to arrange a move for us this evening.'

'What do you mean, someone? Pedro, right? I thought you were going all in on him now?' Linn said.

'Yes, but you can never been completely certain—although that's the way we're leaning.'

'Magnus, it can't carry on like this.'

'I know that—okay, I *think* it's this Pedro, but I can't be one hundred per cent sure yet. I still don't get why he would be after us? Or you?'

'For god's sake Magnus—you're a policeman, you're after him, and what's more you keep popping up like a jack-in-the-box. It's a disturbed man we're talking about. Of course he fucking wants to hurt you ... '

'But ... '

Linn gave him a piercing look.

'Make sure you find him, Magnus. Because we can't take much more of this.'

He stroked her cheek. 'I'm going to start by making sure we get out of here.'

'Thank you. I'm starving and the kids are going crazy.' She got up and put on her dressing gown. 'Can you pick up a few things we need too?'

'Just write a list and I'll sort it out.'

Linn nodded. The swelling around her eyes made her look tired.

'I can do something with the kids this morning if you like, because I'll be late tonight,' said Magnus.

'Why?'

'We're having a meeting and reviewing everything.'

'Yes, but why so late?'

'Ask Arne. What do I know?'

Magnus reluctantly lifted the cheese sandwich to his mouth and bit into it with an unhappy grimace.

'But what are you and the kids going to do?' Linn sat down on the bed.

'We'll go swimming somewhere.'

'That'll be fun, but are you up to looking after both of them while they're swimming? I can come with you if you like.'

'No chance. You have to rest. Anyway, you would only scare people with that face.'

Magnus smiled teasingly and gave her a cheesy kiss that made her pull back.

A few hours later Linn was asleep. She was dreaming about Christmas and uninvited guests complaining about the food. For a couple of minutes, she made anxious shuddering movements, but then she sank into a deep sleep, impenetrable from the outside world. She didn't even notice when Jonas Orling pushed the door ajar to say he was popping to the loo.

64

The prick on her throat made her come to and she turned onto her side whimpering. Soon her sleep deepened and she noticed nothing as her bed was trundled away. She was dreaming about something she hadn't seen for many years. A large green wooden door hiding something truly terrifying, yet also desirable and exciting. They wanted her to come inside to help them. And she had to obey. There was no other choice.

When her limp body was carelessly thrown into the back of the van a couple of minutes later, her hand fell heavily between the doors and was crushed by the door's locking mechanism. She felt nothing. But her assailant—breathing so violently they sounded sick—felt *everything*.

65

The officer on duty, Petra Larsson, tied her chocolate brown hair into a ponytail and looked in the mirror. She looked worn and haggard, far older than her twenty-six years. The dark rings around her eyes could no longer be hidden with make-up and she wondered how much overtime she was obliged to accept. Ever since the start it had only been her and Astrid Flodin taking turns to guard Gunvor Berggren, and you didn't have to be a genius to work out that they were at least a man short.

Petra Larsson pinched her cheeks hard to generate some artificial colour. Then she went into a cubicle and carefully put toilet paper on the seat before sitting down. It felt like the most relaxing moment in hours. She stayed for a little while as she studied her black shoes that matched her uniform.

When she washed her hands, she dreamt of a hot bubble bath with lavender. The thought lingered as she wandered back to Gunvor's room and tumbled down onto a chair outside the door. She didn't even check inside, wanting to avoid a nonsense-filled conversation with the confused old woman.

But if she had deigned to open the door, she would have discovered that Gunvor Berggren was no longer there.

Instead, it fell to an assistant nurse to discover the room was empty some two hours later. Gunvor had reached her final destination by then.

66

Arne Norman trusted Magnus Kalo a great deal. That was why he found what had happened on this Wednesday morning particularly embarrassing.

The relationship with Sofie Eriksson hadn't been planned. A late day at the office and a couple of beers had gone further than he had really wanted. He had always been tickled by the idea—at least in principle—of having a relationship at work, but despite being twenty years his junior, Sofie was no catch—not in his eyes at least.

Arne had two failed marriages behind him and didn't intend to let just anyone into his life. So he probably ought to have put a stop to it at a much earlier stage, he realized now. But he had been flattered that such a young woman could be interested in him. And when Sofie had let her hand rest on his for a moment too long he had been unable to say no. Her mouth had looked sweet and moist, and he had immediately realized what was going to happen. He had been just as certain that he would regret it.

This morning in the meeting room Sofie wrapped her arms

round him and smiled. Arne swallowed hard. Now there was no going back, it had to come out. It was a mistake, he had simply been horny and lonely. But naturally it had to be wrapped up in the most insidious way. He pushed her away from him and began stuttering.

'Look, Sofie ... I'm an old man and I've been married twice. I'm not looking for a new relationship.'

For a brief second there was an icy silence. Sofie's smile vanished as if by magic. He slowly opened his mouth to say something, but just then the door opened and Magnus came in. He looked at them both recoiling in separate directions. For a moment a surprised expression appeared on his face, then he shook his head in exhaustion. Sofie rushed out, her face bright red.

'I hope I'm not interrupting,' said Magnus drily.

Arne remained where he was at a loss—he pinched the bridge of his nose. It was stupid to make excuses, he felt like an ashamed dog.

There was a vacuum of a couple of seconds. Then he recovered and said in a curt and controlled voice:

'And what do you want?'

'Gunvor Berggren's gone.'

'What do you mean? She's dead?'

'No ... well, I don't know. It seems as if someone has quite simply kidnapped her from Danderyd hospital.'

Arne's hand went up to his mouth.

'Jesus Christ!' he exclaimed hoarsely.

'Yes, you might say that.'

'Who was on duty?' Arne looked at Magnus sternly.

'Don't know, we'll have to check.'

Arne leaned against the desk. He was dizzy, as if he had got up too quickly and blood rushed to his head. Dazed, he sat down on the edge of the desk and looked at the floor, unable to express himself. Then he turned back to Magnus.

'We'll have to call a press conference. There's going to be major speculation about how the hell we could be so useless that we let the old woman disappear. It's just as well we tell our story straight away. It's a bloody disaster.'

Magnus nodded.

Arne paced back and forth anxiously, talking to himself, almost as if he were trying to calm himself.

'We'll have to turn it on its head—ask the press for their help. Tell it as it is and hope they are gentle with us. I want more information—then we'll organize a press conference. Make sure forensics get over to Danderyd. Interview the staff and the idiot who was on duty—everyone!'

'Of course.'

'Find the woman, Magnus. Just find her.'

A hopeful look suddenly appeared in his light blue eyes. 'But ... you don't think she might have wandered off on her own do you? She is senile.'

'Unfortunately not. She can barely walk.'

Arne sighed. His arms hung limply by his sides and he look remarkably pale under his tan.

'Are we going to publish the pictures of Pedro Estrabou too?' Magnus said.

'Yes, it's time. But it's important that it's clear we only want to talk to him as a witness, nothing else.'

Magnus mumbled in agreement.

'The problem is we only have old pictures of him.'

'We'll take what we've got.'

67

The atmosphere at the press conference was initially low key. Everyone wondered what the police had to say and when

Superintendent Arne Norman entered there was a momentary silence. But the calm didn't last—soon the questions were raining down. How could the police have lost a woman they were meant to be protecting? Was this a serial killer? If so, who was he after? Who were the Berggrens? Who was Pedro Estrabou? Why did they need to publish his picture?

Arne Norman miraculously managed to avoid the most awkward questions and tone down Gunvor's disappearance. She had dementia and Arne implied that she might have disappeared of her own volition.

The fact that Gunvor couldn't walk remained unspoken.

When he later left the room with a smatter of flash photography hitting his back, he felt satisfied. He had made the case appear incredibly complicated and the police as competent. If he had been a monkey, he would have beaten his chest and done a little dance, but he settled on a broad grin.

Gunvor Berggren's disappearance wouldn't crush him and his team—they would be bruised here and there. At least if they could find her alive.

But it wasn't time to raise the sail yet—they had a long way to go before they had a fair wind and the water was so placid that just a couple of small circles would reveal something hiding in the depths.

68

Linn packed up the few possessions they owned and looked around the bare hospital room. She would have liked to say it was beginning to feel pleasant at the hospital, but she felt nothing but relief to be leaving.

Magnus had said that she and the kids could go early to the safe house if they wanted, and Linn hadn't hesitated for a second. The on-duty officer, Jonas Orling, was carrying the two bags of newly purchased possessions and Linn took the kids in a hand each, then they left.

The apartment in Bergshamra was located in a red brick building, not dissimilar to their own home on Torsten Alms gata in Aspudden. The balconies were made from white metal, and everything appeared to have been built some time in the eighties. In the background she could hear the hum of cars on the motorway.

'You can't go out on the balcony,' Jonas warned as he unlocked the front door.

'I know,' Linn said.

The apartment comprised three rooms and a kitchen. It was sparsely furnished and all the furnishings were made from heavily worn yellowing pine—the sort of things someone had probably wanted to get rid of.

Linn looked around. The soiled grey patterned wallpaper depressed her. The kids had the opposite reaction. Elin and Moa cheerfully rushed around, jumping exuberantly on the worn out sofa.

Moa shouted: 'Mum, are we going to live here?'

'Yes, for a while.'

Linn felt a certain comfort from saying that it was only temporary. They would find something of their own soon, but, she thought as she let her hand glide over her tender nose, the person who was after them had to be in custody first.

Jonas coughed and said comfortingly, as if he had read her last thoughts: 'This is only for a while. Once this is all over, you can move back to Aspudden if you like.'

Linn gave an askew smile. Of course they would catch the murderer.

Later in the evening when Magnus arrived at the apartment, they cooked their first dinner together for ages. Linn felt in a better mood than she had for a long time.

Moa and Elin giggled loudly, clearly influenced by Magnus and Linn's improved state of mind.

Magnus took a big bite of chicken and feta. For a moment he managed to force out thoughts of the missing Pedro Estrabou—and the dark threat faced by his family.

'It feels good to be on our own again.'

'Yes, but I'd rather have a guard outside the door ... '

The anxiety swept across Linn's face.

'It's not necessary. I'm home now—one police officer is quite enough if you ask me.' Magnus smiled.

'But ... '

'No one knows that we are here, relax ... '

A little while later when both kids were asleep, they crept into the kitchen.

Magnus put a pan of water on the hob.

'Do you want some tea?'

'Please.'

Linn sat down on a chair and pulled her legs up to her chest. She was as agile as a gymnast despite being thirty-six and never having trained a day in her life. Limbs like stretchy rubber just seemed to be in her genes.

'Do you remember what I said last week when we were talk-ing about Erik's murder?'

'What?'

'About the perpetrator probably being someone who had been abused and having become a master at shutting down their emotions—someone who has suffered trauma.'

'Yes, of course I've not forgotten.'

'I was thinking about Pedro—he doesn't fit the profile. He's worked as a torturer, he's the child of a rape and ought reason-ably to hate his life.'

'Yes, everything points to him ... '

'No, that's not what I'm saying. But no matter whether it's Pedro or someone else, you have to be careful. This isn't just some generally confused and mentally disturbed person you're dealing with—they're deliberate and disturbed.'

'What's the difference?'

'The planning, the calculating. If the person were completely sick, they wouldn't be able to do these things—not so thoroughly and methodically. Think of the perpetrator as someone with great conviction instead. Someone who wants something.'

Magnus looked quizzically at her. Linn shrugged her shoulders as if she were explaining something obvious.

'You and me, we follow a set of societal rules—based on a normal conscience, like most people have. But this person has a completely different logic. This makes this person even more dangerous than someone acting impulsively, if you see what I mean. The impulsive one makes mistakes, but the methodical ones rarely do ... '

'But what does he want?'

'Well, I'm not entirely sure. It might be redress or revenge ... or some kind of saviour act.'

Magnus furrowed his brow in concern. 'Pedro has every reason to avenge his mother, but how do *we* come into the picture?'

Linn poured the tea.

'Hatred of the police?' she said. 'You have said or done something ... can you think what it might be?'

Magnus ran a hand over his face.

'I genuinely have no idea—I don't even know when we've come into contact. I thought he had been annoyed by me interrupting his murder of Gunvor, but I don't know ... '

Linn went into the larder and fetched a bag of cardamom crisp rolls. Magnus followed her with his gaze.

'What do you think we should do then?'

'Don't know ... have you checked whether anyone else has

been treated for burns to their genitals?'

'Apart from Gunvor, Erik, and Domenique?'

'Yes, there might be other victims. If it's a case of *an eye for an eye, a tooth for a tooth*, anyway.'

'Sofie checked—she only found a report about the burnt dog.'

'Strange,' said Linn, looking out of the window.

The first snow of winter had begun to fall. Heavy, damp flakes plummeted down, illuminated by the streetlights, before landing on the wet pavement below. She usually loved the first snowflakes. They usually filled her with a happy feeling that something was on the way, but not now. Instead, she was annoyed at the almost romantic scene taking place on the other side of the window. And it was far too early for snow, she thought. But it was typical that even the weather was mocking them.

'Find him, Magnus, so that we can bring this to an end ... ' she said quietly.

69

The water streamed down his neck and continued along his skin in a series of unruly rivulets. It was impossible to guess which way they would go before eventually being swallowed by the drain. Magnus pulled back the shower curtain and reached for the towel. He didn't have time for long showers. Gunvor Berggren might be alive, but if she was then it was only just, given her state of health. He didn't even want to contemplate the horrors she might be subjected to before being killed.

Linn pushed the bathroom door ajar.

'You need to hurry. It's already late.'

'Okay.'

'Don't go anywhere today, Linn,' he said pleadingly.

'No, the kids and I are going to sit here all day like animals in a cage, I promise,' she replied sarcastically.

When Magnus arrived at the office around an hour later, Arne was standing in front of Sofie and Roger, his face bright red. For a brief moment, it looked like Arne was going to rush out, but then he let the anger gush out like a stream of lava.

'What the fuck are you playing at?' he shouted. 'You've not found anything! Where the hell are Gunvor and this Pedro? The prosecutor's office has requested that they be kept in the loop and I don't even have time to go to the crapper!'

The two police officers stood there silently. The uncontrolled reprimand was as provocative as if he had hit them with a cane.

Magnus knew what was coming and hurried into his office. The phone rang at the same time as he shut the door.

A couple of minutes later he went back out to the glowing red combatants who were now standing outside his office and screaming incoherently at each other.

For a second he stood in the midst of the gunfire, looking at them. Then he raised his voice.

'If I might interrupt for a moment ... '

Arne, Sofie, and Roger stared at him.

'There's information just in that several witnesses saw Pedro Estrabou in Germany last year and there's no reason to doubt the sources. A couple of the witnesses have even been tortured by him.'

His colleagues quietened down as if they had completely forgotten what they were fighting about.

Magnus continued.

'But it gets better. A Swedish woman says she's seen him in Sweden on two occasions.'

Roger was the first to find a voice.

'When and where?'

'Both times at the shopping centre in Mörby in September of this year. The witness is a security guard, so I consider the sightings to be pretty credible.'

Arne caught his breath.

'Find him and bring him in. If he's in Germany then we'll sort that too.'

'If he's there then it's hardly likely to be him,' said Roger. 'Gunvor disappeared yesterday.'

'Stop whining and just do your fucking jobs!'

The Superintendent turned on his heel and shuffled into his office. Roger rolled his eyes, which made Sofie laugh.

'I know that Arne doesn't think we're getting anywhere, but I think the small pieces are going to turn in a marvellous puzzle soon. With lots of small pieces,' she said with a smile, before continuing. 'By the way, I spoke to the credit card company about that rose sent to Erik Berggren's funeral. It was his cousin who sent it.'

'Annika?' Magnus looked quizzical.

'Yes, but there's nothing odd about her sending a rose to her relative's funeral.'

'No, I suppose not. But why did it say "forgiven" on the card?'

'No idea. You'll have to ask her.'

Magnus turned to the coffee machine and made a watery espresso.

'I'll call and ask her if we can visit. It's usually better than doing it over the phone and I thought I'd check up on the search for Gunvor too. They've put out a nationwide alert, but I want to be certain we're not missing anything.'

'Okay.' Sofie turned to Roger. 'Shall we try and find Pedro?'

'Yes, where should be start?'

'No idea.'

Magnus drank a gulp of the unpleasant coffee and grinned at them.

'Maybe you want to start with Missing People?'

70

Gunvor's disappearance had caused concern not only for Magnus and his colleagues, but also for Linn. When she thought about Moa and Elin's safety, it was as if she was in a deep, dark hole. There wasn't a second she let them out of her supervision, and if they were quiet in their room for a couple of minutes it felt as if her heart was being squeezed with fear.

She hoped the kids wouldn't sense her fear, but realized it was a vain wish. Every time they went to play she would appear round the corner with an anxious 'Hi, what you are up to?' Even with a guard outside the door she felt unsafe.

The man Magnus and his colleagues were chasing wasn't stupid. He had managed to remove Gunvor from hospital without any trouble. This person wanted to finish what he had begun. He was not careless and he would kill them all if he got the chance. She was certain of that.

The sense of powerlessness drained her. Home was supposed to be like a rose-tinted bubble—nothing from the outside world was supposed to compromise the feeling of safety they had. There shouldn't be any evil inside the front door. Yet it was there—nightmarishly creeping in through the cracks—insidious and sinister with only one mission: to destroy.

71

It was a matter of time. No one knew for sure what would happen. Linn and Magnus had put their family life on pause and were living as if they were in a vacuum in the gloomy safe house.

Linn moved restlessly around the apartment, manically cleaning anything there was to clean, sorting her hair, and then cleaning again. All the time she was on the hunt for something to distract her from the person out there—the person who couldn't be allowed to get in.

It was torture knowing that something terrible might happen and they could do nothing to stop it. Of course she trusted Magnus and his colleagues, but still—they couldn't find Pedro Estrabou and the fact was that no one seemed to be able to do a thing until Pedro took his last breath. It was as if all they could do was wait. And something was going to happen—she knew it.

Finally, she made up her mind. She was going to go to the Berggren family farm at Flaxenvik and see where Erik Berggren had grown up with her own eyes. She couldn't just stay in the apartment, waiting. With a little luck, seeing it would help her get a grip on what the Berggrens had been like.

Linn was quite aware that Magnus and the on-duty police officer would stop her if they knew what she was intending to do, but she didn't have any intention of telling them. Then she had the chance she had been waiting for. Magnus was at work and Jonas Orling had offered to come in on his day off to take the kids to the Museum of Science and Technology since Linn was still deemed to be unwell.

She reckoned it would take them at least three hours to get there and back.

Since moving into a safe house, the surveillance had reduced and there was no one checking to see whether she had nipped out for a bit.

It was already quarter past two when she pulled up the hill on David Vidstedts väg. The small farm was grey and sombre in the slushy snow. Linn could almost imagine an old woman clad in grey with a headscarf ambling up the hill with a milkmaid's yoke over her shoulders.

The cottage and barn looked like they were ready to curl up to protect themselves from the surrounding forest.

So this was where they had lived—the Berggrens. Linn stood quite still in the courtyard and stared at the house and branches of the tree threateningly brushing the roof. She breathed in the atmosphere. If she hadn't been familiar with the Berggren family history, she would have thought the buildings were charming—but instead they made her shiver. Somewhere in the distance a barking dog was audible.

It was clear that no one had seen to the buildings in years. The paint on the cottage was flaking and the roof tiles had long given up.

Perhaps it had been a bad idea coming here after all? Magnus and Roger had already been. It was probably stupid of her to believe that simply by seeing the house she would experience some kind of revelation.

For a brief time she stood with her hand on the car door, hesitant, before closing it with a light slam.

It was here that the dog had been tortured. Erik had been in his teens then—was it him who had done it? Linn didn't know what to think, but somehow she knew that these buildings were important.

Had Pedro been here too? Had he met his father?

Linn climbed onto the porch of the cottage—a faint sense of worry gnawed inside her and she listened for the barking. It had stopped. She was alone.

To her relief, she saw that the light penetrated through the broken windows. She took a couple of steps into the cabin. The floorboards creaked precariously under her feet—apart from that she could only hear the wind from outside.

At one time the cottage had probably been idyllic, but now there was a downcast feeling in the house, as if the walls themselves were depressed. It was doubtful that the feeling could even be removed through refurbishment. Linn ran her hand over the old cast-iron stove. Her fingers immediately turned black from the soot. What had the current owners been thinking about when they had bought the place? She supposed its proximity to the sea. Perhaps they had wanted to demolish it and build a new house?

She carried on into the bedroom. It smelled musty and mouldy. The flowery wallpaper had peeled off. She stood quite still for a while, taking in the atmosphere. This was where Mr. and Mrs. Berggren had slept. They had lain side by side, year after year. What had Gunvor been thinking? Had she known what Gösta had done to Domenique? That he had burnt her? She must have known something—or could a person really hide those kinds of desires?

Was Gunvor a victim too? And what had it been like for Erik having a father that evil?

Linn felt the headache flashing through her temples like lightening, and she rested against the wall beside her. Her sooty hand left a mark. She quickly tried to brush it away with her sleeve, but it only made the soot more eye-catching, if that was possible. She looked around for something to wipe it with.

There was a built-in cupboard in the wall. She opened the door. A sweet, suffocating smell made her pull back violently. The smell penetrated into her nose and made her feel sick.

When she had recovered, she leaned forward. The cupboard was empty apart from a tin of dry paint in a plastic bag. Where was the stench coming from?

She prodded the paint can with her foot to see if something was behind it. Nothing.

The cupboard continued round a corner. The walls comprised mouldy chipboard. What was the smell?

On impulse, she stepped into the cupboard, but as she stepped over the threshold a floorboard gave way and she fell headlong into the back wall of the cupboard. The rotten chipboard immediately broke lengthways.

'Shit!' she swore in fright.

She quickly got back onto her feet and gradually attempted to discern shapes and figures in the darkness now surrounding her. The terrible stench grew. The insane thumping in her head made even small movements feel like torture, and the dark was scaring her. It was time to leave.

When she cast a final glance into the cupboard, she could make out a dark void behind the damaged chipboard. Somewhere deep down, she began to realize where the smell was coming from ... She wanted to shout for help, but no one would hear her. Instead, she slowly moved backward out of the cupboard, keeping her eyes on the black nook. Fear spread rapidly through her body—it felt like a paralysing poison preventing her from breathing. She stumbled over the threshold and ran out of the bedroom and out of the house. She tugged desperately at the car door—at first it stuck, but soon she got it open and jumped into the car. The engine started with a splutter and she reversed out of the courtyard at breakneck speed.

Not until she was on the motorway to town did her thoughts become coherent. Her hands trembled and she tried to control them by grasping the wheel so hard that it hurt. She went the wrong way twice, and she felt more and more hopeless.

72

Annika Wirén was coming in later in the afternoon, so Magnus went for a coffee in the café below their office. It was a dated place—unhip and worn out, just the way he liked it. He had never felt very comfortable in the designer cafés serving lattes and ciabattas—it was just one of his conservative tendencies. Sometimes he thought he would have fitted in better in the fifties, long before computers, Twitter and Facebook had taken over the world. He even disliked mobile phones since they meant he was available twenty-four hours a day.

He stirred his coffee. Perhaps they ought to move out to the country and give up the mobiles, TV—the whole works?

He smiled to himself. Moa and Elin would probably hate growing up in the back of beyond, unable to go anywhere unless they were taken. By the by, he didn't even like nature—particularly not now that everyone caught Lyme disease as soon as they put a toe in the woods.

But tick-borne diseases were the least of his worries right now. The smile vanished and he pushed the cup away. As he walked back up to the office he discovered his phone had been on silent. There were seven voicemails—all from Linn. Worried, he hurried into his office, but he hadn't finished dialling before the door opened and Linn stumbled in. She appeared to be on the verge of tears. Her eyes were roaming the room.

'What's happened?'

She shook her head, too worked up to speak.

'Is it the kids?'

'No, no, no!' Linn slumped into a chair and tried to force back the tears. Her hands were shaking.

'But tell me what the matter is!' Magnus's anxiety made him sound harsher than he had intended.

'I went to the Berggren farm in Flaxenvik.'

'What?'

'You heard me. I wanted to see it with my own eyes.'

'Have you completely lost ... ' Magnus's jaw dropped.

'Sorry, I just wanted ... '

'Stop it. We're talking about an insane murderer and you just ... don't get it.'

'I ... '

'What?' Magnus stared at her angrily.

'I think there's a dead body in the house.'

Magnus fell silent and his furious grimace disappeared.

'What?'

'I went into a cupboard and then I fell right into a wall and it broke.'

' ... and then you saw a body?'

Linn looked at him wide-eyed.

'Errr ... no. All I saw was a big void behind the cupboard, but I could smell it.'

Magnus looked sceptical.

'It smelled sweet and horrid. You usually say that's what rotting corpses smell of.'

'Yes, that's right.' Magnus put his hands on Linn's shoulders.

'You have to go there!' she exclaimed.

'That's not how it works. I have to have permission from the current owners, or the Prosecution Authority has to issue a search warrant.'

'But you do believe me?'

'Yes,' he said hesitantly. 'But I have to play my cards right here—it can't be known that you're running around playing detective. If they find out that I've let you see part of the investigation I might lose my job.'

Linn looked at him.

'You'll sort it out somehow.'

Magnus gave her an irritated look and she hastily got up.

'I have to go home, or whatever we call it. Jonas will be back from the outing with the kids soon. It'll be hard to explain where I've been if he gets back first.'

Linn gave Magnus a fleeting kiss on the cheek. She was calmer now, but her face was still ashen. Magnus reached for her hand as she began to leave. He gently placed it against his cheek.

'I love you.'

Linn smiled weakly.

'And I love you ... but please, go and see what's in that cupboard.'

73

Magnus sat down. How could he request a search warrant for a house that the Berggrens hadn't lived in for years? Their first visit to the farm had given no cause for further investigation and Linn's visit could under no circumstances be disclosed.

He bit his cheek pensively. The dentists who owned the farm had said they were welcome to visit, but they hadn't counted on the police breaking anything—whether it was cupboards or walls. Magnus decided to tell a white lie to Arne.

When he reached Arne's office, he was on the phone—but he quickly hung up. It was clearly a call of a private nature.

'Was that Sofie?' Magnus said, sitting down on one of the chairs by the desk.

'What do you want?' Arne said wearily, as if he hadn't heard the question. 'I have so much to do that I've got gastritis. Is this important?'

'I need a search warrant.'

'Oh?' Arne looked hopeful. 'Does this mean you're making progress in the investigation?' He cracked a smile so wide that his porcelain veneered teeth shone brighter than ever.

'Roger and I were at the Berggren family farm a while back, and it just struck me that I noticed a strange smell in the house. It might have been a body.'

'What are you saying?' Arne looked at Magnus in astonishment.

'I think we ought to go through the house and barn again but more thoroughly.'

Magnus hoped it wasn't possible to see him blushing slightly. He realized quite how stupid he was coming across and was ashamed of his poor lie.

Arne was happily just as poor at uncovering it.

'Are you sure?'

'Yes.'

'Then I'll sort it out. I have to talk to the Prosecution Authority anyway. But why didn't you check on the smell while you were there?'

Magnus rifled through his head looking for a good explanation and found the perfect one—precisely adjusted for his boss.

'I was confused after the fire and ... Linn and I had had a row.' He paused theatrically.

'You know how it is with relationships,' he said meaningfully, as if they shared a male understanding that women were complicated. The Superintendent swallowed the bait, barbs and all.

74

The colours of the sky had already deepened and were approaching a blue-grey hue. Darkness would fall early today.

Magnus wiped the condensation off the windscreen and looked at the Berggrens' old farm, which was brooding like a menacing hawk above Flaxenvik Bay.

'It looks just as desolate and unpleasant as last time.'

Roger scratched his unwashed hair and glanced at his colleague.

'Mmm, yes ... did you really notice a smell when we were here last time?'

'Absolutely.' Magnus opened the car door.

'But you didn't say anything?'

'No, it was only faint. I didn't think about it.' The red flames of embarrassment licked up Magnus's throat, but Roger didn't notice. He shrugged his shoulders.

'Shall we go inside and look around?'

'Definitely.'

Magnus pulled on the thin latex gloves, well aware that he couldn't just head straight for the cupboard in the bedroom. Instead, he wandered around the kitchen a bit before routinely slipping into the bedroom. He heard a number of banging noises from the kitchen and assumed Roger was going through the kitchen cupboards.

'It mostly smells of mould, if you ask me,' Roger shouted.

Magnus didn't reply—he had reached the cupboard. The door was ajar and a suffocating smell hit him. He turned on his torch and took a couple of steps into the dark. The light picked out a plastic bag with a tin of paint. He took a big step over it. The hole in the wall appeared. The sickly sweet stench was unbearable and he tried to withstand the impulse to vomit.

'Roger! Come in here!'

Despite having looked into the void, he could see nothing.

He tentatively nudged the suspended piece of chipboard. The wall could be forced. Roger appeared behind him at the same moment.

'Fuck ... how could we have missed this? Is it coming from in there?'

'Yes.'

Magnus took a couple of steps back, then kicked the wall with all his might. The chipboard gave way and revealed an empty void of around a square metre in area. Magnus illuminated the grey stone walls inside with his torch.

'Is that the chimney?'

'Yes, some kind of buffer around it I think.'

'Where's the smell coming from then?'

'Don't know.' Roger looked at Magnus with a peculiar expression.

'What is it?'

'There's something in your hair.'

He carefully reached out his hand to Magnus's hair and held his quarry under the torch. It was a small, white larvae. This realization made him close his eyes for a moment.

'Jesus Christ,' he whispered breathlessly.

Roger and Magnus looked at each other in the glow of the torch. Then they looked upwards.

Lashed to the visible roof joists above them, the body looked almost birdlike. The arms were at right angles to the body and the head was hanging heavily down against the rib cage, as if it was coming off at the neck. But worst of all was that the entire body was moving. The larvae were making the body swell as if the corpse was alive—and in the centre of the maggot-infested face, the eyeholes stared back at them, empty.

Magnus and Roger desperately threw themselves out of the cupboard and threw up. Shock made them lose their composure and Magnus frantically combed through his hair to get rid of the maggots.

Roger leaned against the wall, sweaty and pale.

'Oh my God, oh my God.'

Magnus whispered hoarsely.

'Is it Gunvor?'

Roger looked miserable. His voice sounded breathless when he replied.

'Perhaps. It might be her ... '

75

'This is not Gunvor Berggren, but you probably already knew that?' The forensic pathologist Eva Zimmer seemed unaffected by the maggot-eaten body.

'Well ... ' Magnus looked at what should have been a face in disgust. It appeared to have been pulped into something unrecognisable.

Eva Zimmer turned round and dropped the autopsy scalpel in the sink. It emitted a sharp clatter.

'But it is a woman, and I don't think I'm too far off in saying she's about seventy,' she said.

Magnus looked. The delicate body was twisted into a strange position and the laws of physics no longer applied.

'How did she die?'

'Nothing complicated about that. Someone stabbed her with a knife about twenty times. The knife may have been about the size of a bowie knife.'

Magnus sighed heavily.

Eva smiled cheerfully at him.

'An illustrator is coming later to help me develop a picture of what she might have looked like. It's going to be great fun.'

Magnus looked at her in astonishment.

'It's as if you're in another world.'

Eva smiled benevolently. Magnus couldn't help feeling she was almost unnaturally unaffected. It was as if she solely saw dead people as interesting objects of research.

'DNA?' he asked curtly.

'Yes, just hers, and it's not in our records. We don't have a clue who she is.'

'Her teeth? Can we compare them to dental records?'

'All extracted. You're dealing with an evil little bugger this time.'

Magnus nodded despondently.

'Did you find anything else?'

'No, not yet. Actually, the ropes. She was tied up and hung in the roof *post mortem*. She has no bruises on either her wrists or ankles. And considering how little blood or traces of blood there were at the scene, it's impossible for her to have been murdered in the house.'

'But do you know how long she's been dead?'

'Yes, I do. Look at this larvae.'

Magnus looked unwillingly at the small animal Eva had put in a glass jar.

'A bluebottle. When they get older they become darker and darker—this one is about a week old, I should think. It's rather interesting you know—examining the insects.'

Magnus grimaced in disgust.

'Who lives in the house?' Eva looked curious.

'No one—it's a summer cottage, but it's owned by a couple of dentists called Eva and Per Boström.'

'Dentists—well well!' Eva chuckled.

'They've been in Thailand for the last month and presumably have nothing to do with it.'

'But you're going to interview them?'

'Yes, as soon as they're back.'

Magnus turned back to the body, silhouetted under the sheet.

'You haven't considered working in a more pleasant field such as curing people?'

'But who would be here to help you?' Eva raised an indignant eyebrow.

Magnus regretted his unnecessary sarcasm.

'Sorry,' he said, ashamed. 'I shouldn't throw stones in glass houses. Even though I think it's tragic that there's a new victim, I also see new possibilities with this body. If we can find a link between this woman and Pedro Estrabou, we'll have him. It's going to be very interesting to see what your report and the forensics report say.'

Eva looked at him.

'It's okay, and you know what? In the long run, I think my work makes a difference for the people who have lost someone.' She gave Magnus a sad look.

76

Linn climbed out of bed and left the tangled bed sheets in a heap on the floor. She couldn't sleep. There were far too many things whizzing through her head at night and when morning came it was rather a relief.

She went into the living room and turned on the TV on a low volume to avoid waking the others. The news didn't have anything to say about the woman at the farm, or anything about the murders at all. She turned it off in disappointment and carried on into the kitchen.

It was still dark outside, but the streetlights illuminated the slush outside in an almost dreamlike way. She got a baguette out of the freezer and put it in the oven. In her sleep-induced state, she burnt her hand on the oven shelf and let out a brief scream. It wasn't loud, but it was enough for Magnus to come running like a madman. He looked shaken. His dark hair was standing on end and his eyes were wide open.

'What the hell are you doing?' he exclaimed almost angrily when he saw she was in no danger.

'I just burnt myself on the oven—calm down.'

Magnus lowered his gaze.

' ... I get so bloody nervous ... '

He stopped and put his arms around her.

'Sorry love, are you okay?'

'Yes. Good morning, by the way.' Linn kissed him.

'Morning. Isn't it odd to be waking up before the kids?'

Linn sat down at the kitchen table.

'Yes, but it's nice.'

Magnus yawned. 'You went to bed very late.'

'Mmm ... I couldn't sleep so I checked out some houses online. I don't want to move back to Aspudden, Magnus. Not even if they refurbish the apartment.'

Magnus sat down opposite her. He hadn't had time to think about the future, but now that he did he felt exactly the same.

'No, nor do I. It feels like it's been ruined,' he said.

Linn looked at him.

'Well, we'll have to check out a few areas once this is over. I made a list of what we want—I can read it to you while we eat breakfast.'

Magnus nodded, but when she read it his thoughts were far away. He hummed absently as she listed their wishes.

'Close to a train station, sea view, good day care, red paint-work ... you're not listening!'

'Sorry ... there's so much going on at the moment.'

'I know, that's why I'm trying to think about something else for a bit.'

Linn put away her list and poured a glass of juice.

'Okay, what's happening next?'

'This evening, Arne will give some information to the press—then we hope to receive tips.'

'That might be a good idea. What's he going to say?'

'No details—just things we have to release to bring forward witnesses, if there are any. Photos of Gunvor, a reconstructed picture of what Pedro should look like now and a phantom picture of the woman we found in the cottage.'

'Couldn't you take a photo of her?'

Magnus shook his head and Linn pulled a disgusted expression.

'Was it that bad?'

'Worse.'

Magnus put another baguette in the oven.

'Do you want one or two?'

'That's fine, thanks.'

'I'm only going to say one more thing about this, then we can talk about something else.'

Linn brushed the bangs out of her eyes. 'Okay,' she said cautiously.

'You know how we usually say that mass murderers have gone through some tough stuff as kids, and that sometimes they take it out on people who are weaker than them—like animals?'

'Of course. That's sometimes what happens.'

'Well, I was thinking about something. Do you think there might be anything in those allegations of animal cruelty directed at Erik Berggren? Might he have burnt the family dog and killed it? I mean, with a father that evil he could have been subjected to God knows what and in turn have taken it out on someone else.'

Magnus continued. 'I've always assumed that Gösta is the root of the evil, but what if Erik did something he shouldn't have? Someone might want to take revenge on him?'

Linn looked thoughtful.

'But there are presumably no reports about him?'

Magnus spread out his hands in disappointment.

'No, there aren't.'

He looked surprised, as if his theory had suddenly sunk like a stone into a river.

Linn leaned forward, her gaze intense.

'But that doesn't mean something didn't happen.'

77

The media reports about the murder had a big impact. During the next few days, Magnus and the others were overwhelmed by phone calls, emails and text messages. All sorts of tips flooded in from all corners of the country, but nothing seemed especially reliable. Many people claimed to have seen Pedro Estrabou, but no one could provide any credible information about where he was. A twenty-three-year-old woman claimed to have met him in a bar and had sex with him, but that in the middle of the act he had turned out to be a woman. Another woman from Rotebro was convinced that Pedro cleaned her office at night. A frightening number of calls came from racists who were hung up on Pedro's foreign appearance and felt that that in itself was proof that he must be the murderer.

The sum outcome of it all was that it would take time to go through witness statements—and that was precisely what they didn't have. Magnus was afraid that time for Gunvor had already run out.

Despite the increase in police manpower, it felt like every step forward in the investigation saw another step backward. Roger had red stress marks on his throat and smelled of old sweat. His shoulders were pulled up to his ears and he was rushing back and forth in the corridors like a photophobic rat. Everyone's gaze had suddenly turned on their department and it made it harder to focus.

Magnus's brain did its best work amidst chaos and when it

was up against it. Otherwise he could be quite leisurely. It was a rarely appreciated characteristic, but with the positive counterweight that he could almost always remain calm.

Roger pulled off his T-shirt and changed into a new one from his drawer, as Magnus sat down on the desk.

'What do we have going for Pedro?'

Roger looked at him, perplexed.

'What do you mean? He has motive, opportunity, everything.'

'But what about Erik and Gunvor? Why would he take them out?'

'Well, that's what we're missing. But I think Pedro has been in contact with them over the years and has bothered them somehow. But we have to get hold of him so that we can get some answers.'

Magnus nodded. Pedro was the link between Argentina and Sweden—it was impossible to escape. He thought it was him too. At least he wanted to believe it was.

'Want to go downstairs for a coffee?' Roger asked.

Magnus shook his head.

'No, I've got a meeting with Annika Wirén. It's probably a waste of time. You've spoken to her before, but she's the only living relative the Berggrens have, so I thought it might be worth it.'

Roger suddenly looked greedy.

'Do you want help?'

Magnus looked puzzled.

'Errr ... she's just being interviewed for informational purposes. It's no big thing.'

Roger looked disappointed.

'Of course ... say hello to her from me.'

78

Annika Wirén was already in the interview room when Magnus arrived. She was wearing an orange coat and her dark hair was neatly pinned up in some kind of complicated tangle. Her big eyes looked quizzical. Magnus shook her hand and introduced himself.

'I need to talk to you about your cousin Erik. I gather he had a rather complicated upbringing that I hoped you might be able to tell me more about.'

'I've already spoken to the police once, I really don't think I have much more to say,' Annika said, smiling cautiously.

'Yes, you spoke to my colleague Roger, but we wanted to follow up with a few more questions now that we've made some progress in the investigation.' Magnus looked up from his notepad. 'You sent a rose to Erik's funeral?'

Annika looked perturbed.

'Yes?'

'You sent a card with the word "forgiven"?'

'Yes, that's right. You're probably wondering what I meant by that?'

'Yes, can you explain?'

She gently shrugged her shoulders.

'I meant what I wrote. He wasn't always so nice to me while I was growing up, but he was sort of disabled, so I forgive him. I wanted him to know that. It's not so strange, really.'

'What did he do?'

Annika was silent for a moment and fiddled nervously with her cuticles. Magnus thought it looked like she was going through her options. Finally she sighed and spoke.

'It was more what he didn't do. He didn't help me when I needed someone.'

'What did you need help with?'

'Nothing in particular. You know, there's a lot of stuff when you're growing up—but I'm not accusing him of anything ... why are you asking this?'

Her face was open and vulnerable. Magnus liked her calm manner and replied truthfully.

'I'm not actually sure. Anything could help at this stage. We've found a body at their old farm in Flaxenvik.'

Annika looked at him, shocked.

'Who is it?' she said in a monotone.

'We're not sure yet. I hoped you might be able to give us a clue.'

Annika flinched as if she had been smacked on the fingers with a ruler.

'I've not had anything to do with them for years—I told your colleague that.'

Magnus dropped his gaze.

'But there were some strange things going on in the Berggren household at that time, weren't there?'

Annika shook her head violently.

'I was almost never there.'

'I understand that this is hard for you.'

Annika nodded.

'I saw on TV that Gunvor had been kidnapped from hospital. Why?'

'We're not sure right now.'

Annika got up.

'I'm afraid I can't help you any further. Are we done?'

'Yes. No—actually, there's one more thing. Your mother was Gunvor's sister—did she say anything about the family to you?'

'Mum died when I was seven, and she spent a year in hospital before that. I don't remember her talking about them at all. I don't even remember her, unfortunately.'

Annika quickly looked down at the floor. Magnus realized he

had hit a sore spot and rapidly changed the subject.

'Your Dad?'

'They didn't talk much, apart from when he gave me a lift there in the holidays and so on.' Annika glanced at her watch. 'I'm afraid I have to go.'

Magnus got up and shook her hand.

'We may be in touch.'

He watched her slim figure as she vanished down the corridor. Roger was right. She really looked like a dancer, but somehow she moved clumsily and stiffly—so she was obviously no dancer. And surely she was too old? A career like that was probably over long before thirty?

Magnus shook himself—the chill penetrated everywhere—the corridors and the office. He wondered whether Gunvor was freezing somewhere, or whether she was already resting in a cold grave.

79

When Magnus left the office a little later, he peered through the metro train window and was surprised by how calm everything appeared. The white blanket of snow had somehow subdued the pace of the city and even the sounds of the city were duller and more remote than usual. The buildings in the old town leaned against each other, as if for warmth, and on the water there was already a shiny, thin layer of ice.

He rarely took the car to work any longer, partly because he didn't want to end up in some frustrating traffic jam and partly because he wanted Linn to have access to the car in case something happened—*god forbid*—but today it would have been good to have it. He was missing Moa and Elin. They took up their natural position and it was exactly what he needed right now—something to push away the thoughts about the murders.

There were only a few people in the carriage. When he got on he would usually scan his fellow passengers to work out whether anyone might try to speak to him—anyone who was alone or agitated. If he saw anyone then he would sit as far away from them as possible. It wasn't that he was afraid of being spoken to, he just wanted to be left in peace during this brief period that he had to himself. With time, he had fallen into the same habits as many others on the metro. To avoid letting strangers into his world, he would stare vacantly out of the window regardless of whether there was anything there to see or not. Sometimes, he remembered to bring reading material, but unfortunately he hadn't on this occasion.

The train ran into a tunnel and he could see his own reflection in the window. He bitterly noted that he had wrinkles on his forehead and the hint of bags under his eyes. *It's downhill from here*, he sighed internally and let his gaze sweep over the other passengers reflected in the window—it was a convenient way of sneaking glances at people.

But then he appeared—a man wearing a cap—ten metres away, at the far end of the carriage. Magnus couldn't explain what caught his attention. Perhaps it was the man's build or that he had the cap pulled down so that it concealed his face. In any case, it was the same person he had pursued from Josef Lidhman's apartment. He was completely convinced.

Thoughts rushed through his head. The murderer wasn't standing in the same metro carriage as him by coincidence. He was after him. Had he been followed from work?

Magnus felt every muscle preparing for action. He could arrest him now. Get him here.

He slowly got up and began to move toward the man, taking care to look as carefree as he had done before.

He saw the man freeze for a split second. Then his shoulders tensed and he raised his hand quickly to adjust the cap to further hide his face. Then the brakes squealed and the train stopped at the central metro station with a shudder. People began to step into the aisle.

Magnus pushed forward like a lawn mower through the throng, but it was too late. He hurried off and looked around the crowded metro platform. It was rush hour and people were scuffling to get in and out of carriages. Magnus stood on a bench and looked around. There was no cap bobbing in the masses. It was as if the man had disappeared.

'Crap!'

He wandered up and down the platform a couple of times. He had missed him. *Again.* But now he knew. They were looking for a man. Any thought of the attacker being a woman was dismissed.

But had he seen Pedro Estrabou?

Frustrated, he got onto the next train. Once he had sat down he called Roger and told him what had happened.

'How sure are you it was the same guy you saw at Lidhman's?' Roger said.

'Pretty bloody sure. There was something about the attitude I recognized.'

'But was he after you?'

'What do you think? Of course.'

Roger was quiet for a moment. Then he replied anxiously.

'Do you think he knows where you live?'

'No, I think that was why he was following me—to find out.'

'And you couldn't follow him?'

'He just vanished ... ' Magnus replied despondently.

'I'm trying to pull up surveillance footage. There has to be something. And I'll review your protection as well.'

'Yes, do that. I'd like Orling if possible.'

'The probationer?'

'Yes, I trust him. He's good and I'm not just saying that

because he's helped out with the kids.'

'I'll try. But I think he was being brought in to go through witness statements. But forget about that—go home and take care of your family.'

Magnus put his mobile away in his jacket pocket and looked out of the metro window again. Despite it being cold he was sweating.

Dusk drew across the sky and the pink light made the heavens looks like a Monet. But Magnus could no longer see beauty.

80

The morning sun cast its golden rays over the ice-covered inlet. Jonas Orling stopped, took a deep breath and let the cold air dwell in his lungs. The ski trail had never been as perfect as it was today. He smiled at the thought that he could spend another half hour outside before he had to go to work.

His phone emitted a beep. It seemed unreal that someone could reach him out here. Slightly annoyed, he pulled the phone out and listened to the message.

His heart skipped a beat and when he hung up he sank into a snowdrift and laughed. What fantastic luck.

He poured a cup of hot chocolate and put it to his lips. It was just the right temperature and sweet the way he liked it.

His family would be happy. He called his mother straight away to tell her the news, but was careful not to say which case he was going to be working on. While talking he ate the cheese sandwiches he had brought with him. Not until his fingers were stinging with cold did he end the call.

Damn—the guys would be impressed. A murder case—that was something. Jonas blew hot air into his Lovikka gloves and, his hands fumbling, he packed away his food bag. He was happy. His life lay ahead of him like a magnificent string of pearls full of great surprises and all he had to do was bend forward and pick them up.

81

Linn looked out of the kitchen window at where the slush had been replaced during the night by fresh, powdery snow. To her relief, the street was deserted. She was increasingly getting the creeps even though they had a guard. Despite being happy that Jonas Orling had been given more important duties than being on guard, she was also somewhat disappointed. It had been nice having him there, like a calm teddy bear outside the door. A man of few words but with an aura of goodness surrounding him.

His replacement was a young policewoman called Johanna Ljungblad. She made Linn feel like a rat in a lab. Her first words were that she needed 'advance warning' if Linn or the children intended to leave the apartment, and that she personally would prefer it if they didn't. It took a great deal of self-control on Linn's part not to scream in response. Now she was avoiding Johanna as much as possible, which meant she largely remained inside when Magnus wasn't at home.

Elin and Moa were playing in the bathroom. They seemed quite unconcerned about the situation and had already got used to the safe house. The snow began to fall in big, heavy flakes outside. In the past she had taken the kids outside to make snowmen when the weather was like this, but now she was afraid. She looked down at her hands. *Like hell*, she thought, *like hell are you going to take our lives.* She went into the hall, her jaw clenched.

Johanna Ljungblad wouldn't be happy, but she knew she had to engage in battle. The kids had already been deprived of their home. Now they needed to live as normally as was possible. She pulled the kids' new snowsuits out of the cupboard and began looking for the new gloves that Jonas had bought for them. Once everything was on the floor, she kneeled down and looked at the clothes. For a long time she simply sat there while a battle took place in her mind. It felt like she couldn't move. Then the tears began to pour down her cheeks and she threw everything violently back in the cupboard. She couldn't. She just couldn't.

PART 7

82

There were around thirty-five people at dentist Per Boström's fortieth birthday party, and his wife Eva had just led a toast at the stylish party when the police had rung the doorbell.

On being obliged to leave their guests behind in their Vaxholm home for a trip to the police station, the suited Per Boström had exploded with rage. Insults regarding the deficiencies of the police had flowed out of him like a river. Eventually, Magnus had been forced to tell him to shut up.

Now the couple were seated in separate rooms. Roger had the dubious pleasure of interviewing the angry dentist, while Magnus was sitting opposite the elegant and sequin-clad Eva Boström.

Magnus turned on the tape recorder.

'You are only being interviewed for informational purposes— just so you know,' he said apologetically to the woman in front of him.

'So I've gathered,' Eva Boström pursed her lips slightly. 'We've been in Thailand for a month and got home the day before yesterday, so we've got nothing to do with this.'

'I hope you understand that we have to interview you when we find a dead woman hanging in the roof of your cottage?' Magnus said critically.

Eva Boström didn't reply.

'Is there anyone apart from you two with access to the farm?'

Eva Boström scratched her temple.

'No, not that we've invited. But you know the way things are. There are no locks, it's open all year round.'

'Have you been in contact at all with the previous owners—the Berggrens?'

Eva shook her head.

'No. Well, yes. We met Gunvor, of course—in connection with buying the house. At the estate agent's. But we've not spoken since then, thank goodness.'

'Why do you say that?'

'Well, that house has been nothing but a nightmare since we bought it, so it wouldn't have been a particularly pleasant conversation.' The woman suddenly looked at him indignantly. 'But it's nothing I would murder her for.'

Magnus smiled.

'I didn't think otherwise.'

Eva Boström laughed in relief and showed off a white row of teeth.

'When were you last there?'

'Several years ago. The house is only good for demolition, so we had been planning to sell the whole bloody lot as a plot. We prefer going abroad on holiday to get away from this rubbish weather.' She looked at him anxiously. 'What do you think will happen now?'

'To what?'

'Selling the house?'

Magnus furrowed his brow. 'I don't have a clue. But you'll have to wait until the investigation is over.'

'But the price—no one is going to want to buy a house where a woman has been found dead.'

The corners of Eva's mouth turned even further down, and Magnus couldn't help thinking that in a few years' time they would probably be stuck there for good.

'Do you have to make this public?' she pleaded.

Magnus could feel himself losing his temper.

'This is a murder investigation,' he hissed, and was about to add ... *and I don't give a damn about your bloody house* ... but he controlled himself.

'Please don't visit the house until the investigation is complete,' he said curtly, pushing his chair back. 'You husband is down the corridor with my colleague. You can air your concerns to him.'

Magnus felt despondent as he shut the door. His skin was boiling while he was freezing. He felt close to a breakdown. Shivering, he pulled a blanket out of a cupboard and put it over his shoulders, then rested his head on his arms on the desk and slipped into an uneasy sleep.

83

The trees writhed in the driving wind and Karina Sunfors was glad to be inside in a warm pizzeria. She looked down at her hands. The last month had been an inferno. She had been so close to losing him.

Since the day they had seen Pedro Estrabou at Elgiganten in Arninge, Carlos had been in hospital. But now there was finally light at the end of the tunnel.

The first bite of pizza tasted wonderful—she hadn't realized how hungry she was. The nurse who had forced her out had been right, she had to eat and sleep if she was to get by. Well, at least eat, Karina thought. While she was eating, she looked around the room. The walls were covered in yellowing pine panelling and despite the owner hanging up a random assortment of paintings to lift the atmosphere, it was obvious the restaurant had seen better days.

In a corner there were five youths staring at a wall-mounted TV showing some kind of poker game. After a while one of the boys called out.

'Change the channel! This is shit!'

The man behind the counter switched to the news. The youths didn't seem entirely satisfied with the choice but said nothing. Karina did. She stood straight up and dropped her fork on the floor.

'It's him!' she exclaimed. 'It's him.'

84

The phone ringing made Magnus jump. He had trawled through all the surveillance footage from the central metro station without any results and fallen back asleep at his desk. He coughed before picking up the receiver.

'Magnus Kalo.'

'Hi—it's Jonas Orling. A tip's come in that you have to hear.'

Magnus made an effort not to sound like he had just woken up.

'What?'

'A woman called. She said she knows where Pedro Estrabou lives, and that she's followed him in the car.'

'This isn't some nutter is it?'

'No, no. Pedro tortured her husband. He's called Carlos Fernandez and was jailed by the military junta somewhere in Buenos Aires. He even had a heart attack when he saw Pedro. He's in Danderyd hospital.'

Magnus was silent for a moment, then said, 'Let's go now. You can come with me and fill me in in the car. Meet me in the car park.'

85

Carlos Fernandez was sitting semi-upright in his hospital bed. Karina had brought in the police and now Pedro Estrabou would escape the punishment and suffering he deserved.

Carlos clenched his jaw. People were fickle. He had told her to keep quiet, to leave the police out of it, but as soon as she had the chance she had run off to a pizzeria and called the cops.

He hadn't had time to think—to plan his revenge—and now the opportunity was gone. He had never killed anyone, but he knew he was capable of it. If Karina had been able to read his thoughts right now, she would have walked out of the room never to return. But she couldn't. Instead, she stood there before him, exalted. Pleased to have made her heroic effort.

'How about that? They showed his picture on TV. Perhaps he's not just a witness, maybe he's actually murdered all these people. What do you think?'

Carlos turned his head to one side in an attempt to conceal his anger. His voice was controlled and serious.

'He has killed, raped and tortured. He has removed newborn children from their mothers. Of course it's him. His purpose in life is to bring pain to others.'

Karina looked at him searchingly, her slender shoulders tensed. Why wasn't he happy? The police are going to catch that horrible person and Carlos will be able to put it all behind him. She couldn't understand why he looked so distant. His facial expression was one she was unfamiliar with and she didn't like it.

There were rapid footsteps outside the door. The police were coming. Karina sighed with relief and went to open the door.

'They're coming,' she said.

86

Magnus immediately sensed the man's reluctance. He was lying in bed with his arms crossed and looked generally sullen when Magnus sat down on a stool next to the bed. Jonas Orling was standing in the background, his notebook at the ready.

'How are you?' Magnus asked.

'What do you think? I almost died.'

Magnus pretended not to hear his angry tone.

'We think this man, Pedro Estrabou, may be the key to solving three Swedish murders and a kidnapping.'

Carlos laughed unexpectedly.

'You mean you think he's guilty?'

Magnus grimaced.

'It's possible, but in the first instance we want to get in touch with him.'

'It's him. And you'll be wanting to know where we saw him and how I can be so sure it was him?'

'Yes, please.'

Carlos laboriously pulled his top up. His chest and stomach were covered in thick scars, as if he had been whipped.

Magnus raised his eyebrows and looked at him questioningly.

'Electric cables. The baton was also a favourite of his. I have fourteen fractures in my body—most haven't healed properly. Pedro Estrabou's face has been in my dreams for thirty years. Do you really think I would be mistaken? If so, you're stupider than you look.'

'Sorry ... where is he now?' Magnus asked.

Karina stepped forward from the window.

'I can give you the address. Carlos needs to rest now.'

87

Roger gazed intensely at the beige fifties villa where they believed Pedro Estrabou was hiding. He felt impatient.

'Do you think he's in there?' Sofie put her jacket across her legs to keep warm.

'Perhaps. We have to keep a low profile.'

'Maybe he has Gunvor in there?'

Roger looked doubtful.

'It's hard to drag a body around an area like this without someone noticing. There's always someone looking out of the window somewhere.'

'He may have been lucky?'

'I don't think this bloke relies on luck.'

Sofie pulled out a pair of gloves from her pocket and put them on. Her breath rose like a cloud toward the roof of the car.

'It got cold early this year.'

Roger nodded. Despite the cold, he was only wearing his usual leather jacket.

'It's frustrating that we can't even arrest him ... ' he said.

'Yes, but perhaps we could bring him in for questioning?'

'I don't think we'd get much out of him in the time we had,' Sofie said sceptically.

'Magnus can—if anyone can, it's him. Have you seen him in action?'

'No, but I've heard he's good.'

Roger rubbed his cold hands together, but didn't let the front door out of his sight for even a moment. For a second, he had thought the handle was moving, but it appeared to be just as stationary as before. He leaned back and put a pinch of snuff in his mouth.

88

Magnus looked at the computer screen in surprise. The address in Mörby provided by Karina Sunfors had turned out to be owned by one Marcelo Vidas.

The man had turned up in Sweden in 2003, at the same time the amnesty for people involved in the military junta had been annulled, and it wasn't unlikely that this was Pedro Estrabou's new identity.

Magnus looked at the information he had just received from British Airways. Marcelo Vidas would travel to Buenos Aires a couple of times per year, connecting on to the province of Córdoba in the north, where he stayed for a fortnight or so before returning to Sweden. What was he doing there? Visiting family?

Magnus was so engrossed in his work that he didn't notice darkness falling outside.

While Roger and Sofie were on the stakeout outside Marcelo Vidas's house, he was finding out as much as he could about Marcelo's life. He had already got hold of his bank details, and had noted that Vidas withdrew the same amount every month—four thousand kronor—from an ATM. The money was always withdrawn on the fifteenth. Apart from a salary from a cleaning company, a lump sum of twelve thousand kronor came in every three months. Where was the money coming from?

For a brief moment he looked at the brown carpet, then he picked up the phone and called chief of police Osvaldo Ortiz in La Rioja. Domenique Estrabou's accounts would have to be checked too.

It took around an hour for his email account to emit a beep.

You're quite right, Mr. Kalo. Domenique Estrabou has been receiving a sum equivalent to four thousand Swedish kronor every month for a number of years now. The sender is one Marcelo Vidas.

Magnus smiled to himself. Finally, things were beginning to fall into place. But where was he getting the money from?

89

It happened in the evening. Pedro Estrabou stepped out of the house in Mörby and slipped down the steps like a shadow. He was wearing a grey tracksuit and moved toward his car with rapid steps.

'Is he going to murder Gunvor?' A cynical smile flickered across Roger's face.

Sofie waved him away with her hand.

'Shut up. He's driving away.'

She switched on the engine and slowly followed down the street. They had to keep at a safe distance.

The cars moved in caravan at a stately pace. Pedro took the turning toward the centre of Mörby. He parked by the metro station. He remained in the car for a while before opening the door. The rugged man glanced at his watch and then walked into the station, taking firm steps.

Roger rolled his eyes.

'The bastard might be taking a train. Get out and follow him, I'll call Arne and ask what to do. Stay in touch.'

Sofie nodded and got out of the car at the precise moment the man's back vanished through the wide sliding doors. She upped her own tempo. They couldn't lose him, but things were going quickly now. She began to jog.

The entrance was designed like a small square and led not only to the metro but also to a shopping centre.

Sofie looked around. Pedro Estrabou was gone. Despair grew in her. Where had he gone? Of course, he might have gone down into the metro, but he might just as well be in Ica, Pressbyrån or have headed into the subterranean car park.

She had just dialled Roger's number when she saw Pedro again. Silently, she left the phone in her hand. Pedro Estrabou was in Pressbyrån.

'Hello?' Roger's voice was audible at the other end of the line.

'He's in Pressbyrån—buying pick 'n' mix.'

'Where are you?'

'I'm outside, by the ticket barriers.'

'Keep talking and don't meet his eyes, in case he spots you.'

'Okay.'

Sofie did her best to look like she was engaged in a pleasant conversation on the phone, but it wasn't necessary. Pedro wasn't looking out of the window.

'He's coming out. Hang on.'

Pedro Estrabou put the bag of sweets into the pocket of the grey tracksuit. His facial expression was lifeless and pale. For a couple of minutes he stood quite still outside of Pressbyrån before slowly going up the stairs to the second storey of the shopping centre.

Sofie followed. When she got halfway up, the man began to run. For a split second, it confused her so much that she couldn't bring herself to do anything—then she rushed after him.

Pedro ran into the shopping centre aiming for the lift. Sofie reached the doors at the same time as the digital display showed that the lift had gone down. She panted heavily into the phone.

'I don't know, but it seems as if he ... he must have seen me. He's gone down in the lift.'

'Understood.'

Roger put away his mobile and ran into the entrance while drawing his service weapon. People standing in the way were frightened and surprised and ran away, some screamed and others stood still, as if they were watching a film that didn't affect them. At the same moment as Roger reached the middle of the entrance hall, a quiet scraping sound was audible and the lift doors opened.

'Stop! Police!' he shouted.

The man looked at him despondently, then proffered his hands toward Roger and spoke with a smile.

'Go on, arrest me.'

90

'We've got him, you should be happy.'

Magnus looked at Arne Norman, whose bright red face looked like it could burst at any moment. His words made

Arne change expression—his eyes narrowed and became contemptuous.

'Happy? It was hardly part of the plan for Roger and Sofie to chase Pedro and arrest him. And with weapons drawn—in the middle of a shopping centre. He was supposed to lead us to Gunvor.'

Magnus sighed.

'This is how it turned out—we'll just have to deal with it.'

'We've got six hours, then we have to release him. I'm going to speak to the Prosecution Authority—they might want to appoint their own investigator now we have a suspect.'

Magnus shook his head.

'I'm sorry.'

'For what? I don't want any pity.' Arne tried to sound indifferent, but it was obvious that the outlook was distressing to him. 'Question him straight away, find out where Gunvor is, we can sort the rest later.'

'I'll do my best, but there's a risk I'll fail.'

Arne looked unreasonably crushed.

'Then a cold-blooded murderer will go free. One who knows he should avoid the police. Do you understand what that means?'

Magnus looked dejected. He was quite aware of what it meant, above all for his own family.

91

Linn pulled the black T-shirt over her head. Her face was beginning to return to normal and there were only a couple of pale bruises under her eyes to give away what had happened to her that evening at Gärdet.

The rising anger she felt toward the attacker made her feel strong and energetic. Only occasionally, when she was thinking about Moa and Elin, did the paralysing fear sneak in, whispering with an evil grin: *you don't even have a chance.*

The police had arrested Pedro Estrabou. Linn assumed she ought to be happy, but there was still the uncertainty. What if they had arrested him before they had enough evidence?

What if it wasn't him?

Pedro Estrabou was used to questioning people in the ESMA torture centre—would he really confess to the significantly softer Swedish police? She doubted it. And if they were forced to release him, what would he do next? He might have been a little lax before—a fire, an assault, but now ... he wouldn't rest until he had killed them.

Magnus had promised to call straight after questioning was over and Linn was on tenterhooks. She put an electric heater in the kids' room to ward off the winter chill and sat down in front of the TV. Cold air was blowing through the ventilation grates, and she was freezing despite wearing two jumpers.

She was so lost in her thoughts that it took a good while before she realized she was watching a children's cartoon. She turned off the TV and stared listlessly into space. All along she had thought things would be better once the attacker had been arrested, but now she wasn't so sure. She and Magnus had come apart this autumn. She was alone almost all the time and they never had time to talk to each other properly. She sighed in resignation. No, she couldn't be that unfair. It would be naïve to think that there could be full-blooded romance between them while their family was being threatened. Right now, all that mattered was survival.

She fell back into the sofa cushions and put her feet on the coffee table. It would have been good to flick through some photo albums to revive that family feeling, but all of them had been lost in the fire at the apartment. A few, sad tears ran down her face—then she went into the kitchen to do the dishes.

92

The glass of water was condensing. The interrogation room was cramped and smelled musty. Magnus felt cornered by the walls. He took a deep breath. This was personal. The man sitting opposite him could very well be the person who had tried to burn his children and beat Linn to death.

His heart was pounding. He turned away from Pedro and closed his eyes for a split second.

'Do you recognize me?' he said brusquely.

Pedro's gaze was guarded, but below the surface there shone contempt. His short, greying eyelashes made his blue eyes look hard. His face had deep furrows and everything on him seemed to aim downward, apart from his eyebrows, which stretched up toward the high hairline.

'What do you think?' His voice had a slight accent and sounded slightly pugnacious.

Magnus pretended not to notice.

'Are you Pedro Estrabou?'

The man shrugged his shoulders nonchalantly.

'We can confirm it through DNA testing if you don't tell us,' Magnus lied. 'We're going to swab you later.'

The man looked bored.

Magnus attempted once again and forced a tone of understanding into his voice.

'I'm not interested in your crimes during the junta regime—that's not my department. But I can see if we can do something for you if you're willing to cooperate with us.'

Magnus watched the man who was expressionlessly staring back at him—he didn't seem to be reacting.

'Should I interpret your silence to mean that you are Pedro Estrabou?'

The man nodded.

'But you've also called yourself Marcelo Vidas?'

Pedro looked down at the table in between them and nodded again.

Magnus pushed out his jaw and changed tack.

'How long have you lived in Sweden?'

'Since around 2003.'

'And why did you come here?'

'I don't know—there are lots of Argentinians here and I got a job too.'

'So you didn't come here to avenge the rape of your mother?' he said sharply.

Pedro shook his head.

'Witness has shaken his head,' Magnus said for the benefit of the tape recorder.

'How do you feel about the fact that your mother was raped?'

The man gazed at him with a dark expression. 'How would you feel?'

'I don't know. I had hoped you could tell me.'

Pedro snorted in reply.

' ... but you put money into your mother's account every month?' Magnus continued.

'Yes.'

'Why?'

'Because she needs money to live—is it so strange to help your mother out?'

'No, not at all. But where does the money come from? We've noticed you receive twelve thousand kronor every third month and that it isn't a salary. Where does that money come from?'

Pedro stared silently at him and was about to reply when the lawyer, Johan Rahldin, a thin-haired man of around fifty, stepped into the room and stopped him.

'Yes, hello. Sorry that I'm late.'

'Not to worry,' Magnus gestured at the chair next to Pedro.

'I couldn't help but hear your question—and I just want to point out that this is an initial post-arrest interview.'

'Yes, and ... '

'My client doesn't have to answer any questions in depth before I've arrived.'

Magnus controlled himself.

'I've got six hours—can we get started?' he said, his eyes black.

93

The interrogation felt just as meaningless as bashing your head against a wall. Magnus tried to get at Pedro by all sorts of methods, but the greying man tersely denied all involvement in the murders and in Gunvor's kidnap.

Estrabou's lawyer, Johan Rahldin, also attempted to limit the psychological games that Magnus was playing, although it really made no difference. Pedro was a completely closed book. In the middle of the night, Magnus gave up.

Pedro Estrabou would go free. This was a nightmare scenario.

Linn was awake when he rang.

'I'm coming home love. I didn't get him.'

His voice was hazy with fatigue, but it couldn't conceal his despair.

94

A little while later when Linn and Magnus pressed their bodies close together under the duvet, both of them felt almost sick with exhaustion. Linn rested on Magnus's arm.

'What do you think? Is it him?'

'He's capable and he has motive—at least for Lidhman's murder. But I don't know anything else.'

'How did he respond to the questions?'

'He didn't—it was as if I'd asked him what he usually buys at Ica.'

Magnus shut his eyes. 'If it's him, he'll never admit anything ... I didn't even see any signs that he recognized me.'

Suddenly he felt doubtful. Was it really Pedro?

When he turned to face Linn she had fallen asleep. Her calm breaths were soporific and he felt himself slowly drifting off. The dreams that received him were calm and beautiful, as if they wanted to tempt him deeper into a better world. The smell of freshly cut grass, the sight of Moa and Elin on a flowery meadow.

But during the night the dreams would turn against him and he would wake up drenched in cold sweat, feeling as if he had inhaled something poisonous and suffocating. There was something evil out there and it was just waiting for an opportunity.

95

Not everyone was having trouble sleeping. Jonas Orling slept well at night—but then he always had done. Sad thoughts struggled to penetrate him.

Some envied his calm, safe personality—others thought it made him boring. No matter what people thought, it was hard to dislike him.

He was like his father—reliable and responsible. Those characteristics would soon attract a woman. His mother was convinced of this as she sat opposite him, eating lunch in the restaurant. A daughter-in-law would mean she would have to share her son with someone else, but it would also provide her with the grandchildren she dreamt of. It was worth the sacrifice.

'Is work going well?' she asked, pushing her glasses onto her nose.

'I think so. We've arrested a man. He was questioned last night, but I don't know how it went.'

'Is it him—the mass murderer?'

Jonas rolled his eyes.

'Not a mass murderer as such, and he's only under suspicion. If we don't find anything on him he'll be released.'

His mother looked at him anxiously.

'You will though, won't you Jonas? Sometimes what you deal with seems so nasty. You will be careful?'

'I'm just a probationer, Mum. I review tips and things like that with a manager. Stop being so jittery.'

Jonas took a bite and chewed frenetically while he looked at her in irritation. Sometimes she really got on his nerves with all her worrying.

Later, when he left her and headed back to the office, he felt relieved. Her anxiety was sometimes suffocating. He should probably have marked his independence earlier, but he didn't like fighting and he didn't want to hurt her. It was easier to withdraw when it was all too much—that was what his father had always done and it had worked very well, so far as he could tell. That was why it would be a while before he visited his parents again, he reflected.

96

The DNA samples and fingerprints from Pedro Estrabou gave them nothing. Neither did the search of his house. All that remained was an examination of his computer, but that would take time.

Magnus and his colleagues sat at the meeting table reviewing the situation. There was an atmosphere of disillusionment in the room.

'What we can hope is that he leads us to Gunvor,' Magnus said. Roger snorted.

'She's probably already dead. Why would he keep her alive?'

Magnus smiled feebly. 'Roger Ekman, the eternal optimist.'

'Yes, but you do get it don't you? She'd only be a burden.'

Sofie looked at the others.

'Roger's right. If Pedro is guilty then he really should want to get rid of Gunvor and all the evidence now.'

'Yes, but I'm not entirely convinced it's him any longer,' Magnus said quickly.

'Why?' Arne looked perplexed.

'I didn't recognize him ... and he didn't recognize me.'

' ... but you haven't seen the murderer properly,' Arne interjected.

Magnus shrugged his shoulders.

'I merely said that I wasn't entirely certain that it's him.'

'Anyway, it would have been good if we had pushed him harder while we had him,' Arne said.

Magnus shook his head.

'We had nothing on him—we had no other options. Of course, I could have handed him over to the war crimes commission, but if Gunvor is alive it would be plain stupid to have him locked up.'

Roger looked serious.

'Who's watching him?'

'Right now it's Orling. Sofie will take over in an hour or so.'

Arne nodded to Sofie who got up and disappeared through the door.

Magnus rubbed his eyes.

'The National Forensics Centre team are going to search every corner of Pedro's computer. If there's anything there they'll find it. I just hope he isn't so high tech that he's managed to delete everything.'

Arne pushed his hands into his pockets.

'Let's just hope that he's not so unaccustomed to computers that he doesn't use them at all. I'll call National Forensics and see if I can hurry them up. If we're lucky, he might have searched for a member of the Berggren family or simply have Googled Lidhman. That wouldn't be so stupid.'

'Do you know how many investigations have gone cold or become completely worthless while we waited for forensics?' Magnus said.

'Of course,' Arne said. 'But you don't have to worry about that for now. This case is as top priority as it gets—even at National Forensics.'

97

Pedro Estrabou had gone straight home after questioning had ended. When the front door slammed behind him, he had leaned against it and sunk to his knees. Why weren't they leaving him alone? Why did he have to keep on fleeing? Here, back home in Argentina, everywhere! Angry tears flooded down the furrowed cheeks like rivulets on a dry riverbed.

Now he was sitting on the hall floor, a shadow of his former self, far away from his children and grandchildren. His body ached with exhaustion.

Life is toying with me, he reflected, thoughts whirring through his head until it felt like the whole world was against him.

He pressed his sweaty hands against his thighs and dark patches of sweat formed on his grey trousers. Then he stood up with a heave and stumbled into the bare kitchen where he opened the cutlery drawer.

The bread knife was serrated and dull, with a worn wooden handle. Slowly, he rolled up his shirtsleeve and placed the edge against his lower arm. He knew exactly where to put the knife, because he had seen his mother ready with a knife more than once. Now it was him, standing there and letting the blade rest against the thin skin. He pressed gently so that blood oozed out in small pearls, but he didn't cut deeply.

He stared at the red matter, then dropped the knife on the floor. There was a loud metallic clang as it hit the stone tiles.

Pedro leaned over the sink with his arms around his head. His face was grey. His thin lips let out inconsolable sobs. Since he was unaccustomed to crying, the noise sounded contrived and guttural, almost as if he was giving birth. But all that was being born was a new plan. A new idea for freedom.

PART 8

98

Gunvor had met Gösta the summer she turned twenty-five at the church Saturday coffee morning. He was a few years younger than her and very beautiful—but she was too, with her long, golden hair and her silken skin. Her father used to call her heaven's most beautiful angel, but Gunvor was quite a long way off being an angel. She was a full-blooded egoist, at least until the day Gösta came onto the scene. After that, she didn't only think of herself, but also him. Her heart lay naked in his hands, but she had no idea how hard he would hug it. Sometimes it would feel as if sharp nails were clawing at her insides. He broke her down, controlled her, but it wasn't all one-sided. Sometimes it felt like they were fighting to the death. As if they were destroying one another.

At first she thought it was flattering that she could evoke such strong emotions in him, but as time passed, his jealousy became increasingly disturbing. Perhaps she should have left him, but she couldn't now. It was as if he had radar built in. If she had the slightest doubt about their relationship, he would immediately smother her in intense declarations of love until her head was once again completely turned.

Out and about with people, Gunvor would be dressed decently so as not to arouse desire in other men, but at home she often wore provocative outfits—and sometimes nothing at all. All according to his wishes.

She did everything he asked of her. And he asked for a lot.

They hadn't been together for long before he wanted to engage in more advanced experimentation. Most of all, he wanted a prostitute to participate in their games, and he used to pick up women in Stockholm while Gunvor was left waiting at home in Åkersberga. Gösta had a lot of ideas—and he convinced her that what they did with the girls was something that unified them—something they were doing together.

But that wasn't what Gunvor was dreaming of in the cold cottage. She was dreaming of her son and those dreams were filled with grief and remorse. The thoughts in her sleep were painfully clear despite her dementia. She whimpered anxiously on the camp bed. Soon she would open her eyes and then reality would be far worse than her nightmares.

99

The cold hovered around Pedro Estrabou as he hurried out of his house. As the drive was covered in rubbish bags, his car was parked on the other side of the street. He had a hunted look in his eyes and looked over his shoulder nervously. Sofie and Jonas watched him. It was dark and the light from the street lights made the snow almost appear as if it was taken from a story. Pedro was only wearing a thin blue sweatshirt and both Roger and Sofie assumed he was fetching something from his car or quickly jumping inside to drive away.

They were wrong. Pedro stood behind his car, bent down as if he was unlocking the boot and vanished. Later, Sofie would recollect that a car had slowly driven past them as they had waited for Pedro's head to reappear, but by then it was too late.

They had lost their prime suspect.

100

The plastic mug of boiling hot tea hit the wall like a projectile and the yellow liquid flowed down the fibreglass wall.

'Fucking shit!' Magnus bellowed, pounding his fist against the desk. He threw himself into his chair, but got up again almost straight away and picked up the mug from the carpet. He threw it angrily into the overflowing waste-paper basket, whereupon it fell out.

'Shit.' He kicked the mug with his foot. Then he sat down and tried to calm himself.

There was no point in shouting at Sofie and Jonas. What was done was done, but whose car was it?

Sofie's description of the car was, in spite of everything, good. A bright green Ford Fiesta, with a registration number she hadn't been able to see in the dark.

He would get Jonas to search for all green Ford Fiestas registered in the area, but it might be a tricky or downright impossible task. There were probably thousands of cars like it in the Stockholm area.

He leaned forward and rested his face in his hands. Pedro's co-conspirator had to be someone who was sufficiently mixed up in it all to help him escape from the police. But why? They hadn't been able to hold Pedro—was he worried he would be re-arrested?

Magnus dragged his hands through his hair in resignation. His face was chalk white and suddenly just one guard outside the door didn't seem like enough.

101

Gunvor Berggren was freezing and when she opened her eyes, she realized why. It was snowing outside the window, and she was completely naked. She was still too tired to talk. Instead, she lay there, staring. Stared in wonder at the plastic covering the walls and floors. At the shiny, sharp objects on the chair beside her. The fondue fork. The plastic gloves—like the doctor wore. It was all so strange. She called out in a low voice: 'Gösta, are you there?'

But there was no reply.

WEDNESDAY 19 NOVEMBER

102

The dead woman in the cottage was still a mystery. Who was she?

Despite a massive review of missing elderly women, there were no matches for the fragile body.

Magnus stared at Eva Zimmer, the forensic pathologist, who was leaning over the body. For once, the November sun was shining outside and its rays sought their way through the window. Magnus noticed the small particles of dust sailing around the light autopsy room in a dreamlike state. He was glad he had already eaten lunch before visiting, because he didn't count on having much of an appetite after Eva's briefing.

'And there's nothing to go on?' he asked.

The pathologist smiled hesitantly.

'Well, she was stabbed from the front and judging by the angle it looks like she was sitting down. Perhaps it happened in the morning, because there was only some yoghurt and cereal in her stomach. That's probably breakfast, if you ask me.'

'No one seems to have reported her missing.'

'No, I heard. A pity isn't it.'

'Yes.' Magnus turned round to leave, but as he reached the door Eva called after him.

'You must be wondering why I wanted you to come?'

Magnus raised an eyebrow slightly.

Eva continued. 'Well, I've X-rayed the body and noticed that the woman has a hip replacement.' She cleared her throat. 'I've naturally opened her up for a closer look.'

'Why? Is it unusual or somehow identifiable?' A streak of hope jolted through him.

'Yes, exactly. There are different manufacturers, different hospitals use different suppliers. This one is an Exeter plastic—here's the number that was on it. Find out who uses them.' She passed a note to Magnus.

Magnus almost laughed out loud.

'That's fantastic!' he exclaimed.

A smile tugged at the corners of Eva's mouth.

'Mmm ... well, this gives your desk officers and probationers something to do for an afternoon. I'll send you a report with more information about the prosthesis so they can get to work.'

103

There were still plenty of witness statements and notes to keep Jonas Orling and the others awake all night, but the new information about the hip prosthesis pushed the other tasks to one side.

Jonas was seemingly the most cheered up by the news. Pedro Estrabou's disappearance had made him bury himself in shame in the hopeless search for the green Ford, but now he saw an opportunity to make up for his past misdemeanours and he didn't intend to miss out.

The room was filled with expectation and soon phone calls to various hospitals and clinics created a lively hubbub in the room.

Magnus was at his computer. He didn't dare count his chickens before they hatched, but deep down he hoped the dead woman's identity would emerge. What if there was a clear connection between the dead woman and Pedro? Then he would finally be able to quash his doubts and he would know who was trying to murder his family.

Pedro had been gone for almost a day and the police had now placed their faith in the public. The pictures previously shown in the media hadn't been much good, but now they had fresh photos from the interview. The picture would be published in every newspaper and on every TV show they could reach. Pedro would be sought as a witness, like before, but this wasn't a problem, as the police hadn't released the news that he had been brought in for questioning.

Magnus looked out of the glass door. Roger was loitering by the meeting table. He was wearing a faded yellow polo shirt and a pair of jeans that had seen their best days. Combined with several days of stubble and ruffled hair, he looked like he needed a holiday.

Magnus observed him for a while before spotting the dark bags under Roger's eyes. He sighed. They were all working hard. He quickly decided to take Roger for a beer in town—they probably both needed one.

A little while later they stepped into a sports bar on Södermalm.

There was a flat-screen TV on the wall and a bunch of ice hockey fans were braying with delight as the Swedish team scored. The two colleagues soon found a hidden corner in the busy venue. Magnus snuck glances at the patrons while Roger fetched two beers from the bar.

It was mostly young men squeezed in by the tables, with an occasional woman here and there. They seemed so frivolous and unconcerned that Magnus felt a pang of jealousy. It was a long time since he had been able to let go and feel as relaxed as they did. He thought about Linn and the kids and the threat they faced. His responsibilities weighed down on him. He had dragged them into this and he had to make sure everything turned out okay.

'I got you a large one—you need it,' Roger growled, setting

down a foaming beer glass in front of him.

'Yes, I do.'

Roger became serious.

'You mean a lot to me, Magnus ... I want you to take it easy.'

Magnus raised his eyebrows slightly. He felt like he had been caught off guard. Roger rarely said anything emotional—unless it was because he was angry. Not that they weren't friends, it was just they had never previously expressed it in as many words.

Magnus nodded, partly moved and partly embarrassed.

'Right,' Roger said, 'what do you think—will we find out the woman's identity?'

Magnus pulled over a bowl of peanuts and made a gesture of resignation with his other hand. 'What do you think?'

'I think there's a good chance, but there's one thing I know for sure.'

'What?'

'That bowls of peanuts left on tables are terrible. They did a study in a pub once and it turned out it contained traces of thirty-six people's urine. And there are a bunch of people who have norovirus right now.'

Magnus grimaced in disgust and pushed the bowl to the other side of the table.

'I guess only norovirus is missing—then hell is complete,' he mumbled.

Roger laughed and his stout belly jumped in contentment under the table.

Magnus leaned back. This might be a good night.

104

A few kilometres away, on the shore of Lake Mälaren, there was a man standing in the darkness staring out onto the ice. His hands were trembling and his rib cage was rising and falling as if he was crying.

Then he began to walk out onto the frozen lake. His steps crunched in the snow as he slowly went further and further out onto the lake. In the end, he was barely visible, standing by the edge of the dammed fairway.

He stood there for a long time, as if thinking about something, while the water gurgled incessantly and uneasily against the sharp edges of the ice. Then he put his hand in his jacket pocket and pulled something out. A pistol. He had almost forgotten it in the car. He leaned gently forward and let it drop into the open water glittering so alluringly in the moonlight. Once it was gone, he quickly turned on his heel and walked back across the ice. He went through the forest, unconcerned about the drag marks left behind by the body in the wet snow.

By the car he looked around, then he opened the door of the neon green Ford and got in. Instinct told him to leave straight away, but he knew there was one more thing he had to do. Fumbling, he grabbed the rags and cleaning spray from the glove compartment and got out. There was a faint clicking sound when he opened the boot, and he looked sadly at the dark patch of blood.

105

Jonas Orling was already at work by the time the sun began to rise. He had always been a morning person. This morning, he had woken up at around five, eaten his porridge and a cheese sandwich, done the dishes and got dressed. Instead of turning on the TV and killing time, he had decided he might as well go to work. Today they would have a list of older women with Exeter plastic hip prostheses and hopefully just a few would be the same height as the victim. He wanted to be there.

Furthermore, every available police officer was now searching for Gunvor Berggren. What if it was him—Jonas—who came up with the decisive information that saved her? The one to heroically stop Pedro Estrabou just before he killed again?

A broad smile spread across his face. He had already received a tip the day before that he particularly wanted to check out. An abandoned cottage in Brottby that had suddenly come back to life.

He jotted down a quick note to Magnus and put it on his desk, pulled out his car keys and headed down to the car park. Then he got in the car and drove off on the most important journey of his life.

106

The news that the police had released Pedro Estrabou had felt like a punch in the face. The pain and humiliation had been just as demeaning as the lashes he had received in the juntas' cellars. Why had they let him go? It was an insult to him and everyone else Pedro had tortured—all the mourning relatives.

The Swedish police were shit—they had released a murderer, a monster, but they didn't care.

Carlos Fernandez looked down at his hands resting on the kitchen table. Karina could never know anything, that much he knew. This man had already taken so much from him, but now it was over. Never again would Pedro Estrabou affect his life. As of now, it was over and he wouldn't spare another thought for him.

Carlos shut his eyes and breathed in the cold air coming through the leaky windows.

Karina's happy voice was audible from the bedroom.

'It's so good to have you home. I slept like a log last night. Did you sleep well too?'

His voice was rough when he answered.

'Yes.'

'I thought I'd do some shopping—is there anything you want?'

Carlos opened his eyes and gazed dreamily out of the window. There was a new tone of relief in his voice.

'Yes, buy a bottle of champagne. I think we should celebrate tonight.'

107

'You couldn't have smelled anything at the cottage!' Arne said, a little louder than usual, as he stepped through the door of Magnus's office.

'What do you mean?' Magnus's stomach dropped.

'You and Roger were at the cottage ages ago—long before the woman was put in the roof.'

Magnus looked at his boss, an uncertain man in disguise with a cocky attitude. His brain searched frantically for an out. Anything—Linn's visit could not be discovered.

At last he found what he was looking for.

'I went there again.'

'What?'

Magnus gave a diplomatic smile.

'Yes, I wanted to soak up the atmosphere, have new ideas. The dentists had said it was okay if we checked the place out.'

Arne felt his lust for battle flowing away. He nodded.

'Next time I want to know what you're up to, and that applies to the rest of you too,' he said acidly. Then he turned on his heel and vanished with his head held high.

Magnus swallowed hard. He felt like a liar and discovered to his surprise that the conversation had made him anxious, but he hadn't given himself away and that was what counted.

He immediately picked up the phone to tell Linn, but she didn't reply. For a brief moment he experienced a sense of unease in his stomach, but then he remembered that Linn had said she had an appointment at the hospital that day. Relieved, he breathed out and looked around the office. The forensic examination was complete and the report was waiting for him on the windowsill. There was one thing that particularly interested him—the examination of Pedro Estrabou's computer.

It wasn't common for NFC to work this quickly and Magnus made a mental note to thank Sofie who had been nagging them on a daily basis with her phone calls.

He picked up the stack of paper and put it on his desk.

Before he started he needed a cup of coffee—and not the poison from the vending machine. The first time he had drunk it he had experienced serious abdominal pain and he suspected there was something hazardous in the black muck.

The snow fell relentlessly outside the window and for a

moment he wished he were sufficiently self-important to send one of the probationers out for the coffee. A couple of minutes later he was standing in the café downstairs, brushing the snow off himself.

He treated himself to a Danish pastry and turned up the collar on his jacket and went back outside into the blizzard. A plough drove past him, scraping the tarmac at a deafening volume.

Only now that he returned to his office and put his frozen lips to the paper cup did he see the note from Jonas. He coughed and coffee sprayed across the desk.

'Bloody hell!' he snorted, while brushing the liquid away in confusion with his sleeve. Arne would go mad. He rushed out of his office into the bare corridor.

Jonas wasn't in the probationers' office. Nor was he anywhere else. Magnus traipsed back to his desk and re-read the note.

Hi, I got in early. We received a tip about an abandoned cottage in Brottby, Vallentuna, from an old lady. She sounded credible. I'm going to go check it out. Back around 8.30.
Jonas

It was already just after nine. Magnus hadn't forgotten Linn's visit to the cottage in Flaxenvik, and even if it was good that she had gone there and noticed the smell of the corpse from a certain perspective, he didn't like these kinds of spontaneous outings.

Magnus liked Jonas. He was calm and cheerful and there was nothing uncertain about his behaviour. He might be a little naïve, but he had all the qualities necessary to become a good policeman. That was why he decided to relax and not fly off the handle when he got back. Jonas would receive a stinging warning, but he would carry on working on the investigation. Linn would also be mad if Jonas was removed from the case, which was a major reason for letting him off lightly.

Magnus smiled slightly. He couldn't take out the only reliable babysitter they had ever had.

He opened the forensic report and had just pulled the cap off his pen when there was a knock on his door.

Roger looked unhappy when he appeared in the doorway.

'Where's Orling?' he grunted.

Roger read the note that Magnus handed over and whistled.

'Oh really? What are you going to do with him?'

'Just scare him a little.'

Roger looked sceptical. Magnus rushed to the defence of the probationer.

'He's a good guy.'

'Yes, but that doesn't mean he can go off on his own, does it? He might bodge it and ruin everything. We don't want any bloody solo raids.'

Magnus gave him a look as if to say that he had heard enough.

'I'll deal with him.'

Roger nodded.

'I actually came to find out what the lab had found.'

'I've not had time to read the report yet.'

'Okay, let's have a meeting after lunch. Perhaps you can summarize it for us then.'

'Sure. But could you find out which tip Orling is following up on? I don't like that he's not back yet. Call him on his mobile.'

'Of course—but I'm sure he's fine.'

'Yes, but there's a whole lot of snow. He might have gone off the road or something.'

'Surely he'd call if he had?'

The furrow between Magnus's eyebrows deepened slightly.

'I just want you to check,' he sighed.

Roger snapped as he moved back to the door: 'Yes, yes—I'll do it. I said I would.'

108

The heavens seemed to have opened and it was a challenge to keep the car in the narrow tyre tracks in the snow. As soon as they ended up even slightly off the track, the rear wheels skidded and hissed furiously. He bent over the wheel and struggled to make out anything in the whiteness, but he couldn't see more than ten metres ahead.

Jonas turned on the traffic bulletin on the radio. There was a class two weather warning and anyone not yet on the roads was encouraged to stay where they were. Should he turn back? It was already past nine and he had wanted to be back before the others got in to work. But it was too late now. For a moment he was worried—he wasn't quite sure his initiative would be appreciated.

But what if the tip led them somewhere—what if? Jonas smiled and took the Brottby turning. The winding forest roads were covered in thirty centimetres of fresh snow.

Eventually, he didn't dare drive further. He might get stuck if he was unlucky and this deep into the forest there were unlikely to be any ploughs. But it didn't matter—he knew he was close. He turned off the engine and put on his green-and-white-striped beanie hat. Then he took a deep breath and stepped into whiteness.

The snow was lying heavily on the pine branches and it was as quiet as a cemetery. The ice-cold air sank into Jonas's lungs and moved around like an icy fan.

Now he was where he felt happiest. A steaming warm cloud formed as his breaths met the chill.

He could feel the folded map in his pocket but he didn't need it—he had already memorized it and knew which way to go.

The freezing cold bit at his nose and cheeks as he trudged onwards. His jeans would be soaked, he thought. But he steamed on and when the road forked he chose the right-hand option. There were no other sounds apart from his own crunching steps now that the wind had died down. Soon he would be there, but he didn't know what he would see. He didn't know that his path would soon reach its end.

109

The cottage looked idyllic, bedded down in a deep bank of snow. Jonas was reminded of the brown timber cabins he would stop in when hiking in the mountains.

Below he glimpsed the road between the trees. The source must have been driving along it when they saw the lights on in the cottage. But right now it was dark.

Jonas pressed his nose against the window. He couldn't see a thing. The yellowing lace curtains inside concealed all. He looked down at the ground. There wasn't a single footprint around the house, but as it was snowing heavily it was hard to tell whether anyone had been here recently.

He dried the snot dripping from his nose with his Lovikka glove. Then he went round to the back. He had snow in his shoes and his feet were beginning to get wet.

When he had done almost a full lap of the cottage, he suddenly stopped. There were now tracks outside the door. Had they been there before? He took off one glove and anxiously put his hand in his pocket looking for his service weapon. Once he felt the cold barrel he felt calmer.

He walked to the door and bent down. The tracks led away from the door—but to where? Suddenly, it was as if the air had changed somehow. As if the realisation made everything taste of blood. The tracks led into his own. *They were following him!*

He quickly looked over his shoulder, but it was too late.

Jonas fell to his knees and looked down at the snow. It was

already red. He barely felt the next stab—his face was buried in the red snow and his eyes stared at the crystals of ice in astonishment, then they saw nothing.

110

Jonas Orling's mother was sprinkling sugar on her cereal when it happened. Suddenly, it felt as if her body was going to fall apart. Somehow, she knew that Jonas was dead and it tore her to pieces. When she fell onto the kitchen floor, she screamed. The animalistic cry came from deep inside her and it carried on and on. When her husband came rushing downstairs he thought she had gone mad. It would take some time before he buried his face in his hands and screamed the same way. Before then he would be flung between hope and doubt until he felt like he was losing his grip. He would shout to his wife wandering around the house like a shadow. Tell her off for losing all hope. As of now, their lives were broken and the grief would divide them. The sight of each other would always remind them of Jonas and they wouldn't be able to live with the pain. But he didn't know this yet.

He was going to call Jonas's mobile, then he would call his home phone, and finally his work. They would hear his voice, his sigh of resignation and explanation that he was fine—that his mother was imagining things. At least, that's what his father thought as he picked up the phone.

111

As Magnus skimmed through the dry forensics report, he tapped the edge of the desk with his biro. They were dealing with a thorough attacker—that much was clear. But they had found things like a fingerprint on a saucepan, footprints and fibres from a blue top. Magnus was about to make a start on the pages about Pedro Estrabou's computer when the phone rang. The sound made him jump.

'Hi, this is Jonas Orling's father—Nils Orling—sorry to call you like this, but is Jonas there?' His voice was pleasant but Magnus could clearly discern the worried undertone.

'No, he's out on assignment.'

Nils Orling went quiet and breathed heavily down the line.

Magnus had met Nils a couple of times. He was a fair size with a reddish beard and round glasses, and he radiated the same kind of calm that Jonas did. Magnus had liked him at once.

'Was there something in particular you wanted?'

'No ... ' Nils Orling dragged the words out as if contemplating something. Then he said apologetically: 'We tried to reach his mobile. My wife is a little worried, that's all. Tell Jonas to give us a ring when he gets back.'

'Yes, I'll do that. Bye.'

When Magnus had hung up he felt downhearted. Why would Jonas's mother be worried? Had Jonas told her about his plans? He tried to dismiss the thoughts, but the unpleasant feeling remained. He got up and went to Roger's office.

'Have you found the tip?'

'No, Jonas must not have put it in the register—and he isn't answering his phone.'

Magnus grimaced.

'We've got the note at least. Is Brottby especially urban?'

'No, completely rural. A cluster of houses by the motorway and they've got a shop and a pizza place, I think. But the rest of the houses are spread out in the forest.'

'Is it a big area?'

'Yes, really big.'

Magnus bit his lip.

'If Jonas still isn't picking up and hasn't been in touch after lunch we'll have to start searching.'

Roger looked sullen.

'Stupid kid,' he said. 'What did NFC say?'

'Nothing out of the ordinary, but I was about to read the file on Pedro's computer. It'll be interesting to see if there are any emails or searches that might connect him to the victims.'

Roger nodded and returned to staring at his computer screen. Magnus felt uneasy when he sat back down at his own desk. He hoped that Jonas was just taking the opportunity to do some fishing while he was out there—but something told him that wasn't the case.

He reached for the phone and tried calling Jonas's mobile again. There was no ringing. That meant it could no longer be tracked.

112

They searched everywhere. The helicopters whirred around like anxious flies above the woods in Brottby. Police knocked on cottage doors, stood outside the Brottby branch of Ica, asked questions and ran amongst the trees with torches—but no one had seen Jonas Orling.

Later in the afternoon, Arne and Magnus called a press conference and once again the glare turned on their problematic investigation. It was unwelcome attention and it bothered them all.

A female reporter from one of the evening papers stood up. 'What is your view on the police managing to lose two people in such a short period of time—with one of them being a policeman?'

'You mean Gunvor Berggren and Jonas Orling?' Arne replied slowly, while fumbling for a good answer.

'Yes—who else might I mean?'

'Jonas Orling has left a message stating that he was following up on a tip in Brottby, and that's obviously positive for the investigation.'

'Who gave the tip?'

'We're looking into that now, and you're welcome to write in your papers that we'd like the person who made the tip to get back in contact.'

'What was Jonas Orling working on?'

'As I said, he wasn't working on anything sensitive—he was reviewing tips relating to the people we're looking for.'

'Shouldn't probationers be accompanied if they're out on assignment?'

Arne hesitated, then replied drily. 'Yes, hmm ... with regard to the investigation, I can't give any details. But all available resources are being used, so I'm convinced that both Gunvor Berggren and probationer Orling will be found.'

The blonde woman snorted.

'Alive?'

'I'm sure that both you and I understand that we can't make those sorts of guarantees.'

Another voice came from the swarm of reporters.

'Will Missing People be searching for them?'

'You'll have to ask them that. It's an independent organisation, so I can't say.'

The blonde reporter stood up again.

'You previously asked the press to circulate pictures of a witness, Pedro Estrabou, and a reconstructed picture of an unidentified murder victim. Have you made any progress? Why do you want to find him? And have you discovered who the murder victim is?'

Arne held his hand up as if steadying himself.

'Calm down, one question at a time. In relation to the man,

the answer is no, we haven't found him yet.'

'But what does he know? Is he suspected of something?'

Arne hesitated for a moment before replying.

'No, he's not a suspect. But I can't say more at the moment.'

'What about the woman?'

'We're hoping to identify her shortly.'

'Thanks to the involvement of the media?' the woman said.

'No, thanks to our forensic pathologist. If you don't have any further questions about Jonas Orling, we'll end it here.'

A dull murmur spread through the room and the female reporter sat down in dissatisfaction. Just before Arne turned round, she shouted across the crowd.

'What if he's dead though? What'll happen then? Are you ultimately responsible?'

Arne looked unwell. His answer was partially swallowed up by the rattle of chairs and hubbub of journalists.

'Yes, it'll be me who has to face the consequences.'

113

Linn was curled up on the sofa watching the news on TV. Tears burnt her eyes. She felt completely numb.

Jonas had touched her with his kindness and his calm. How many people of his age were so considerate of others? He had had his whole life ahead of him, but now he was gone.

But he was used to being outdoors. Maybe he had had engine trouble and had sought shelter somewhere? Or perhaps he had gone off somewhere and forgotten to tell anyone? The last option seemed unlikely, he was probably much too diligent to do that.

She curled up even more and held her arms tight around her knees. There was something missing in her train of thought, something important. Pedro certainly fitted in with her thoughts about the murderer: childhood trauma, withdrawn and definitely disciplined enough, but there were a lot of other things that didn't fit. Like the tortured dog and why Gunvor and Erik had been mutilated sexually when the dead woman in the cottage hadn't been. Then there were the attacks on their family, carried out with the same attention to detail, but without any sexual dimension. The patterns and approaches varied, and the differences felt like they were the result of different motives. A vague, almost unidentifiable idea began to form in her consciousness. She had to talk to someone who had known the Berggren family.

114

Early on Friday morning they found Jonas Orling's car in a ditch in the forest. Not in Brottby—instead, it was just outside Rimbo, near Norrtälje.

It was buried under a thick layer of snow and was impossible to see from the air. Search parties and door-to-door inquiries were set in motion, and continued until darkness fell, but to no avail.

Arne Norman scratched his nose with a toothpick.

'Is there any stone we haven't turned over?'

Magnus shook his head in resignation.

'Forensics are going over the car. We suspect it's been moved. It seems to have been driven into the ditch on purpose and was found just two hundred metres from a bus stop.'

Arne sighed despondently.

'What else are you doing?'

'We're continuing to search Brottby too since that was where Jonas was going. We're mapping all the houses that could be considered to be cottages, and organising search parties and door-to-doors.'

'Good.'

Magnus suddenly looked concerned.

'I wonder whether it's such a good idea to use the media any longer—they're keen enough as it is.'

Arne looked at him incredulously, so he continued.

'They won't help—they'll just press for more details about the murders, and we don't want the background material to end up in the wrong hands. If we catch the murderer, he shouldn't be too well informed about the investigation.'

Arne cocked his head to one side. He could see the logic in it, but didn't like Magnus questioning his authority. His voice became chilly.

'I'll be careful.'

Magnus thoughtfully scratched his scalp. They couldn't release too much information to the journalists, but the press still had an important role to play in reaching the source Jonas had spoken to.

'Repeat what you've already said,' he said. 'Tell it like it is. We have nothing to indicate that Orling's disappearance has anything to do with the ongoing murder investigation.'

When Magnus left the office, he felt weak. He realized he had forgotten to eat or drink all day. His mouth was so dry that he could barely swallow and small drops of sweat ran underneath his T-shirt. There was something about this case—it felt like a sticky dough that he couldn't get a grip on. And now Jonas was gone.

115

Moa and Elin were playing with Lego in their room when Magnus got home and were so engrossed in their game that they barely looked up when he came in to say hello. So he went into the kitchen to see Linn instead. It was good to see her. She was reading a magazine and her blonde hair had fallen across part of her face.

When he came in, she raised her eyes and looked at him expectantly.

'Haven't you found him yet?' Her eyes were sad and he could see she had been crying.

Magnus shook his head. Before he had gone home, he had had to call Jonas Orling's parents to tell them they still hadn't found their son. It had been Jonas's mother who had answered.

For a long time she had listened to Magnus's awkward attempts to comfort her, then she had said in a voice filled with anguish: 'He's dead. I can feel it. There was a connection between us ... I can't explain it ... ' Then she had fallen silent again.

Magnus hadn't known what to say. There was a big risk that she was right and it would have been an insult to her to insist that her son was alive when he didn't actually know.

Instead, he had ended the call as quickly as he could.

Now he kissed Linn on the cheek.

'We don't know anything,' he said curtly. 'Is there anything in to eat?'

'Yes, there's spaghetti in the fridge. We had to eat before you came home because I thought Moa and Elin were going to go through the roof they were so hungry.'

Magnus took the food out of the fridge.

'Have you had a good day?' he asked in an attempt to block out thoughts of a dead Jonas.

Linn knew what he was thinking—it was visible in all his body language that he was somewhere else. His shoulders were tense and he moved stiffly on his legs. They had been together for a long time and she was familiar with how every part of his body moved.

'We've had a good time. Moa and Elin have been playing on their own almost all day. I cleaned. It's been fine,' she replied, while sipping a glass of juice and looking at him.

Magnus put the plate of spaghetti Bolognese in the microwave.

'Shouldn't we talk about Jonas and the murders instead? That's what you're thinking about,' she said.

Magnus sat down opposite her.

'There must be more information about the Berggren family,' she said.

'Such as?'

'I'm not sure yet, but I want to get to know them better. I'd like to talk to the only person who was in closer contact with them—Annika Wirén.'

Magnus's facial expression hardened.

'I would get the sack if I let you run around talking to people involved in this.'

Linn smacked her lips demonstratively.

'I know that. I'm not an idiot. I want *you* to talk to her. Find out what I want to know.'

Magnus blinked.

'Oh?' he said hesitantly.

'I want to know why Erik and Gunvor were mutilated

sexually, because it's what connects them to Lidhman. I think there's a common motive for all three of them.'

Linn took a deep breath and then let the air back out slowly.

'Please, Magnus. I just want to know what they were like ... ' Linn gave her most appealing smile. 'It can't do any harm.'

Magnus wasn't so sure. Of course, he trusted Linn's analyses, but he didn't want to risk losing the investigation.

He took a bite of spaghetti while he thought. He had good reasons to keep Linn out of this—she was already in too deep. Every media company out there was now carefully watching the investigation and one mistake could have dire consequences. Not only for him.

At the same time, it might be time to try something new. Everything was at a standstill. Gunvor had been kidnapped. Pedro had disappeared. Jonas was suddenly gone. Magnus groaned. No one apart from him needed to know what Linn's conclusions were. What did he have to lose?

She reached out a hand and put it against his unshaven cheek.

'Come on, then,' she purred.

Magnus grumbled quietly.

'What do you want me to ask her about, then?'

Linn smiled. The battle was won.

116

As the sun began to rise above the treetops, recently retired Agneta Schiller fed her cat, Siri, a mixture of dry and wet food. Then she sat down at the kitchen table made from yellowing pine and called the police. She was soon connected to a guarded policewoman at the police station.

'Sofie Eriksson, CID.'

'Hello, I've seen on the news that you're looking for me,' she said cautiously.

There was silence at the other end of the line.

'And who might you be?'

'My name is Agneta Schiller. It's about the missing police-man. It was me who called him before. I spoke to him.'

'It was you who spoke to him?' The voice at the other end suddenly sounded more alert.

The cat jumped onto the table and Agneta Schiller gently scratched her behind the ears.

'Yes, I think so. I didn't give much thought to the name. I just wanted to tell him about that cottage in Brottby that's been abandoned for so many years, and then suddenly there were lights on.'

'Yes?' The voice encouraged her to continue.

'Well, I think I was put through to the homicide unit. Well, it's nothing serious as such, but you are looking for a missing assailant, and that foreigner Pedro whatever his name was ... well, I thought he might have broken in there.'

'Pedro Estrabou is only being sought as a witness.'

'Well, whatever you say. Anyway, the young man I spoke to sounded most interested,' she said in a more prudish tone.

'But why on earth didn't you get in touch sooner? We've been looking for you for days!'

'I didn't want to get mixed up in a serious police matter! I just wanted to make a tip. You're surely supposed to be allowed to do that anonymously if you want? Isn't that a right?' Agneta Schiller unexpectedly raised her voice a couple of octaves.

'Okay, okay, calm down. Where is the house?'

'Near the Yesterdays palais de dance in Brottby. There's a small road. I don't know if it has a name. It must be the only house on the road and as I said, well, no one has been there for a decade or more and now ... all the lights on. I often pass it on my way to buy cat foo ... '

'Are you calling from your home phone?'

'Yes.'

'Do you have a mobile too?'

'No, what do you ... '

'Thank you.'

Click. Agneta stayed where she was looking at the phone in astonishment. Those police officers didn't seem to have many manners—that much was clear. She picked up Siri's empty bowl and filled it with mashed fish.

117

Sofie put on her coat. Of course, Agneta Schiller might be another let-down, but Sofie's intuition told her that Agneta was the one they had been looking for.

She looked at her note with directions on it as she hurried down the corridor to Roger's office.

An hour later, Sofie and Roger were trudging through the forest in the wet snow. It was six o'clock and the sun had set long ago.

She shone her torch, but despite the LED light they kept stumbling over snow-covered tufts of grass, branches and rocks. Roger was poorly dressed in a black leather jacket and trainers. His feet ached with cold.

Sofie glanced anxiously in his direction. As usual, her colleague had his hands jammed in his pockets. She couldn't see his facial expression, but he was panting like a bellows and sounded like he was about to have a heart attack.

'Are you okay?'

'Yes, yes ... '

'Should we call for backup?'

'A car's coming from town, but it'll take a while.'

Sofie smiled in relief, but since the dark had covered them like a dense blanket Roger didn't notice.

They walked for another fifteen minutes without seeing anything except snow-laden pines and firs.

Roger began to wonder how cold his toes could get before he needed medical attention. He looked at Sofie trudging on like an elk ahead of him.

'Do you have to amputate frozen toes?' he said with a grimace, before clenching his jaw. The cottage was suddenly right ahead of them. It was in darkness and the brown paintwork meant it was almost impossible to see in the dark.

Sofie put a hand on his arm to silence him. It wasn't necessary. Roger was on edge and neither of them moved a millimetre. Sofie had turned off her torch, and all they could hear was the sound of cars on the motorway in the distance.

As if they had reached a silent agreement, they began to creep toward the cottage.

When they were five metres away, they separated, each one of them going in a different direction. Roger could no longer feel the cold. His body was as light as a feather as he rubbed along the wall of the house and tried to see through the black windows that were like empty, gaping eyeholes. He had his weapon in his hand and was holding his arm straight against his body. The faint crunching of Sofie's steps on the other side of the house calmed him down. But then he heard Sofie violently draw breath and whimper. The adrenaline pumped through him. His arms trembling, he raised his weapon and took a few steps along the wall, then rapidly rounded the corner with his weapon in front of him.

Sofie was crouching on the ground.

'What happened?' he said in a low voice.

Sofie signalled that he should come. When he reached her, she held up a handful of snow.

'Blood,' she whispered.

'Are you sure?'

Roger bent down over her hand. It was blood.

'Tell backup to hurry.'

Roger pulled his phone out of his pocket, but a faint popping sound from inside the cottage made him stop. They quickly looked at each other. Then they crept as quietly as possible to the cottage door. They knew what they had to do, but they could never have prepared for what was waiting for them inside the brown cottage.

Roger raised his weapon and kicked the door in.

118

It had got warmer again and the snow had transformed into a slushy mess on the roads. The brown snowdrifts by the verges appeared to contain enough gas and dirt to poison a whole barracks. Magnus wound down the car window. The previous owner had been a big smoker and despite the car having been valeted repeatedly, the odour of old cigarette smoke had never quite disappeared. He blew his nose audibly.

Just my fucking luck to get ill, he muttered as he drove into Norrtälje.

Darkness had fallen and he was glad he no longer had to drive on the unlit motorway.

Unfortunately, Annika lived a few kilometres outside of town and it took a few minutes for him to reach the darkness on the other side of town.

He was staring through the dark looking for the sign for Vissbole. When at last it appeared over the crest of a hill, he gave a sigh of relief. He had only driven a few hundred metres along the smaller road when the yellow wooden house appeared, surrounded by snowy forest and arable land.

The house looming up ahead in the forest wasn't big, but more than enough for someone single like Annika. Actually, now he came to think of it, she had mentioned a boyfriend. He hoped he wouldn't have to meet him. They had serious matters to discuss and he wanted her to speak freely about her visits to Gösta and Gunvor.

There didn't appear to be space by the house for cars, but a couple of hundred metres away the road was wide enough for two cars, so Magnus parked his car there.

It was hard to avoid the sodden slush on the road and he gratefully stepped onto the path winding between knotted apple trees.

In daylight the trees probably looked idyllic, but in the dark they cast skeletal shadows over the small garden. A big greenhouse prevented him from seeing through the windows, but he could see that the lights were on inside the house. Magnus sighed with relief. Annika was at home. He hadn't bothered calling before setting off since he hadn't wanted to give her an opportunity to reject a visit. Linn had a point—if there was anyone who could see the connection between Erik, Gunvor and Josef Lidhman, it would be Annika.

Magnus ran his hand across his face. He was dead tired and in reality he hadn't wanted to head all the way out to Norrtälje tonight, but it was typical of Linn to get him to do idiotic things like this. He should have said no straight away.

Magnus nervously brushed his hands over his rib cage, as if he was worried about having a heart attack there and then. Then he reached out for Annika Wirén's gilded doorknocker.

119

Linn was lying on the sofa when the phone rang. It made her wake up with a jump. She quickly rolled onto the floor and grabbed the mobile off the coffee table. She didn't want the noise to wake the kids.

Her voice sounded wheezy as she answered.

'Darling?'

'Oh ... no. It's Arne Norman.'

Her senses immediately sharpened. The last thing Magnus had said as he left was that she shouldn't tell anyone where he was.

'Oh, hi ... Magnus is at the shops.'

'At this time of night?'

'7-Eleven. We ran out of milk.'

Linn bit her lip. What a bad lie. She really should have checked who was calling before picking up.

'I've tried his mobile, but I'm getting no reply.'

Only now did Linn notice the tension in his voice.

'Has something happened?'

'Yes, ask him to call me as soon as he gets back. It's important.'

Arne quickly hung up and Linn stared at the phone. What should she do now? She paced back and forth nervously in the small apartment while she dialled Magnus's number in vain.

'Damn!' she exclaimed. There must be bad coverage at Annika Wirén's house. She left a brief voicemail for him.

'Hi darling, Arne just called. He wants you to call him. He said it was very important. Call me too.'

She threw herself back onto the sofa. What had happened?

She waited for five minutes, then another five. Worry spread through her like a virus. What if there was something wrong with the mobile network? Why had she asked him to go tonight?

She pulled out her mobile and called again but there was still no answer. With her hands in a knot on her lap, she stared at the worn out lino. She stayed there for a long time, before getting up. She would just have to go and get him. She could always call him on the way and turn round if he picked up.

120

Annika Wirén looked surprised to see Magnus on the door-step. For a moment, there was a hint of fear in her eyes. She was wearing a white dressing gown and her dark hair curled down onto her shoulders. She quickly pulled the dressing gown tighter around her, as if she wanted to cover herself.

'Sorry to disturb you so late.' Magnus smiled apologetically.

'Yes?' Annika showed no signs of comprehension. She was holding the door handle, as if contemplating shutting it.

'I take it you remember me? We need to have a talk. Can I come in?'

For a second he thought she would say no, but then she quietly opened the door while forcing a smile onto her troubled face.

'Isn't it rather late to be working?'

Magnus nodded, unsure of how to respond.

The hall was small but nicely decorated in a light, rural style. On the wall there were black and white photos of cats. He looked around.

'Could we sit down somewhere?'

'Yes, we can go in the living room if you like?'

Annika led him into a similarly stylish living room. Every-thing was white—even the floor. A white Howard-style sofa and two white armchairs to match were positioned around the open fire. There wasn't a TV in sight.

When Magnus sat down in an armchair, he hoped his blue cords wouldn't leave any marks.

'I'm just going to put something on.'

Annika disappeared out of the room. She soon returned wearing a black tracksuit that accentuated her curves.

'Sorry,' she said in a low voice.

'Not to worry.' Magnus leaned forward and gave her a

friendly smile. 'It's your relatives that I want to talk to you about again. You are, after all, the one who knew them best, and I need to know everything you know—whether it's important or not.'

'I don't know if I've got much ... ' Annika curled up on the sofa.

'Give me what you've got.'

For a moment something desperate and frustrated seemed to pass through her eyes, then her gaze changed and became vacant.

Magnus sat there in silence. Waiting to see what happened. Why was she so reserved? He struggled not to look too interested and nonchalantly cast his gaze around the room.

It was all frightfully tidy, as if no one lived there. There was an open book on the table and a knitted blue jumper hanging on the back of a chair. Otherwise there was nothing lying around. He turned back to Annika. The last thing he wanted was for her to back away and clam up. Unfortunately, that was precisely what was happening.

Annika squeezed out an apologetic smile and spread her hands.

'What has happened is sad, but I have no explanation.'

The change of attitude surprised him, but he soon realized why. Through the window, he could see that a car had parked on the road, out of which climbed a man with powerful shoulders. As there was no street lighting, Magnus couldn't see his face and he raised his eyebrows quizzically.

'That's Stefan—my boyfriend,' she said.

'Do you live together?'

'No, he comes and goes as he pleases. He doesn't like being pinned down.'

'Oh right ... '

She rolled her eyes slightly.

'He's a supply worker at different care homes. It's hard to ... well, you know.'

Magnus pursed his mouth. He was silently cursing that they had been interrupted. But he wasn't going to give up—not yet.

121

Linn rushed down the steps, car keys in hand. The officer on duty, Johanna Ljungblad, had loudly protested as she swept past and asked her in passing to keep an eye on Moa and Elin, who were sleeping in their room. But she didn't care.

'Don't worry, I just have to run an errand—I'll be back soon!' she half-shouted from the street door, before it slammed behind her.

A couple of minutes later she pulled out onto the street. If she drove quickly, Magnus would be able to call work within an hour. That would have to do. She put her foot down.

122

'Do you mind if I use your toilet?' Magnus got up.

'Go ahead. First door on the right in the hall. Do you want anything to drink—some tea perhaps?'

Magnus could see how reluctantly the offer crossed her lips, but he nodded.

'Yes please.'

Linn had told him to build trust, but it certainly wasn't easy.

Annika glared at him as if he was a stinking dung heap. It was obvious that inspiring intimate conversation was not his thing. Disillusioned, he went into the bathroom. He had just put up the toilet seat when he heard the key turning in the front door and Annika cooing lovingly outside.

'Hello love. The police are here.'

There were a couple of moments of silence. Then a slightly nasal voice.

'Where?'

'In the toilet?'

Magnus couldn't identify the sound he then heard. A cupboard was opened. Footsteps disappeared into the house and then he heard nothing.

He washed his hands and when he opened the door he was faced with Annika's fiancé, Stefan.

Magnus's appearance made the man freeze like prey before a hunter. They looked at each other for a brief moment.

The man's appearance confused him. He was tall and powerful, but his face was as smooth as a baby's bottom. The tip of his nose pointed slightly upward and his chin was feeble and feminine. Somehow, he looked like a child with distorted features. His brown hair was shoulder length and in a ponytail. Magnus held out his hand.

'Sorry to bother you. I ... '

The man smiled and displayed an uneven row of teeth.

'You're here to talk to Annika. I won't disturb you. She's in the living room.'

123

Linn had driven more than halfway when her mobile rang again. She fumbled in the red fabric bag on the passenger seat while trying to keep her eyes on the road. Paper, pens, old receipts, a black cardigan and a couple of Lego cars made it impossible to find the phone in time. She hoped deep down that it was Magnus calling, but was disappointed when the display showed Arne Norman's number.

'Fuck!' She put the mobile in the cup holder between the seats and sped up. She felt stressed. Magnus couldn't lose his job because of her and her ideas. He was most welcome to stop being a policeman, but it had to be his own choice. He would not on some melancholic occasion, in any case, get to blame the end of his police career on her.

The phone beeped. Arne had left a message.

124

It was at the threshold to the white living room that Magnus realized, but it was too late. The syringe penetrated between his shoulder blades and took immediate effect. It made him lose his balance and fall to his knees. Arrows of pain shot through his arms and shoulders. For a moment, everything went black, then the fog descended. As if in a dream, he saw someone coming toward him, bending down and contemplating him.

He was like a captured animal, throwing his body carelessly around to get free. He lifted his arms, but they wouldn't do what he asked of them. He attempted—in vain —to reach for the syringe hanging from his back like a rocking feather, but the room was no longer following the laws of physics, but was instead swaying in all directions.

He waved and fumbled with his clumsy hands. A sweat broke out on his forehead. He had to get up—he had to get up and fight, but his body wouldn't. A moment later, he gently fell onto the white rya rug and curled up like a child.

125

Roger was slumped on a stone staring vacantly into the slush. The harsh glare of the work lights made the snow look dreamlike. He was tired and upset, but he had got forensics there and they were already in full flow.

'Where's Sofie?' Arne shut the car door behind him and his

voice sounded more jittery than he had intended.

'I told her to go home. She was in shock.'

'Does she have anyone to talk to?'

'Her mother was going to come over, I think.'

Roger ran his hand through his hair. Only now did it become visible that his entire body was shaking.

'How are you feeling?' Arne said.

'Not so hot. I think this is the worst fucking thing I've ever seen.'

'What's it look like?' Arne looked toward the lighted porch.

'Well, what can I say? This is a sick person we're dealing with. The inside of the house is completely covered in plastic: the floor, the walls, the furniture, the table she's lying on ... and there's a whole bunch of knives in there ... and a fondue fork. Forensics are dealing with it.'

'Gunvor Berggren?'

'Yes, she's bound, naked and burnt.'

'With water on the genitals, like the others?'

'Yes, but more accurately. As if the murderer had more time. It looks like he cut the edges with a knife to make a neater shape. The face, on the other hand, is completely obliterated—as if he's beaten her completely indiscriminately.'

Arne swallowed. Next was the question he didn't want to ask.

'And Jonas?'

Roger shook his head.

'Dead, stabbed in the back.'

Roger breathed heavily.

'There was ... blood outside ... I think he was attacked there and then dragged in. He's lying in a corner of the living room. Like a bag of rubbish, as if he didn't mean shit.'

'Do you think the murderer knew Jonas was a policeman?'

'He definitely knows now. His wallet was lying next to him, so he must have seen his credentials.'

Arne held his hand to his forehead. Now they were dealing with a murdered policeman too. He groaned.

Roger saw the anger in his eyes, but misinterpreted it as outrage at the waste of Jonas's life. He got up and put a comforting hand on Arne Norman's shoulder

'This makes it even more personal,' he said with obvious disgust.

Arne nodded in agreement.

'Yes, enough is enough.' Arne looked back toward the cottage. It was time to take a look at the killer's work.

126

Roger drove them back. Arne was still weak after that experience. He cursed himself for wanting to see the murder scene with his own eyes. Whoever had done that was no human. There was nothing humane about what Gunvor Berggren and Jonas Orling had been subjected to. Nothing.

Roger cleared his throat.

'Where's Magnus?'

Arne winced.

'I've called him several times. It's a real nuisance being unavailable in the middle of an investigation this serious.'

Roger hung his head.

'Keep calling. We need him back in,' Roger said.

'Of course.'

'I'll find out who owns the house.' Roger sounded resolute.

Arne Norman covered his face with his hands. 'Are you up to it?' he said. 'I can ask someone else to make the call.'

'No, I'll do it. We have to catch this bastard Pedro now.'

127

The car beeped unnervingly, as if it wanted to induce a psychiatric disorder in its driver. It needed petrol and it needed it *now*.

Linn could feel her stress increasing and she desperately stared through the windscreen looking for a petrol station. As if on cue, a filling station appeared right by the road—illuminated like a colourful lighthouse in the darkness. Big signs enticed customers to buy fresh coconut balls, but Linn didn't see those. She could only think about Magnus.

While the fuel flowed into the empty tank, she kept dialling his number. At last, she gave up and listened to Arne's message instead. What he said made her gasp.

'We've found Jonas Orling and Gunvor Berggren dead and seriously burnt at a cottage in Brottby. Tell Magnus to call us *now!*'

When Linn slumped back into the sagging driver's seat, she couldn't stop the tears from pouring down her cheeks. It couldn't be true. Not Jonas.

With great effort, she forced herself to stop. She rested her forehead on the wheel. Deep breaths. Of course she had feared the worst, but deep down she had still hoped she would be wrong. She had hoped so dearly.

She dried the tears away with her sleeve and switched on the engine. Where was she? How far was there left to go?

She shook herself to try and return to her senses.

There was a map in the glove compartment—she would probably have to check it once she reached Norrtälje.

As she drove, she thought about Magnus and what might happen if his outing became common knowledge. She couldn't trick Arne with the 7-Eleven story any longer. They would be wondering why he wasn't calling now that they had found

Jonas. The feeling of shame made her eyes fill with tears once again.

She picked up the phone and called Arne.

'Hi, it's Linn Kalo.'

He sounded stressed and not particularly pleasant.

'Where's Magnus?'

'He's at Annika Wirén's.'

'What?'

'Yes—he said he wanted to interview her again.' Linn served up the lie as calmly as if she had been serving him fresh waffles with jam and whipped cream.

Arne grunted in displeasure. 'He is needed here and now.'

'I'll do what I can. Where did you find ... Jonas and Gunvor?'

'In a summer cottage in Brottby. I can't give you any more information, but it was Roger and Sofie that found them and they'll probably be in therapy for months.'

Linn felt the wave of nausea rush through her and she tried to forget the visions of a dead Jonas.

'How did he die?' she asked in a more subdued tone.

'He was stabbed with a knife, but it was probably a blessing in disguise. I can hardly describe what Pedro has done to Gunvor.'

'What has he done?'

'I can't go into detail, but let's just say that she doesn't have much skin left. It's awful. Absolutely awful.'

Linn fell silent. The words overran her. Sank into her consciousness. It was hard enough to grasp how someone could cross the line and kill, but this level of desecration was incomprehensible.

'Do you think it's the murderer's house?' she said in a low voice.

'We don't know. Roger's looking into it. Right, that's enough. I've already said too much. Ask Magnus to call me as soon as you hear from him.'

'I will.'

Linn hung up. Knowing that Jonas was dead hurt. And she knew the same grief would soon hit Magnus. Tears slowly began to run down her cheeks again and this time she let them.

128

The pain that woke him was frightful. Magnus was tied up in a grotesque backward arch, and his limbs felt like they were tearing apart. Thin rope had been used to lash his wrists and ankles together, and he could taste a thick, bloody copper flavour at the back of his throat.

He groaned in agony and opened his eyes. The dark surrounding him was compact, but he soon grew accustomed to it and dark shadows began to slowly appear.

He was lying in the middle of the living room floor. He looked around desperately, but there was no one to be seen. Some way off he could hear a sound that was like someone digging through a cutlery drawer.

He tugged hard at the ropes and they dug into his wrists with renewed vigour. He stifled a scream. He tried to work at the ropes round his feet, fumbling with his fingertips while listening to the nuances of the sound behind him. Then he realized what the sound was—someone was choosing their tools in the kitchen. Something to use on him—something to kill him with.

Fear overwhelmed him and he felt his nerves give way. He shut his eyes to regain control. His memory was coming back in fragments. The man with the childish appearance, the syringe rocking between his shoulder blades. Magnus made an effort not to shout. For some reason, he understood what this man was waiting for. He wanted him to be awake when he killed him.

Then he thought about Annika. Was she in on this? Or had

he already killed her? His eyes wandered in the darkness. She wasn't anywhere to be seen. He made a new attempt to get free and managed to grab hold of the robe wound round his ankles with his fingertips, but however hard he pulled, the knot just seemed to get tighter. His feet were beginning to go numb from lack of blood.

I have to get out! Magnus could feel that he was beginning to hyperventilate. *Think!* The clanking sound had stopped and that terrified him.

He pretended to sleep, trying to make his body look as limp as possible despite the strange position. Through his eyelids he could see that the light had changed. Someone had turned on a light somewhere far away and the rays were now sneaking into the dark room. Light steps approached, stopping for a moment before continuing to get closer. Magnus heard someone walk round him and then stop close by. He tried to breathe calmly, taking deep breaths, as if he was sleeping.

A cool finger suddenly brushed his cheek and continued to probe down on his throat. He could feel his blood pulsing. Don't wince, don't move!

'I know you're awake, so you might as well open your eyes.'

The voice was teasing and soft. He recognized it immediately. Reluctantly, he opened his eyes and, blinded by the light, tried to see the man crouching beside him. His eyes filled with tears and he blinked repeatedly. Soon he could see the man's features in the weak light. His eyes looked calm and melancholic, but before Magnus could say anything, he got up and left the room. The light was turned off.

Magnus groaned, his body shuddering in a fit of shivering. The longer he lay in this position, the weaker he would get. Lying on his side, he braced himself and tensed his body as best he could. The gruesome pain made his eyes black out, but nothing happened. Despite trying to relax his muscles as much as possible in the twisted position, he was beginning to get cramp in his thighs. He sobbed.

He began calling for help, but inside himself he knew that there was no one there. At least, no one who wanted to help him.

129

Arne Norman leafed through a few pages of notes. He was surprised to say the least.

'You see,' Roger said, 'the woman who owns the Brottby cottage has a prosthetic hip—an Exeter Plastic—exactly the same model as the dead woman at the farm in Flaxenvik had.'

Red patches had spread up Roger's throat and were beginning to work their way up toward his face.

'Can we confirm this is the same person?' Arne said.

Roger shook his head in exhaustion.

'It'll take time.'

' ... and we don't have that right now. We have a police murder on our hands.' Arne leaned back into his chair.

Roger looked serious.

'I think we can assume she is the mystery victim.'

'What's her name?'

'Rigmor Metzén. And listen to this: a couple of weeks ago she was taken home from the nursing home she lived in. Her thirty-six-year-old son, Stefan Metzén, was going to take care of her at home, he said.'

Arne whistled.

Roger shrugged his shoulders impatiently.

'Exactly how common is that? And she has Alzheimer's.'

'Find the son as quickly as you can. He has to be questioned. And for the love of god please get Magnus Kalo *in here*.'

Roger headed for the door. He was grateful that the surname

Metzén was unusual—it wouldn't be hard to find any relatives. He called directory enquiries and was immediately given the number of an Anna Metzén in Bromma.

130

He heard a pitiful whimper from diagonally behind him. With painful effort, Magnus rolled onto his other side. Pale clouds obscured the moonlight, but now he was used to the dim light and it didn't take him long to discern the body lying on the sofa. Judging by the sound it was a woman and he assumed it was Annika. Unlike him, she wasn't tied up with nylon rope— Annika was lying there quite comfortably asleep with a warm duvet up to her neck. It appeared to be an anxious slumber that kept making her twist and turn, but she seemed otherwise okay.

Magnus didn't know what to do. Had Annika come in to lie down recently? Had she been lying there all along? Was she friend or foe? His thoughts were interrupted by rapidly approaching steps.

'You and I are going for a little trip soon.' The soft voice cut through the darkness.

When the man had come some way into the room, Magnus could see him clearly from his grotesque position on the floor. The man was holding something in one hand.

'What are you holding?' he asked.

The man giggled.

'Something for you and something for my beloved to help you sleep soundly.'

'Why are you doing this?' Magnus felt fear taking hold of him.

'You should never have come to my barn ... or to Gunvor's,' the man said curtly, his eyes shimmering with pure hatred.

Then he bent over Magnus, smiling. Magnus's eyes were

dimming and the man brushed so close that he could smell him. Sterile, sweet, a mixture of hospitals and pick 'n' mix sweets.

'When you next wake up you'll see where I grew up, but you won't be depressed because I'm doing great now. Really great.'

The man held up a syringe in front of him.

'Wait! Don't!' Magnus's voice revealed more fear than he had wanted. He wanted to plead for his life, but he knew it wouldn't help.

The mortal dread made his eyes fill with tears and when the man put the syringe against his throat he closed his eyes in a final prayer. But the sting didn't materialize. The sound of a car engine outside made the man rush to the window in surprise.

'Help! Help me!' Magnus shouted for all he was worth and his voice cracked into falsetto. The man took two huge steps toward him and as the sharp pin penetrated into his throat he could no longer hear the engine. He wondered fuzzily whether the car had driven past. He could dimly see the man's face hovering expressionless above him and the way the stony eyes were making sure that he was slowly slipping out of consciousness.

131

Linn parked behind Magnus's car on the gravel track and reached for her bag on the passenger seat. She wondered whether Magnus would be angry at her for turning up, but things had happened—Jonas was dead—and there was every reason to have come to bring him home.

Annika Wirén's house was dark apart from a small lamp in the window. It seemed strange that it was so dark.

For a brief moment, Linn felt a pang of unjustified jealousy. Magnus was good-looking. She shouldn't be sending him to the homes of single women at night. Not that he would do anything, but ... She brushed away the thoughts. The jealousy was only inside her—Magnus had never given her any cause to distrust him.

It's time I packed in all this negativity, she thought to herself in irritation as she pushed open the car door.

132

The pines surrounded the garden like a massive wall, while a blanket of wet snow covered the lawn. The cold was piercing. The raw air felt like it was seeking its way under her winter clothing and carrying straight on into her pores.

Linn shivered and put her hands in her pockets. The garden path to the house was just as slushy as the muddy grass, and she carefully raised her feet to avoid the worst of the puddles. She suddenly stopped mid-step. There was a broad-shouldered man standing on the step, watching her.

'Hello—can I help you?' His voice was cheerful.

Linn assumed the man was smiling, but she wasn't sure.

He was at least fifteen metres away and the light from the small lamp in the window wasn't bright enough for her to see his face properly.

'I'm looking for Inspector Magnus Kalo!' she called out in a half shout.

'He's gone.'

For a moment thoughts whirred through her mind. She had just seen Magnus's car further down the road.

She squinted as the man came down the step.

His stance looked peculiar. His shoulders were tense like a cat waiting for a bird.

His hands were fists by his sides and his steps were far too quick. Linn stopped. Something was wrong. She saw him approaching and felt the fear creep in. Now she could make out the man's facial expression in the moonlight and it made her recoil violently. There was something twisted about his face. What she had initially believed to be a smile was actually a sick expression. She had seen the same look before on some of her patients and she knew what it meant. Yet she had never seen anyone as terrifying as the man now smoothly hurrying toward her.

Instinctively, she turned round and began to run—at first awkwardly and then quicker. Panic welled up inside her like a deep and ancient force. All sense of logic was gone.

Soon she was racing across the slippery grass with just one thought: *Away—must get away.*

She could hear the steps behind her getting closer. Heard him shout.

'Come on—stop. Stop, you fucking whore!'

Run. Run! Linn felt the fear lifting her legs from the ground. The bare winter branches of the apple trees whipped her face, but she felt nothing. Onto the road. Twenty metres from the car. She could hear him panting, getting closer and closer. She wouldn't make it. She was going to die. She understood that now. In despair, she saw Moa and Elin's faces in front of her.

Sharp nails dug into her skin as she pulled away from the coarse hands.

'Let go of me! Leave me alone!' She writhed hard in an attempt to get away, but when she turned round to flee he threw himself over her. She kicked frantically to get free—she felt light, weightless, as if her body had a will of its own. Her heart was bolting along like a startled hare in her chest.

Shortly after, she stumbled, and the man straddled her kicking legs. His face had hardened into a distorted parody of a human and his rough hands strained to reach her neck.

Once his grip round her throat tightened it would be too late. With all her might, she pulled her knee up between his powerful thighs and she hit him in just the right spot.

The man bellowed like a wounded wild animal and fell heavily on top of her. She lay there for a split second waiting to see what would happen—but nothing happened.

With one last effort, she rolled the unconscious body off her, turned onto her stomach and got up on all fours. Her nausea could no longer be ignored and she threw up on the grass. Her throat was burning like fire. It was as if her throat had been destroyed and she coughed violently as she stumbled toward the house on wobbly legs.

'Magnus!' she shouted, her voice filled with doubt. 'Magnus, please!'

Stumbling, she entered the dark house. Her trembling hands wouldn't obey her as she sought out the light switch by the door. Exhaustion made tears run down her cheeks.

'Magnus!' she called out, pleading. She turned round and looked out at the lawn. The man was still lying there. Once the light was on, she ran into the kitchen on a whim. Her voice was barely more than a whimper. 'Please, where are you?'

She went back out into the hall again—the light was spilling into the dark living room—and there he was.

Linn gave a cry. Lifeless and tied up in a grotesque manner, Magnus was lying in the middle of the floor. She rushed forward.

'Darling, wake up!' she begged, while shaking his shoulders hard. He was warm. He was breathing. It was okay. She closed her eyes for a moment. *Calm. You have to stay calm.*

Magnus's hands were blue and swollen. She looked desperately for something to cut the ropes with. She ran into the kitchen and opened four drawers before she found a big pair of scissors.

Panic rushed through her as she began to work on the ropes round his limbs while sobbing. She prayed that it wasn't too late. She sobbed, and it felt as if time had stopped as she hacked through the centimetre-thick nylon ropes, but then abruptly she ceased. The feeling that she wasn't alone made her slowly turn round.

A dark-haired woman was sitting on the sofa watching Linn with an overwrought expression. Linn held the scissors tightly in front of her.

The woman opened her mouth to say something, but then closed it again without saying a word.

'Annika Wirén?' Linn said cautiously.

The woman nodded without taking her eyes off the scissors Linn was aiming at her.

Annika didn't look dangerous. In fact, she looked scared to death.

Linn didn't know what to do. Was Annika a perpetrator or a victim? Could she be trusted—could she ask her for help?

The sound of steps in the hall interrupted her train of thought. The man had woken up.

133

Now that the man was standing in the doorway, Linn saw for the first time what he actually looked like. The light feminine features formed a strange contrast to his big, honed body. Most prominent were his eyes, which had an odd shimmer in them. The distorted facial expression he had had recently was gone. Now his arms were hanging loosely by his sides and his face was covered in grief. He held his hand out in a pleading gesture, but it wasn't Linn he directed this to—it was Annika.

'What's happening?' Annika looked terrified.

'I did it for you. To free you.'

The man took a couple of steps closer, his hand outstretched. It was as if he was begging, as if everything depended on her reply.

Annika looked at him in silence for a couple of seconds then confusion took the upper hand. She laughed nervously—almost hysterically.

'For me? What do you mean? What have you done?'

'I made them suffer just as much as you did.'

Annika fell back into the sofa, her eyes filling with tears.

The man walked toward her, with his hand still outstretched.

'They didn't deserve to live. You told me that once—do you remember? And I thought about—I thought about what you said a great deal. It was people like that who wanted to destroy everything beautiful. What they did to you in the barn, it'll never ... '

Annika was holding her hands to her mouth. Her eyes were wide and filled with bottomless fear.

The long silence felt as tense as the string of a violin.

Then she whispered: 'You're sick, Stefan. You're not normal ... '

Linn looked at the man. He hadn't expected this. He had been expecting something else—gratefulness, worship. The moment he was shattered was as clear as if it had been replayed in slow motion. His face contorted into a grimace of pain and his eyes filled with sorrow and then anger.

'You love me.' His voice cracked.

Annika looked at him with a frightened expression, but said nothing.

It took him less than a second to reach her, and he shook her shoulders making her head fall backward. He shouted like a wounded animal.

'You and I are unique. Different. Just us—no one else. Do you understand? They were bastards and deserved to die!'

'Let go of me. Please ... let go.' Annika was like a rag in his grasp—she was sobbing hysterically.

'Shut up, bitch!'

Now all that was audible were her gasps for breath and the guttural sound of her neck being violently pushed back and forth.

He smashed Annika's head into the windowsill hard.

Her eyelids fluttered. Her body collapsed into the white sofa, lifeless.

Linn screamed but he didn't notice her. Instead, he looked at Annika in shock and awkwardly patted her bloody cheek.

'If anyone ought to understand that you don't do this to me, it would be you. You stupid ... Don't you get it?' he said, sobbing.

Linn felt paralysed. Every cell in her body was telling her to flee, but she didn't want to. She couldn't leave Magnus.

After a while the man turned his head. His eyes were heavy with grief and hatred.

'It's your fault—it's your bloody fault,' he hissed as he slowly got to his feet. Linn was still holding the scissors in a vicelike grip in front of her, but she didn't stand a chance. In less than a second, the man charged at her like a raging bull and rammed her with all his might.

The weight of the attack made her fall backward and she hit her head on the floor. The powerful fists grabbed her throat once again, squeezing it tighter and tighter. She was spinning into darkness. But then the pain faded and Linn felt herself vanishing—life itself was losing its colour. *Moa and Elin. Where were they? Were they sleeping?* She wanted them there with her.

Then she danced up to the light. Her lungs felt as if they were on fire as the air was drawn into them. The man lying across her was heavy. She gasped for breath. The scissors were wedged so deeply inside his chest she could barely move them, but she didn't dare let go of them. She lay there for a while, uncertain what would happen. Then she pushed him away and began to cry loudly and uncontrollably.

The man was lying on his back with his hands over the

wound. He took a deep, wheezing breath, but he soon stopped making any noise. The silence was absolute.

With great difficulty, Linn rolled away and began to crawl toward Magnus, crying, while still holding the bloody scissors in a vice in her hands. Her voice was pleading and barely audible as she put her head on his ribcage.

'Don't leave me ... please.'

Magnus groaned weakly, then fell away again. But he was breathing. He was alive.

Linn attacked the ropes with the bloody scissors. When she finally got them off, she collapsed next to Magnus's limp body in exhaustion.

They lay in that position for a long time before the clattering sound penetrated into the room. A helicopter was approaching. At first it sounded distant, but then the noise got louder and louder. Soon she could hear shouts and running steps on the garden path outside.

Linn began to laugh. She couldn't stop.

134

Roger was the first officer on the scene. Standing in the doorway of the semi-dark living room, he stared at the scene before him in shock. Then he shouted.

'Call an ambulance for Christ's sake. Call one now!'

By the time the horde of police officers were pushing through the doorway, Roger was already sitting by Linn holding her trembling body in his arms. The shouting and general din around him seemed distant and unreal.

'My God, Linn ... ' His voice was barely above a whisper.

'How did you know ... ?'

'Stefan ... he ... ' Roger nodded at the man on the floor. 'He has a sister called Anna. She knew he was at his girlfriend Annika's in Norrtälje. We put two and two together.'

'But why? Why did he do it?' Linn's eyes reflected her confusion.

'Linn ... ' he said softly. 'Stop talking.'

Linn slumped onto his chest. Fatigue made the voices around her seem like an impenetrable carpet.

'Magnus ... How's Magnus?' she mumbled.

Roger shook his head.

'I don't know. I really don't know ... '

135

Gravel crunched cosily under Linn's clogs as she carried the tray of coffee into the garden. The air was still cool, but the birds were twittering expectantly, and the rays of the spring sunshine were warm.

'Can you get the milk too?'

The shout came from Magnus, who was sitting reclined in a sun lounger with his face turned toward the sun. His eyes were shut and he didn't notice that Linn was already sitting opposite him.

'I already did,' she replied cheerfully.

Magnus jumped, then smiled and looked around.

'Where are Moa and Elin?' His voice immediately sounded anxious.

'They're hiding under the tree. Relax.'

Magnus breathed a sigh of relief.

Linn looked at him and knew what he was thinking. The same struggle was taking place inside her. A battle they had to win.

'It's over now,' she said with determination.

'Will you ever forget about it?'

Linn shook her head with a melancholic smile.

'No, I took the life of another person. I'll have to live with that for the rest of my life.'

Magnus looked at her, sitting there in his fisherman's jersey that was several sizes too large for her. She had small wrinkles around her eyes that reminded him that they were getting older, and somehow it made him love her more, as if he understood that time was short.

'I've already said it before—it wasn't your fault that Stefan died. He would have killed us. He even killed his own mother and hung her up in the roof.'

Linn bit her lip and nodded.

'I know, but it's still tough.'

She raised the cup to her lips and sipped the hot coffee.

'But why did he hate the police so much?'

Magnus looked confused.

'I'm not sure. His mother did time for drink-driving when he was thirteen, so he spent six months in a foster home. Perhaps that was what started it?'

'And then you turned up and got in his way.'

'Yes—in the middle of his mission of love. You know, if I had arrived at the care home ten minutes later that day, we would probably have steered clear of this hell.'

'You can't think like that.' Linn looked at him in concern.

'By the way, how's Annika?' she said.

'She's trying to learn to speak and walk again. It's taking its time, but I've managed to get a lot out of her.'

'The fact that the doctors found serious burns around her genitals ... '

'Yes ... ' Magnus stared down at the grass.

'Can they do anything about it?'

'I don't actually know. I'm not even sure the doctors know.'

Linn shook her head sadly.

'Imagine being sent away to your relatives during the summer holidays and being raped and ... it's so dreadful.'

Magnus stirred his coffee.

'Yes, it's completely sick how that trio—Gunvor, Gösta, and Josef Lidhman—could set upon a fifteen-year-old girl like that.

But why did they force Erik to watch them in the barn?'

Linn shrugged her shoulders.

'No idea. Maybe they wanted to humiliate him? Maybe they were ashamed of his special needs? Or maybe they even hated him?'

Magnus made a gesture of resignation.

'All of it just makes me want to be sick.'

Linn carefully put her cup down on the table.

'At any rate, I think it was Erik who killed the dog as a way of striking back. His home life was probably pure hell and he must have felt completely powerless. He could control the dog. It was probably a way for him to deal with what he had experienced.'

Magnus was silent for a while. His gaze fell on Moa and Elin who were putting pine cones in a bucket. They seemed quite unconcerned. He smiled.

'Stefan Metzén probably didn't have it easy either. His mother clearly had issues with substance abuse ... '

Linn cocked her head.

'It's a bit too simple to say that everyone who carries out evil deeds had a tough upbringing, but Stefan must have had some issues with his mother given what he did to her, and he probably saw a kindred spirit in Annika. They were both broken-winged. Damaged goods.'

Magnus helped himself to a cake.

'I talked to a therapist who had seen Stefan a couple of times last year. She had told him to process the darkness inside him to reach the light. She said he looked pretty bloody strange when he left, apparently. Then he never came back. She got the impression that he misinterpreted her.'

Linn poured the rest of her coffee onto the grass.

'That was probably crucial,' she said firmly.

It took a while for the pieces to fall into place. Then he sighed deeply.

'If we hadn't fixated on Pedro Estrabou we might have caught him sooner.'

It couldn't be denied. Linn looked toward the pine tree where Moa was peering out and laughing.

She turned back to Magnus.

'Do you still not know where Pedro disappeared to?'

'No, but the computer we examined showed that he had been blackmailing Josef Lidhman for years. He had been sending the money to his mother in Argentina.'

'Well, I suppose there was a kind of justice in that. But the question still stands—where is he?'

'No idea, but I don't care. It's not my department,' Magnus replied happily.

For the first time in a long time, he felt really happy. He had barely felt any twinges in his leg lately and they had found their dream home. A green wooden terrace by the sea. The kids were playing at being pixies and it was spring. Life was good.

Linn looked across the lawn and thoughtfully chewed on her bun. She was sleeping more soundly at night now—but how was the man who had been tortured by Pedro Estrabou? Could he sleep while his old tormentor was still at large? Linn bit her lip anxiously.

She would never know that Carlos Fernandez was sleeping peacefully every night for the first time in decades. Lying in the arms of his love, he was content in the knowledge that his problem was buried in the dark waters of Lake Mälaren forever.

For more information, visit us at www.worldeditions.org.